The Junk Lottery

Mickey Getty

Orchard House Press
Port Orchard • Washington

The Junk Lottery
copyright 2006 by Mickey Getty
published by Windstorm Creative

ISBN 978-1-59092-184-5
First edition August 2006
9 8 7 6 5 4 3 2

Cover images by Mickey Getty.
Design by Buster Blue of Blue Artisans Design.

This is a work of fiction. All of the characters in this story are products of my imagination. Any resemblance to persons living or dead is coincidental.

All rights reserved, including the right to reproduce this book or portions thereof in any form whatsoever, except in the case of short excerpts for use in reviews of the book.

For information about film, reprint or other subsidiary rights, contact:
legal@orchardhousepress.com

Orchard House Press is an independent press dedicated to publishing timeless books and games across all genres. The orchard and house logo is a trademark of Orchard House Press.

Orchard House Press
7419 Ebbert Drive Southeast
Port Orchard, Washington 98367
www.OrchardHousePress.com
360-769-7174 ph

Library of Congress Cataloging in Publication Data available.

For my sisters
both kin and kindred spirits
and all our daughters.

Acknowledgments

For Johnny Payne, author of *North of Patagonia* and *Kentuckiana,* professor and teacher extraordinaire, I am grateful. This book wouldn't exist without you.

To Becky McEldowney, sister in spirit, author of *Manual For Normal, Guardian Devils* and *Soul of Flesh,* I am forever indebted. Your patient reading and rereading, editing, critiques, and unconditional support are without measure. Without you, I may not have persevered.

Aimee Levitt, my sister-in-writing, your insights have been invaluable.

Jane Reeves, you started it all when I didn't have a good enough answer to your question: "Well, why *don't* you write a book?"

Thank you to Doug Arnold and Rick Bell for reading my proof pages.

A heartfelt thank you to my publisher Jennifer DiMarco, Senior Editor Cris DiMarco, and the staff at Windstorm Creative for believing in this story.

> And Lou, my husband,
> my bulwark of strength,
> thank you.

To Eriko,
Keep on writing those stories. They are important!

The Junk Lottery

Mickey Getty

Mickey Getty

July 2010

1

My Dear One,

How strange to write them words that I can't say out loud, but I can't let words pull me from what I must do today. I always thought a man uses his strength and wit to live as a man, as the one to feed and fight for the family. I am not a man no more.

I am a survivor. That's what I told myself. I never told you how I was beaten and pushed aside as a kid. I wouldn't die. I didn't believe I was stupid, or bad, or worthless. I fought for myself every day. I was afraid of nothing, of no one. When they wouldn't feed me, I found my own food. Rabbit, squirrel, snake, berries, roots, crab apples. I watched the animals. When Paw wouldn't let me in out of the cold, I built tree houses. My strength has always won out. Until now.

I was a weird kid, folks said, always in the woods. But you didn't know why. I needed the safety of the forest, the trees, the fire from their kindling. They were my family, my home.

I hated Paw that day he threw the chain saw into my arms. Flat on my back in the mud, arms and legs pinned under it, I spit the dirt from my mouth and decided to show him I was no 'fraidy cat. I wouldn't cut my arm off. I wouldn't need him or anyone.

Turns out, I loved the chain saw, big, yellow, obedient, with its muscle shaking into my arms, shoulders, back. It was powerful, I was powerful, stronger and bigger; the beatings stopped.

I asked for nothing. If I couldn't do for myself, I did without. An abandoned shack was home. I quit school. Learned good enough to make money. Finally earned my keep, Paw, and more. Our land, our house.

Lived lean, grew vegetables, hunted for meat, venison my favorite. I survived, steel to wind, rain, frost and pain. I could handle anything.

You know, something happened when I had money. I was afraid of losing it. That's why, like the squirrels and bees, I stored up.

I trusted no one. Not even you, my beautiful one—breakable, sweet, smelling like a meadow. Flaming red hair, clear blue eyes, always smiling. Eyes that see only goodness. Eyes that trusted. Your eyes saw me, loved me, believed in me. I was afraid to love you.

As I write, the pen is heavy, my breath comes short. I need rest, but I must finish this.

I taught you all how to survive. The land, the trees, the stream that runs through our land, and ourselves: These were the only things you can count on. My land, it answers to my spade. Little saplings, you seen them, they refuse to do anything but grow. Wild flowers bloom in dry rocky cracks, bees live in the shelter I made. Insects buzzing, Cardinals whistling in the home I grew. The air sweeter than honey. I needed more trees, every kind, lots of them. Planted them for the pleasure of the planting, the growing. And the harvesting, even though I knew it made you sad to see a tree fall.

What a nut I was, Alma. Like a crazy man, I chopped that wood, piled it up. Waste, you know I could not waste anything. If I had been even a little generous, seen what you are always grateful for .... A woman needs to feel gentle touches, to hear soft whispers. Children need to be hugged. But no, instead I planted, chopped wood, split logs for my family. Saved up.

We celebrated Harvest. Remember? A restaurant dinner. All day, we laughed and sang and had fun. That fun, that laughter is what I should have been stashing away, Alma. Those happy moments were worth more than all the junk I collected.

Sickness took my strength. I am back to being hungry. The food I need doesn't come through a tube cut into my *belly. I need to walk outside to look at my land, to be in the garden, to start the chain saw, or chop wood, or load the hunting rifles. It is not enough to hope the way you do.*

You're always sure I'll get better. I see you tired. Why put you through more? What if I became more of an invalid? I want to end it before I lose even that ability. I want to do it where the trees are thickest, but the path is too slippery with ice and I am too weak.

I do this for both of us.
M.

2

Blood red geraniums glowed in the morning sun—tiny tear-like petals with an unfortunate fragrance. She drew a slow deep breath. The warm, fresh air relaxed her, it always relaxed her, it was going to relax her now. Another deep breath. "You can do this, Alma," she coaxed herself, not believing it. She glanced over at the laundry, empty clothes, a tumbled pile near the basement door. She hadn't been able to go down there since it happened. Today, after the dishes. Petra would help.

Today would have been their anniversary and the weather was very much like the day she and Mack married. She twisted the sun flowered dishtowel into a tight coil, scrubbed her hands with it. But that day, instead of feeling shaky and driving off the sound of sirens in her head and looking to see if there was blood on her hands, instead of smothering that chiding voice inside, instead of all that, on her wedding day she felt beautiful, like a fairy princess.

And you created a knight in shining armor to match.

It had been a perfect day for a wedding. A cool spring breeze shook the morning dew from the trees onto the bride and groom—a blessing, it seemed, from the heavens. Sunbeams spotlighted the wedding decorations: Fragrant and colorful mountain laurel and forsythia. Music tendered by a chorus of cardinals and robins, and the song of the wind. A tree felled by lightning was their altar. The lush carpet of pine needles cushioned the steps of few guests: Petra as the maid-of-honor, Alma's mother. The Town Clerk performed the ceremony.

Smoked venison, fresh vegetables and fruit from the garden, berries from the forest, and the store-bought cake Alma's mother brought: The day's feast. Mack killed the deer and prepared the meat himself in a smoker he found and restored. He was proud of the fact that the entire meal was produced through his own efforts, except the cake which he refused to eat.

Such a romantic, Alma thought then, when Mack insisted the wedding be held in his hideaway, his favorite place, beside a creek in the Shwangunk mountains. He'd cleared this spot when he was a kid, and built a shanty — today, their honeymoon suite. When he was ten, he added scraps of wood, tin, discarded shingles, fallen branches, cardboard for insulation. Later he enlarged it, replaced cardboard with plywood, added roofing beams, a wood floor, a real door, a wood-burning stove. It was small, about twelve square feet, one window, no electricity or running water. Weirdo, the townsfolk said. Good hunting, fishing, he said. Strong, Alma thought, self-sufficient.

You didn't allow yourself to wonder why a ten-year-old would build a shanty in a deeply wooded area so far from his home.

Mack had dressed up for the occasion of his wedding: chinos, a-button-down-short-sleeved shirt, sky blue, black loafers, a leather belt. Thrift-store bargains he'd bragged to Alma about. So frugal. He saved everything for the house he was building for her. Their house. He was her shelter, her protector. She was grateful for that. Strong Mack, standing beside her in their forest chapel, promised to let nothing hurt her. He smelled of pine and fresh-cut wood and smoke from the hearth.

Later, preparing to receive him, Alma plunged her hands into the icy stream water that filled the dishpan. She shivered from the shock and forgot about the flutters in her stomach for a moment, only a moment. She poured hot water from the kettle into the pan and shook a few drops of oil into the heated water. The room filled with the scent of lavender. The kerosene lantern flickered playful shadows chasing light about the cabin. The sun hadn't yet set, but it was neither daylight nor dark. Petra had just left, her wishes for a happy honeymoon still in her retreating headlights. Alma thought about bathing in the stream to be fresh and clean for the first time she gave her body to Mack, but though purified by nature, the water was still too cold for her.

She could hear Mack chopping wood for the stove to heat the cabin, to boil water for tea. It would be a while before he joined her. Still, she hurried lest she get caught before she was ready. Long had she waited for this night, saved herself, read all the magazine articles about how to do it, about what to expect, that women were disappointed the first time, in fact were usually unsatisfied. It will be different for us, she thought. She'd so often been tempted to yield to Mack's touch. Waiting made it all the more important that it be perfect, that he be pleased, that her longings at last be gratified. She'd always had such strong impulses that she'd been taught to deny, to offer up as a sacrifice, but no more, not after today. She was at last free.

She removed her wedding dress, hurriedly, fumbling with tiny, slippery buttons and loops, with fingers that refused to be calm. She hung it on a hook, white sequins that she'd sewn on herself, dancing, delicate against the rough timbers of the wall. Alma carefully pulled white satin and lace from her duffel bag. It slid through her hands onto the dirty floor. Shaking it, she dropped it again. "Stay," she said as she smoothed the nightie on the bed to brush the grit off. Then she smoothed the bed and sprinkled some lavender on the pillows after she fluffed them for the third time.

Her hand shook as she sponged herself. The warm water chilled quickly; her skin responded, her nipples became erect. She touched them, curious about what she'd feel. She cupped her breasts with her hands and pushed them toward each other, shoring up her otherwise absent cleavage. Woefully inadequate for that sexy nightie, she thought. That won't matter. I'll slip the straps off and it will slink to the floor. At least in her imagination it did that, slowly revealing her body, soft clear skin, a deep navel, tightly coiled red hair, slender thighs. She drew her hand across her breasts, over the slight round of her belly to the mound between her legs. It should be dark and thick, not red, she thought. Her fragrance was earthy, pleasant, but she continued her bathing, intent on smelling like a midsummer's night. As her fingers and the moist, rough sponge moved down and beneath the fringe, she found herself aroused by her own touch. She yielded, grateful that tonight she was free to indulge herself. The pleasure erased the guilt she'd felt for not being the virgin Mack expected.

She slid into her negligee as she noticed the absence of chopping sounds. Quickly she positioned herself on the bed. No, that wasn't right. How would she get the nightgown to slither off her? She stood by the stove. Lord, no. I'm liable to catch fire. Alma moved to the chest at the foot of the bed and sat, alluringly. This isn't right, she decided. I want Mack to get the long view. She moved to the back of the cabin, her back to the door so that when he entered she could turn slowly, let him feast his eyes for a moment, then when he caught his breath, release the shoulder strap. She stood there, glancing about the cabin, straining to hear foot steps. For fifteen minutes she fidgeted, shifting her weight from hip to hip, tiring.

The cabin door opened. She looked over her shoulder. Mack stood there wrapped in a towel, his hair dripping. How sweet, she thought, he bathed too. She turned slowly.

Alma shook the memory away. That was a long time ago. Earlier this morning, as every other morning for the last twenty-seven years, she lingered at the sink washing the breakfast dishes. The kitchen was her favorite room of the house, even though the soft, warm scent of bread baking, and the sweet smell of jam cooling, were only memories.

The only sort of memories you'll allow.

Some mornings there'd been stacks of dishes and glasses and she'd had to collect them from all over the house. Her oldest son, William, tall, lank like his dad, his straight dark brown hair stubborn with cowlicks, gulped his breakfast in his room while he rushed to finish his homework. Fix it, correct it, make it perfect, never really getting it the way he wanted. Anything less than an A was unacceptable. Her two daughters, redheads like her though not yet graying, piled dishes and glasses near the TV and in front of the bathroom mirror. Each girl had crystal clear blue-green eyes like Alma's, though hers were not fringed with mascaraed lashes. Why they wanted to cover up their beautiful faces with greasy makeup, Alma didn't understand. But she saved loose change for them whenever she could, so they could buy the stuff; Mack would never have approved the expenditure. They were only having fun, and that wasn't wasteful. Alicia, the youngest, was the only one who occasionally remembered to bring her dishes into the kitchen. And Mack ate and drank only at mealtime. He sat at the head of the table.

Today, there were only her own dishes.
Needing someone to talk to, she stepped out onto the back porch where the cat slept in the sun. "What a beautiful view, OJ," she said. "I am one lucky lady. So much beauty." The muscles in her jaw worked. She said these words every day. It was almost like the Indian ritual of saluting the four winds—drawing strength and nourishment from the universe. Never had she needed it so desperately as in the last year and never had it failed her so miserably as today.

Another breath. Slow, deep, full. She waved her right hand as if brushing away the blood spattered images that hovered at her shoulder. She could smell the sun-drenched earth, the heavy sweetness of the lilacs, and the manure aging behind the hen house. The breeze pushed quietly through the trees. She could hear the water burble over the rocks in the stream that flowed through their property, her property now. Another breath as she tried to recreate her fantasy. The lush, green grass led to her own private little forest. Unusual warmth and generous spring showers nurtured luxurious growth. Seemed like only yesterday many of them were the saplings Mack planted. He watered and fertilized them in their infancy. Parented them as if they were his offspring, like other fathers nurtured their children. As they grew, he'd staked and pruned them so they'd grow tall and straight. Now look at them. Tall pine trees, the kinds most people see only on post cards. Majestic maples, that grew at his command. The brilliant white of the birch reflected the sunlight. And the hemlocks, she lingered there for a moment, they never lose their leaves, no matter how cold the winter. The trees were outrageous show-offs in the fall, flashing brilliant shades of red, orange and gold, but Mack didn't seem to be as impressed by their beauty as by their obedience.

From the back porch she could see the wood pile along the north property line, a blemish on the landscape. Two huge trees book-ended the tall stockpile of perfectly cut fireplace-size logs, this cache the largest of five. Mack loved the wood. He cut it, stacked and stored it, set it ablaze.

He used the chainsaw to fell a tree and cut the biggest pieces, then he wielded the ax. She closed her eyes. She could still see his body long and lean. The muscles in his arms and back danced to the whoosh of the ax through the air, relaxed on contact for an instant, then undulated, as he heaved the ax upward for another blow. He thrived on physical exertion; he reveled in the chainsaw's power. His power.

"I love the smell of the wood, fresh and clean," he told her, "and the feel of it under the chainsaw. Did you know the rings tell a story? Look, count back and this was the last World War. This one here tells about a drought."

"Why do you cut them down?" she'd asked him once.

"They serve our needs like the vegetables in the garden do. But the blighted trees serve no purpose—they have to be eliminated. You are too sentimental about them. Good thing you didn't know my father." The resounding crack his axe made as it shattered a limb from the trunk concluded the conversation. Mack seldom mentioned his father.

It seemed an act of violence to you, Alma. But you refused to wonder about that then.

A family of deer sauntered out of the trees and brought her back to the present. They munched crab apples and grass. She adored the deer. Some came very close to the house. Every season, like an expectant parent, she looked forward to the new arrivals.

"Ah," she exhaled a twinge of sadness, her own family scattered across the country. Grace, she thought, where are you? Her daughter, her second child, so like a thorny, wild rosebush that grew beside the stream, bristled at Mack's sanctions and fled from home when she was seventeen. Worry sculpted an image of Grace that often floated into her mind—fiery red hair, eyes tropical-blue-green ice, crumpled body lying in a ditch.

Stop! Alma admonished herself; your imagination, that's all. Focus on the beauty. There's lots to be grateful for if you were willing to look for it. She drifted again into the memory of her wedding night and the gratitude she'd felt that she wouldn't experience the nervousness and the awkward fumbling of a novice. Grateful, too, that they'd waited until they were man and wife.

She'd been so involved with preparing herself, she hadn't noticed the rain until Mack opened the door of the cabin. Lightning flashed behind him. Thunder rumbled distantly. He moved into the spare room as if propelled by magic. His white towel, wrapped low, covered little. His body glistened with wetness, the muscles of his flat belly looked chiseled. Dark hair coiled above the towel. She opened her mouth and licked her lips as if in anticipation of something delicious. His breath caught. His towel dropped to the floor as he closed the door behind him. Alma could see the desire she felt, in his body. He was ready. She released the straps and her nightie slid down, catching on her hard nipple. In one fluid motion, he approached her and released the strap. He took her breast into his mouth for a moment, her muscles contracted, her back arched in response, then he stood back and looked at her saying not a word. He picked her up and carried her to the bed. Standing over her he stroked her body with his rough hands. She reached eagerly for him to guide him into her, impatient to have him inside. He was hard and moist and as eager as she. He pulled her to the edge of the bed and lifted her close. The rain pounded on the roof of the cabin as if it were a drum roll heralding a crescendo. Pain, searing pain made her push him away.

Alma rolled away from him, burying her face in the pillow. As the pain subsided, shame replaced passion. This is what I deserve, she told herself. Aloud she said, "Give me a minute. We'll try again."

"Wait," Mack said, "I have something that will help." He reached under the pillow for a tube of lubricant. "First time . . . your body is tight. I got some thinking . . . I . . . But . . . You were just so . . . Here." He handed her the tube.

Alma had never seen him so hesitant. And though her heart flooded with love, her desire had been extinguished. She applied the cool, clear salve to herself then reached for him, with slippery hands, teasing, stroking, until he regained, even surpassed, his previous passion for her. Even with the lubricant, her pain was greater. Mack was unable to penetrate, unable to come, the pain like a dousing of cold water for both of them. On the third attempt, she used the lubricant on Mack and her hands to bring him to orgasm. Satiated, he turned from her, but not before Alma glimpsed a fleeting look of disappointment as if he'd found black spots on the long awaited tomatoes in his garden.

Yes, looking at the family of deer, but not really seeing them, yes, there was always something to be grateful for. Grateful that Dr. Galvin, her doctor since childhood, was in his office the day after her perfect wedding. He knew her. He knew her mother and her unsavory reputation. Grateful that he would not allow Mack to be present while he examined her, saying he was the old-fashioned country doctor type. Later, he'd told Mack he snipped her too thick hymen. "She'll be fine in a few weeks. You'll need to be careful, though. She'll be tender and need gentle stretching." That day he'd seemed like a confidant, no, more like a father than her doctor.

The phone startled her. She rushed into the kitchen, grimaced at the pile of laundry and grabbed the phone.

It's not the laundry you need to face.

"Hello." She was relieved to hear her friend's voice.

"Are you ready to tackle the basement today? I have a few hours free."

"I don't think I'll ever be ready, Petra. But today is a good day to start. Come on over. How about a run first?"

"Procrastinating again? You've got to face the basement sooner or later."

"Promise. Today's the day. But, a run first, okay?"

"A run or a marathon?"

"I'll mix up your favorite muffins and we'll run while they bake. How's that?"

"I'll be right there."

Alma had just finished mixing the batter when Petra let herself in the front door.

"Okay, here I am. Pop those muffins in. How long to bake?" As if in answer to the question in Alma's mind, she added, "I was just down the road. I called from my cell phone."

" Oh, cell phone, that's right," said Alma, sliding the muffin tin into a hot oven. She didn't have one, wasn't planning on getting one. She set the timer. "Two and a half miles, tops, at your speed." Despite her years, Alma had the body of a runner—lean, muscular, supple in her shorts and tank top and muddied running shoes.

"Two and a half miles! Are you trying to kill me? Remember me? You were the super-mom track coach. I sit in the office on my butt all day being the blond divorcée computer expert. We're going the back way this time. I'm not up for that hill," said Petra, puffing on a cigarette.

It was true, Alma had coached for the Community Center's girls track team, thinking more about salvaging her relationship with her teen-aged daughter than winning races.

"Track coach, ha! They lost every meet after I became coach, Pete. Sure you don't want to go up that hill?"

Steep Hill Road deserved its name. Alma loved to run up the hill. Instead, they turned to the left and ran along a tree-lined winding road and over the bridge. Alma let Petra set the pace, though she wanted to run faster. She needed those endorphins if she was going to tackle the basement today.

"What a mess, Pete, it'll take months to clean the stuff out of that basement."

"I could never figure out why Mack saved all that junk. I mean, he made good money." Petra was already finding it difficult to talk. She gulped greedily at the air. "Him, rummaging through the town dump." Breathless as she was, she still managed her what-a-jerk look.

"He didn't care who saw him." Alma brushed her hair back from her face as she remembered the day she'd gotten the courage to tell Mack how embarrassed she was.

He'd come home that day looking particularly disheveled. His face and hands were dirty and his shirt torn. The knees of his green work pants were dark with wetness. The back of the truck was filled with a tangle of unidentifiable objects.

"What do you have to be embarrassed about?" he'd said. "Who cares about what anyone else thinks, Alma? We could sell these things, if we ever needed money." As if they were golden, he showed her an old cider jug and a chair with one arm missing and the cane back damaged. "What if the economy got so bad after we retire and the pension and savings were not enough for us to live on? What if there is no Social Security?"

"I care what people think. It's humiliating to know people see you rummaging around the dump. It doesn't make any sense."

"It doesn't make any sense to buy lottery tickets either,

and lots of people in this town do. I wouldn't waste my money on that. All this junk, as you call it, makes more sense to me ... something I can fix, hold on to, put on a shelf, pack in a box, save. Things are more real than a chance to win millions. A person can recover his investment with this stuff— have a garage sale or something. This," he said lifting the broken chair and making a sweeping gesture with it, "all this stuff, that's my lottery ticket. Do you think I'd still be driving this truck if it weren't for junk. No car payments, think about that."

"You never told me that," said Petra. "You haven't talked about him very much. Deciding to go down there—the basement—has loosened your tongue?"

Petra was slowing down. They waved to a passing cyclist. The road curved to the right. The air smelled like pine and cherry blossoms. Petra sneezed twice.

"He was very frugal," Alma said.

Petra stopped running and placed both hands on her hips, gasping for air and then clutching her chest. "Frugal? For God's sake, Alma, ... it's time you faced reality instead of twisting it. The man didn't want to spend money on food, because ...," she panted, " ... he could grow his own. But who did all the work? Let's turn around. There's another hill ahead

... I'd have to crawl on the way back."

Petra's like that, blunt, thought Alma, and I appreciate that. I never have to guess what's on her mind. "Yeah. It was hard work. The garden got bigger each year. But I liked growing our food. The chickens! They were the worst."

Those stinking chickens, Alma thought. They pecked my hands bloody whenever I collected eggs. As much as I hated them, I couldn't kill them. Mack, he'd twist their scrawny necks as easy as if wringing out a washrag.

I'll never forget the day I sold those damn chickens.

It was the hottest day of the summer. The stench of chicken shit in the hen house was so potent it made her eyes water. No one shoveled the stuff off the floor, so it was thick and moist. The rooster immediately attacked her, as he did every time. She swung at him with a rolled up newspaper. She was ready for him that day.

"It's you or me, rooster, and it's not going to be me." She whacked him over the head and he went running. Instead of being scared of her, the hens became aggressive. They charged at her, pecked at her arms and legs. They made a racket, feathers flew.

She sparred with her paper sword, but things only got worse. Now the rooster resumed his attack. Sweat rolled down her forehead into her eyes, stinging and blinding. Knowing she couldn't win, Alma quickly filled her basket with as many eggs as she could get. Her wrists were bleeding; the sitting hens wouldn't give up their eggs without a fight. The rooster charged at her again. She slipped, tossing the basket in the air, in an attempt to gain her balance. She landed on a mixture of broken eggs and chicken shit. It was in her hair, on her arms and legs. On her face.

"That's it! I've had it with chickens." She left her paper sword on the foul floor and went to get another weapon—the phone.

She called Hap Hapner, the red-cheeked chicken farmer who'd offered to buy the chickens a number of times. Mack had refused, but he wasn't home now. Hap was there in an hour. He and his son rounded up those chickens in less time than it had taken Alma to wash the chicken shit out of her hair.

When Mack came home, he was livid. "You had no right to sell my chickens," he raged.

"Your chickens? The only notice you took of your chickens was when you were eating them."

"You probably didn't even get a good price for them. What did you get? How much?" He paced the floor, threw his hands in the air. His voice raised to just a notch below a shout.

"Three dollars each."

"He robbed you. Three dollars each. The going rate is five for good layers."

"Not bad, Mack, considering you didn't pay anything for them. They were William's friend's 4-H project gone wrong."

"Where's the money?"

She gave him one hundred fifty dollars.

Alma and Petra stopped running somewhere in the midst of Alma's chicken sale reverie.

"That's the best thing I ever did, get rid of those chickens. Mack was so mad at me. First time I ever did something behind his back. First big thing, anyway." Alma smiled. She remembered the satisfied feeling she had as she watched those pecking menaces being carted off. How extravagant the cash in her pocket felt. She'd sold them at five dollars a piece.

"But the garden," she nodded, "I enjoyed growing vegetables."

They were silent while Petra fought for her breath. Mrs. McEvoy honked a greeting as she passed in her car. Alma knew a lot of people, but Petra was the only friend she spoke to regularly. The mountains were visible in the distance. Not a cloud in the sky. Petra was sweating profusely. Alma's forehead was a little moist and she breathed easily.

"The vegetable garden was one thing . . . Stop. Walking now. It's supposed to be slower than running," gasped Petra. "Let me catch my breath. . . . You filled your freezer," she wheezed, "as full as you packed those Kerr jars with preserves. You had a veritable grocery of home-grown vegetables. . . . A freezer full of freshly killed chickens and venison. Cookies too, bread and muffins." She stopped, bent forward, put her hands on her thighs to ease her back. "My point is, you make the unwonderful seem wonderful. I used to go along with that, but after what he did . . ." Petra shook her head as they turned into Alma's driveway.

The gravel crunched noisily under their feet. OJ

bounded off the front porch to meet them, her orange stripes contrasting with the green lawn, making her look like a sprinting tiger lily.

"Don't forget who you're talking to," Petra said. "I've been in your kitchen when it was 120 degrees and you were drenched with the strain of canning those vegetables. You weren't having fun then. Pregnant. Babies crying. Jars boiling."

"I remember how good the apple butter tasted."

A fresh baked aroma greeted them when they opened the front door.

"Mmm. Those muffins smell great," said Petra. "Sure, we all liked the apple butter, but look what it took out of you and the kids," said Petra, looking around the kitchen. "Wish this was my kitchen—everything neat, in its place."

Alma slid the muffins out of the oven and filled the tea kettle.

"Ice water, that's what I want. No! Caffeine. Got any coke? Hey," said Petra noticing the empty shelves. "What did you do with it all? All those jars of veggies and applesauce... gone."

"Gave it away a few weeks ago," said Alma. She put the steaming muffins and a dish of ice cold butter on the table.

"Gave it away? See, there's the difference between you and Mack. He'd never give anything away. Sell maybe, but never give away."

"There is this family, you know them, the O'Reillys, six kids, no money. I gave them the chicken from the freezer, too. I threw away the venison though—buried it actually."

"One thing about Mack. For all his faults, he did make this property beautiful with the trees," said Petra opening the door to the back porch but stopped short of stepping out. "Buried?"

"I wouldn't cook that venison for him." She shook her head remembering the deer that visited this morning. "After a while I stopped baking his favorite cake. I told him the butter and lemons were too expensive." Alma was quiet for a moment remembering that he'd been unable to eat it when she'd baked it again to coax his appetite when he was sick.

"He didn't get it, Alma. You were too docile, too agreeable, always the peacemaker."

"I felt bad for him, Pete. He was afraid that some tragedy would leave us wanting. He prepared for the worst. And anyway, what was I going to do with three kids? Get a job? Move out ? He'd never let me go any more than he'd been willing to relinquish the chickens." The butter melted on her hot muffin. She bit into its soft, moist center, soothed by the sweetness. "He had his tender moments. In the spring, he'd bring me huge bunches of wild flowers."

"Wild flowers, right, Alma?" said Petra. "Then he decided he wouldn't spend money to buy clothes."

"Oh, but that was fun," Alma said more out of habit than conviction. "We made our own. Much better than store-bought. And Alicia, don't forget her." Her youngest daughter was so good at it she got a scholarship to study dress design."

But she's right, Alma thought. When they were young, the kids accepted that version of why they didn't go shopping for their clothes. But as they got older, resentment grew. I heard William fighting with Mack. He wanted a "cool pair of sneakers" like the other guys in his class. Mack said no. "You'll be glad we saved money if this country has another great depression like the one you're studying about," he'd told William.

Alma kept her thoughts to herself.

"Okay, you turn everything inside out. Only the benefits show. I envy that. Maybe I wouldn't be alone now if I had been able to see only the good parts and make them the whole. But I can't, there's all that nasty stuff still left inside. So, enough of that. Let's get to the basement. Hey! Today's Grace's birthday. Twenty six, right?"

3

It isn't one of those spring showers that appears out of nowhere and disappears as quickly. It has been raining for days. Just now, as she walks along, all her possessions packed into a pillow case, the rain beats down on her. The lightning seems to come off the mountain and intersect the earth yards ahead of her. She doesn't care, so demanding are the emotions swirling within her. She might as well be generating the lightning herself. Cast away like a well-worn sweater that has become unraveled, that's how she felt. She even forgot it is her birthday, her seventeenth birthday—her one more year to freedom day—until today.

He's ignorant, my father is a moron, besides being a mean person. You should know that better than anyone, *mother*.

Her face screws up, her head shakes mockingly, as she repeats words her father said: "Why does he need to study English? He already speaks English. Learn how to repair a car, that'll make him some money."

How stupid can he get, my father? Raoul is a poet, not a mechanic, or a cesspool digger. That's why he, the Mighty Mack, hates him. My father couldn't possibly understand the sensitive soul of a poet. No one's soul, not even the concept of soul, could he understand because he doesn't have one.

Shoulders and the arm holding the umbrella heave and punctuate as she makes her points to the wind that blows the umbrella inside out, then rights it. Grace doesn't notice the umbrella.

I love him and he loves me. Love, there's another thing Mighty Mack wouldn't understand. He doesn't love anybody. Not me, that's for sure, not you Mom. What he loves is to control everyone and everything. Money, that's what he loves, not spending money. Stashing it away so no one can use it. And all that crap in the basement, that's what he loves. Why do you always side with him, my mother? You never come to my defense. How can you stay with him? He might as well beat you, all of us, the way he rules over us, the way he hurls his pronouncements at us. That hurts just the same as a beating.

It would serve him right if I was run down and killed, she thinks, as another car slushes past. Then they'd be sorry. Better yet, broken bones—then he'd have to spend precious money for the hospital bills.

She edges closer to the shoulder as panic slashes through her. He wouldn't pay the bills, would he? You wouldn't dare write a check, would you, mother? Your penny jar? Ha!

Raoul would never hurt me. He'll be glad to see me. He'll wrap his big, strong arms around me. "Don't worry my little Chica," he'll say, kissing me with those warm, fat lips of his, licking my lips, that place where they turn into moist velvet, swirling his tongue in my mouth. Her breath catches. She starts to run, now. "We have each other," he'll say. "We'll get married and be happy." Happier than Alma and Mack. I'll stay with him, work on the farm, save money. I'll help him with his poetry and he'll love me always.

A soggy coated dog sidles up alongside, tries to share her umbrella. Grace neither greets it nor shoos it away.

I know how *not* to raise children. Raoul and me, we know how to treat kids, how to love them, how to be gentle, how to let their spirits grow. That's what Raoul says is so important for his poetry—freedom to let his spirit soar. We will free each other. Our children will be free.

Grace climbs Steep Hill Road without effort or awareness of the sharp incline. The thought of Raoul thrums in her body. A car speeds by so close the umbrella jerks to one side. Mud splashes on her, drenches her pillow case. Alarmed, she shakes the mud from the crude satchel and opens it.

My track medals. I hope they won't rust. She places the

umbrella on the ground and stands on the strap to keep the wind from whisking it away. She rummages through the bag for something dry to wipe them with. The t-shirts and jeans rolled up in the bottom of the pillow case were wet. *My* clothes. Not the ruffles and lace you'd dress me in, mother. Why can't we buy clothes at Sears, like normal people? Finding nothing dry to wipe her medals with, she holds them in the rain until the mud washes off. More scholarship money, maybe. She pushes them into her jeans pocket.

Mud ripples along a plastic bag stuffed alongside the wet clothes. She quickly removes it from the soggy pillow case, slides it under her jacket.

They're safe. The poems he wrote just for me, confessing his timeless love, no beginning and no end. They're safe. How could I have not gone to him that night. You didn't know that, did you, mom? Didn't even suspect, did you? It was easy to sneak out after everyone had gone to bed.

He's not too old for me. He is the only one who gets me. What does my stupid father know about being too old? He doesn't even know me . . . know how mature I am for my age . . . that I'm a woman. Raoul unfolded my beauty, brought the woman in me to the surface. And I in turn lit his soul with my essence. That's what he told me that night. I am his muse, he said. What does the Mighty Mack know about muses?

Soaked now, she rushes along, eager for Raoul. He will take me in his arms, smooth the wetness out of my hair. I'll let him take my jacket off, then my blouse. He'll loosen my bra and toss it aside. He'll wipe the rain from my breasts with his fingers, lick rivulets as they roll over my nipples down my belly. I'll wiggle my jeans off and he will dry me tenderly, each fold, each crevice carefully explored, warmed by his hot tongue, chilled with his cool hands, warmed again. And I will open myself to him but he will refuse. "Too soon," he'll say, pulling my breast into his mouth as he . . . .

Mrs. McEvoy drives up the hill as Grace walks down the other side of Steep Hill Road. She stops.

"Do you need a ride, Grace?" she asks as the car window slides down. Her windshield wipers fling clumps of cold rain in Grace's face. "You really shouldn't walk in this weather, with this lightning. You're hardly visible. Here, get in."

"No. I'm going the other way."

"I can turn around."

"No. I don't want a ride."

"Be careful." Mrs. McEvoy raises her eyebrows as the car window slowly rises in front of her shaking head.

Should have taken the ride. Maybe she'd have taken me all the way to Raoul's. No, you don't need to take anything from anyone, especially not from her. She thinks she owns the world just because she owns the grocery store. That whole family thinks they are better than anyone else. Cashmere coats and leather boots, that's what her grand daughter wears to school. Grace felt a satisfied sneer creeping onto her face. But I'm the one who got the scholarship, and she's the one who's well dressed, but dumb.

A pair of Nikes, the only decent thing she owns, sloshes around her feet. Ice water squishes between her toes.

They were probably gifts too, that cashmere coat and leather boots. But I didn't get gifts from my parents. A gift for me could have been a ride to the drugstore. But no, I had to stand out in the freezing cold, sleet, snow, to catch a bus to town so I could earn my own gift. Sneakers. One fucking pair of sneakers. A gift from you my saintly mother, could have been you not backing down when you said he shouldn't demand rent from my puny paycheck. I never heard you raise your voice to Mack. Until today. Everything changed today.

"She only makes . . . ," you were shouting as William and I stepped into the living room, arms full of firewood and noses drippy from the cold. But you stopped short as if reluctant to continue in our presence. I could see your lips pressed tightly together, you would wait until we stacked the wood and were ordered to do another chore. But then you stood up and walked right over to him, pointing your finger at him. "NO MORE TWENTY PERCENT! LET GRACE KEEP WHATEVER SHE EARNS. ALL OF IT. IT'S HERS. SHE WORKS FOR IT." You did it. I couldn't quite grasp it. Oh, how many times had I wished for you to come to my defense? And you did it today. You were disturbing the peace today.

"So do I. Who pays my bills? It costs to heat this house, you know. She'll give over her whole check."

Thuds and bangs echoed through the rugless room, as logs tumbled out of my arms. "Would that be my paycheck you're talking about?"

"Look, she's bought her own shoes. Now *you* don't have to. Grace will use her money wisely."

"Wisely? One hundred dollars for a lousy pair of sneakers." He raised his hand to heaven. "Ever think to go to K-Mart? You could have bought shoes for your brother and sister, too."

"I wouldn't wear them," shouted William as he dropped his logs on the hearth in front of the wood burning stove. He opened the latch and threw two logs in. They crackled and hissed as they hit the heat. "I'd get a job too, but you won't let me. I'm your personal slave, doing all the work around here."

"Stop," shouted Alma. "That's enough."

"What did you do with the rest of the money? Spend it on that spic?" Mack never moved or changed his expression. A black pipe with a curved stem clenched between his teeth held the stub of a cigar. It stank even though it was no longer lit.

"I'm saving it for school clothes."

"Clothes!" He rolled his eyes and stood to his full height looking from you to me. "Wisely, huh? Your mother and you make enough clothes. Hand over that money, Grace." In one long stride he was beside me, his dirty, calloused hand extended palm up. "You'll pay more rent now."

Mack never struck any of us, but I backed away.

"No!" I didn't disguise the hatred in my voice.

"You'll do as I say as long as you live under my roof."

Mom, you stood with your hands covering your mouth, eyes wide, head shaking a loud but silent NO.

"That makes it easy, then."

Too late, Mom.

The wind shifts, the rain pelts her as she runs along. To Grace, it seems as if the wind and the rain are trying to come between her and Raoul, just like her father tries to. A picture pops into her mind: The fierce North Wind of nursery rhymes, lips pursed, the strain of blowing showing in its red eyes.

Three more miles. I can do that. Easy for me, track star on the best team in the county, right, Mom? If you were just going to mess up, why the hell did you volunteer to help when coach Rudy broke her leg? Just because you run every day doesn't make you any kind of coach material. What made you think you could coach a group of girls? Because you were already teaching 4 H girls to sew? My perfect sister Alicia is really into sewing, she and you are like best friends. *The Girls,* always working on some sewing project or other.

William, what a weirdo. He wanted to sew too, but the Mighty Mack said no, made him take wood shop. Made him take his friend's chickens when that kid, another weirdo, quit 4 H. Free food, free labor: The house that Mack built was never finished.

But then Grace remembers her mother hadn't wanted to help the track team.

"Why?" Her hands on her hips, chin pushing forward. "Why won't you do it? You don't care about what I like to do. Sewing, sewing, sewing, that's all you care about. Well, I don't like to sew. I run. If you don't help us there will be no track team."

"Grace, I don't want to spoil it for you. I don't know anything about track."

"You run. None of the other mother's run."

"Well, maybe, if you help me. I suppose it's the same thing as 4H. Head Heart, Hands, and Health. I'm a sewing coach and the girls have the ribbons to show for it."

They have ribbons all right and I am like a member of another family. That's why I joined the track team. Better than feeling left out at home.

"It's not like sewing, Mom. GOD!" Grace yanked the rubber band from her pony tail. "We compete, we're out there to win. WIN! We have to be tough. You don't teach those wimpy 4H'ers to win. You're all mushy and wish-washy."

"I help them to believe they can do it—make something beautiful. That will work with track too."

"We aren't beautiful, Mom. We sweat, we stink, we fall and get bloody, we throw up sometimes. Coach Rudy is tough, practice five times a week. Every person on the team has to be there, has to run, limp, hobble whatever. Injuries are no excuse. Your period is no excuse. You? You'd be giving us first aid and showers."

"Grace, if you want me to do this you'll have to help. Tell me what I need to know. You be the coach and I'll be the adult leader. The only reason I'd consider volunteering is because I know how much the team means to you. But we need to do it together."

"They won't listen to me. I'm not one of the popular ones."

"You're the best runner. Coach Rudy told me that."

"So."

So as the sun rose the next morning they huddled against each other on the track at the high school. 5:30 AM! The icicles dangling from the trees didn't even drip. Alma brought jugs full of hot chocolate and marshmallows to put in the mugs.

"No marshmallows," objected Grace. "Hot chocolate is bad enough."

"I'm sure the girls don't eat breakfast before practice. You never do."

"That's not the point, Mom. You're babying them, already, on the first day. You have to be tough, like Coach Rudy. She tells us to eat breakfast, to bring our own drinks. If we don't, that's our problem."

Coach Rudy had no mercy. She expected nothing less than excellence, nothing less than one hundred percent from everybody, no exceptions. Coach Rudy required practice five times a week. And insisted the girls run every day. Every day. And we did.

Tara was late the first morning. But it really doesn't matter, said Coach Alma. The girls just drank the hot chocolate instead of running, except for me and Rose Ann.

"Mrs. MacCallum," said Rose Ann, "make her run an extra two miles and do fifty pushups. Those are the rules."

"Well, this morning we won't have time for that."

"By this time, coach Rudy would have put us through drills, Mrs. MacCallum. After we'd run five miles around the track. Drills like running, stopping, turning, running again, supposedly to help us get off the starting block faster." Rose Ann gave Grace that God-doesn't-your-mother-know-anything look.

The rain continues heavily as Grace runs across a meadow, sloshing in ankle deep puddles. Through a stand of trees she sees Raoul's car in front of the shabby cabin where he lives on Reed's Farm. He is a modern day Thoreau. Nature inspires him. Besides, it's convenient; he is a farm hand and the rent is cheap. He's taking a year off before starting college again, saving for tuition. She'd met him in the drugstore. She'd lent him money a couple of times to get his prescription filled. Pain killers; he has a bad back.

She hears voices inside, hesitates for a moment wondering who was there. Why isn't he working? Friends stop by all the time, any time of the day or night, whether he is home or not. Now that I am moving in, my friends could visit any time, too. I didn't bring food or beer like I'm supposed to. Well, it'll be okay this time. It's different this time. I'm going to the man I'll spend the rest of my life loving.

The wire spring on the screen door hums a tune when she opens it and reaches for the inner front doorknob.

4

Alma reached for the basement's antique doorknob. Mack retrieved it, years ago, from a demolition site. He was searching for discarded fixtures to install in their nearly finished house. He'd cleaned and polished it. She protested when he put it away in a box with other treasures he never looked at again. Save it, he'd told her; it could be valuable, even though it was defective. The knob itself was white porcelain, probably handmade in the 1800's. Tiny cracks wandered across the surface forming a web leading to a circle of delicate pink flowers in the center. But in the dim light of the hallway, the cracks were hardly visible. They made the doorknob more interesting.

She imagined the craftsman who created it. What was he like, she'd wonder? Alma envisioned him tall, silver-flecked hair, bent over a workbench in a shed behind his farmhouse, straining to see under the light of a single candle hung in a battered metal container. Another candle flickered on his littered workbench. Maybe this was a hobby enjoyed at night after he worked the fields all day. Did his wife yell for him to come inside, and stop wasting candles? No, she wouldn't. So great was her love for him, and so fully did he return it, that she'd be concerned only that it was damp and he might catch cold. His hands were warm and supple, though callused, with long fingers, perhaps covered by gloves, the ends cut off so he could feel every nuance as he went about his work. And his art, like his wife, would have responded to his gentle, imaginative touch. He must have had a sensitive soul to create such a beautiful object. One that should be admired and appreciated, flaunted even.

Mack had cussed and grumbled the whole time he fastened it to the basement door. He'd sworn up and down she destroyed its value, that use would chip and stain it, muttering that the old brass fitting couldn't be adapted, would never work right. She was ruining it. He said he'd never show her anything again. She persisted, resisted the temptation to deny her sensibilities once again. Yet, standing up for her opinion, she'd felt quarrelsome and inconsiderate of Mack's feelings.

Now, as she stood here, reaching for the doorknob, she was glad she'd insisted. That doorknob made her smile every time she noticed it, one of her small pleasures.

Except maybe today. Today, her trembling fingers curled around the doorknob. Her heart pulsed in her throat. Moisture formed on her nose and in the space between her breasts. The coolness of the white knob arrested her breathing. Jerking back, away from the door, Alma slammed into Petra, who grabbed her friend's shoulders. She pulled away from Petra.

"Alma. Stop. You have . . ."

"I know, I know." She slumped against Petra, allowing her friend to steady her. She rubbed the place between Alma's shoulder blades, patted her head as if she were a child. Moments passed in silence. Her heart slowed. Breathing resumed. A noisy fly buzzed at the screen door, trying to get in. Or out?

"Do you want to do the laundry?"

"No . . . Yes. It's just that . . . I see pictures in my head . . . of what happened . . . as if it were happening again, now. If I go down there, they'll get worse, they'll never go away. But if I don't . . ."

"Just open the door. That's all. Then decide."

Alma's hand moved toward the door. She pulled back again.

"Do you want me to open it for you?"

"No."

Alma reached for the doorknob with her right hand and with the left released the slide bolt. She noticed the band of white skin branding the middle finger of her left hand. She'd taken the ring off, flung it into the toilet and flushed it away. In a surge of guilt and shame, she thought to call a plumber, but in this small town, it wouldn't be long before tongues wagged.

The door creaked as if it, too, were resistant. A damp, musty odor floated toward her followed by the biting stench of gasoline or maybe kerosene. The stairs disappeared into darkness, a sturdy handrail pointing steeply downward beside narrow steps that were placed too far apart into parallel two-by-eights that sloped from the first floor to a crude landing flush against the cinder block wall of the basement. Then two more steps on each side of the landing. The basement was on the right, the garage on the left. The only division between the two spaces was the ladder-like stairs suspended from the first floor, but they hadn't always been there. The basement smelled like home then—before the stairs.

"This is home for now," he said. Mack built the foundation, adding electricity and plumbing, before they were married. The weather turned cold as he put up the floor joists, hefty pieces of lumber, two by ten by fourteen feet, to hold the first floor. He was in a race with winter, getting that first floor in place. It was their roof; they spent the winter in the basement of their new home. The bathroom was the only enclosed space. Alma had never appreciated running water and a toilet so much—a real toilet, with no spiders and no outhouse stink.

They'd lived in the shanty, more like a style-less box-shaped cottage now. She didn't mind some of the hardships. It was like an extended camping trip, she told herself. Mack built the outhouse just for her comfort. And a barbecue pit for cooking. He even bought *new* lanterns, a gas camp stove and a second-hand bed. Just for her, to make the place like home. No one had ever done so much for her.

Alma admired Mack's determination. He'd done most of the work himself, nights and weekends. Reluctantly, he'd had to hire someone to dig out the foundation and another person to pour concrete for the floor. A friend helped from time to time, when Mack found it impossible to do something himself. Someone he'd known since he was ten, George. Another friend helped, a co-worker. Mack had helped him dig a septic tank the year before and repair his roof. The owner of the lumber store in town offered to help. So did other townsfolk.

"Don't need them," was all Mack said when Alma urged him to accept their offers.

And this basement apartment did feel like home compared to the room she'd been renting when they'd met—a bed, a chair, a shared bathroom, the odor of grease and cigarettes seeping under her door. A landlord who visited too often in the evening. She never had a real home. Her mother was single. Her father abandoned them before she was born. Alma and her mother had lived in apartments, rooming houses, and with friends, moving frequently, most times to avoid paying rent. Until her mom met a man who stayed.

Mack was building a house for her. It would be a big house with lots of windows and a beautiful slate fireplace. She'd imagine herself sitting in her living room, a blazing warmth radiating from the fireplace, rocking her firstborn as she nursed him. They'd be so happy.

Mack won the race with winter the day he moved their bed from the shanty. "Just in time," he'd said. "The roofing paper's on. We're sealed in, ready for snow."

He wore a cotton turtleneck sweater and a black windbreaker. Heavy black leather boots laced up well past his ankles. Jeans were tucked inside. No gloves or hat. He never wore a hat no matter how cold it got. And that day it was thirty-seven degrees. He'd been working outdoors all day, first on the roof and then moving their belongings from the shanty, and chopping wood. He added logs to the pile beside the wood stove. There was another stack in the corner and more under a tarp just outside the door. "I'll chop more. We might need it if a blizzard shuts the power off."

"Let me help, then. I can use an ax. We'll..."

"No. That's my job. You unpack the boxes. Put the dishes away."

Though he closed the door quickly behind him, a draft of cold air chilled Alma. She wanted to follow him out. Tell him they were a team, they could work together. None of this his job, her job stuff. Making a home was something they'd do together. Something she'd wanted all her life. She wanted to be near him, closer, even, than when they had sex, to feel his warmth in the things they did together, know his thoughts. It wasn't just a matter of unpacking. She wanted to ask him: Wouldn't a couple of overstuffed chairs look nice in the living area? Where did he think the table should go? She wanted him to need her at his side, but it seemed like he'd drawn away from her after they'd married.

But she didn't tell him these thoughts. Instead she told herself not to be so silly. You don't want to chop wood. We *are* happy. Things *do* change after you're married, that's to be expected. There's a lot to do to get the foundation ready to live in. Why are you being so ungrateful? You're selfish, thinking only of yourself. Look around you, this is your home. Put a little color in this drab place instead of wanting to go out in freezing weather and chop wood. Dress up those cinder block walls. Candles, lots of candles. Be thankful for hot water and the furnace that keeps you warm in here. Set up your sewing machine. You love to sew. Now that you have electricity make something nice for Mack, a tweed sport coat. And stop wondering why he needs so much wood, too. Pick, pick, pick. Aren't you ever satisfied?

She didn't feel like unpacking dishes. She put her down parka on, leather boots, scarf, hat, mittens and went for a walk.

McEvoy's, the only store in town, owned and operated by the McEvoy family, was a combination post office, grocery, dry goods, hardware store, and gossip central. This particular Saturday afternoon, it functioned more as the latter. In the one corner around the pot-bellied stove, sat

Alfy Stodder, Herby Fortner, and Clyde Baker, who was stinking up the place with a cigar and gesturing wildly as if they'd been arguing town politics. All of them town relics. Their heavy jackets were slung over the backs of the chairs. The men wore overalls, except for Herby who wore green work pants, a flannel red plaid shirt, and wide orange suspenders. Picking over some fabric scraps were Alfy's wife Hildy, Herby's sister Wanda, and Frieda Baker who was in charge of the gossip. No doubt they were discussing the County Quilt Club versus their own and surely far superior small group, or the state of somebody's marriage, or hair-do. All conversation stopped as Alma entered.

"Nice to see you out, taking some air," said a voice from behind her. Alma'd walked in, smiled at the women, but moved on quickly to the Post Office window without making eye contact.

Alma turned to see Frieda Baker and groaned inwardly. Frieda was the sort who got right into a person's space. She had this syrupy-sympathetic look on her face. Sappy really, her head tilted to one side. Her whole body said, Oh, you poor thing. You can tell me all your sorrows. I'll understand. Alma could smell her cigarette breath and unwashed hair.

"How are you, my dear?" She looked right at Alma's bulging stomach. "Anything new?"

"I'm fine, thanks, Mrs. Baker. And you?"

Frieda stepped back to better assess Alma's figure. "Nothing new with you, hey? I see you're building. Planning to live in the basement, are you?" She continued her survey of Alma's enlarged profile. "Just happened to drive by and notice Mack capping the foundation. No one around here's ever done that kind of thing before."

Alma knew the house couldn't be seen from the road.

"Yes, we are," replied Alma, reluctant to give her additional information

"Well, aren't you the clever one. You in your condition, still living in the shack in the woods?"

"It's a cottage, Mrs. Baker, not a shack."

"Oh, then you've put in running water, and a bathroom."

"No, Ma'am."

"Well, that's a shack then. Living in a shack. Mack lived there before you, you know. Strange kid, that one."

"Alma," Petra shook her gently. "You going to daydream forever?"

They were still standing before the open basement door. One dim bare bulb lit the staircase. Petra led the way.

"Petra, be careful," Alma said, "these steps are dangerous. They're so cluttered."

Something that sounded like an empty tin can tumbled down the steps, thumping here, clanging there, until it reached the bottom, chinked against the cinder block, and stopped. Bottles, jars, jugs, stacks of magazines, newspapers, rusty old cans of paint, and tools filled the steps so that they were nearly impassable.

"Oh God, look at this mess," Petra said as she started down. "So dangerous. So inconsiderate. No more room in the basement to store his junk so he loads up the stairs," she said, grabbing an armful of newspapers. "The first thing we're going to do is splurge on a brighter light bulb and clear off these steps."

The washer was on the right, in the basement, but to get there they had to negotiate the stairs. "No. Laundry's first."

"It's tempting to just kick this garbage off the stairs and let it fall through the spaces onto the floor," said Petra.

"Don't. I don't know what's in those jars."

"At least let's pick up the newspapers and magazines. Put them in the barrel to burn. Okay?"

Petra tossed the newspaper bundle up into the hallway. "Here grab those cans. Just put them in the hallway and we'll figure out what to do with them later."

Petra made her way backwards down the stairs. Back and forth, handing things to Alma, as she cleared a wider path through the center of the stairs. "We'll get more on our way up. This handrail is still like new, steady as the day

Mack put it in. That man sure could build anything he set his mind to."

Down the stairs and out of sight, Petra shouted, "Where's the detergent? Is it still in your car? No, hold on, there's some here." Alma heard a loud bang. "It's one solid clump," she said as she dropped the box on the floor then slammed it against the steps. "It'll do."

Alma remained on the upper level, hugging the bundle of sheets and towels and clothes. The laundromat's not so bad, she thought. You don't have to do this. Just tell Petra some other day, you'll do it next week, that you're not ready. She could hear the water splash into the washer. She was surprised at how welcome it sounded.

"All right," Alma whispered, expelling all her breath with the words, "It's okay."

She encouraged herself down one step, arms filled with dirty clothes, then stumbled. She sat on a step. I used to run up and down these with a baby on my hip, she thought. Mack took them two at a time.

"Daddy, Daddy," William's voice was so excited. "I'm going to help Daddy," he announced with a grin so broad all his teeth showed. "Daddy said I could hammer with the real hammer." Toy hammer in hand he ran past her, to the open basement door, those skinny little bruised legs in blue shorts going as fast as they could.

"Hurry up." Mack's voice came from below. "I'll have the job done by the time you get here."

"Wait. Wait for me, Daddy."

"Slow down, William. Stop running," said Alma.

"I'm in a hurry, Mom, but don't worry. I be back soon's I'm done." His dark hair so long it hung over his forehead and into his eyes.

Alma remembered the sound of his body, thumping, banging, and bumping as he tumbled down the stairs.

"My arm, my arm." He screamed with the pain. "It hurts."

Alma flew down the stairs. Mack scooped William up in

his arms. He took the steps two at a time, ran into the kitchen and carefully sat his son on the counter beside the sink.

"My arm," the boy screamed, unaware of the blood oozing from his face, the right side scraped raw by the cinder block wall. Alma winced at the sight and turned her eyes away for a moment.

"It looks broken, Mack," said Alma, crying too, wanting to hold her son. "His arm. It's bent, funny. Looks curved."

"Kids don't break bones, Alma. Now hold still," he said to William, "while I clean off your face. And don't make a sound. Shh. That's enough out of you." He positioned himself between the child and his mother.

William whimpered, screwing up his face, lips pressed tight together, as he tried not to cry. Mack gently rinsed the boy's face with water, the child's shoulders heaving with swallowed sobs. Slowly, with care, Mack cleaned the wound quietly making shushing sounds.

He's good at this, thought Alma. Better in a crisis than I am. He can be so tender and gentle. This is the Mack I love.

"Shh, Shh," Mack's voice a soft whisper. "You'll be okay. This is too big for a Band-Aid, son. Hold the paper towel against your face till it stops bleeding." Mack didn't ask Alma to do it; he knew she couldn't handle blood.

"I can't. My arm hurts." He started screaming again, holding his arm against his body with the other one, the blood dripping on his red and white striped shirt.

Alma forced herself to hold the paper towel in place.

"Let's call the doctor, Mack. It should be x-rayed."

"He'll be all right. Doesn't need a doctor. It's just bruised." His arm was turning a bright shade of purple just below the elbow.

"Here, give me your arm, I'll wrap it up for you."

"No, don't touch it," screamed William." Then regaining control, "It'll be okay in a few minutes, Daddy."

"That's a good boy."

But it wasn't okay. Alma took William to the emergency room at two in the morning, so painful and swollen was the arm.

"We're lucky he didn't fall off the side of the stairs or between them, onto the junk you have under there. I want you to enclose the stairs or at least put a handrail up."

Mack refused.

"He needs to toughen up," he'd said.

Toughen up, Alma thought, as she stood up again, pressing the laundry to herself and tried to regain her balance on the basement stairs. He was only four. "Well, he's tough enough now, she said to Mack, as if he could hear her. He hates you."

Petra's voice rose from below, "You all right?" Not waiting for an answer, she asked, "Where's the laundry?" She said it as if it were any old day in an ordinary week. Petra's cavalier attitude made Alma feel annoyed at herself. That propelled her down the remaining steps.

"Well, here you are," Petra said. "Still living and breathing. Let's do it, woman. Don't you think it's about time you bought yourself a dryer? Three kids and no dryer. Still hanging the clothes around the house in the winter, are you?" Shaking her head in disbelief. "You are the only person I know who doesn't have a dryer or a dishwasher. Do you know we're in the twentieth century? And what is that god-awful stink down here? Smells flammable to me." Petra rattled on as she moved to the left side and opened the garage door, leaving Alma on her own.

No sirens sounded in her mind, her hands didn't feel wet and sticky with blood. I *am* still living and breathing. Today is *today*. Not another day. Not *that* other day. Alma focused on the washing machine and the laundry. Not by habit, but by thought and intention, she sorted the dirty clothes into piles, refusing to allow herself to think about anything else; whites in the machine, darks on the floor there, colors here. But that other day trickled in, despite her efforts to concentrate.

Last time she'd been down here there'd been policemen. Sirens wailed outside, her daughter, Alicia, screamed. She wouldn't let herself think about that now, wouldn't see it again, wouldn't hear those sounds, or remember those feelings. Not now. It's a different day. It *is* an ordinary Tuesday, spring-time. Laundry day.

5

Alma reclaimed her basement. Fear, she decreed, would never paralyze, never drain her energies, again. Several trips to the town dump and the stairs were relieved of their stowage, nothing was spared. She was ruthless, dauntless in the disposal. The laundromat? Ha! She waved the thought away with the back of her hand.

Petra helped, but only on weekends. They cleared a path through the basement and garage. Newspapers and magazines disintegrated into black smoke as they burned in barrels. Unidentifiable pieces of wood and furniture parts met the same fate.

Today, Petra churned up a dust storm in the garage; Alma was on the other side. They'd worked for a few hours.

"Alma, I think if we do nothing more today, we ought to move this stuff to the tool shed," said Petra. "There's kerosene, gas and paint thinner. I think some of it's leaked into the concrete floor. What the hell was he thinking when he stored these chemicals here?" A sound like a crude steel drum tossed aside echoed through the garage. "That one's empty. It looks like this red one could be acid." Another thud. "The oil tank has a leak. I think that's what smells."

Alma heard Petra's voice, but the words floated by. The only light seeped into the far side of the basement through the open garage door and two small windows close to the ceiling. The air was rank. Spider webs clung to her arms and stirred her skin as if it were crawling. The washing machine sounded reassuringly normal.

The basement was packed as full as it could be. Metal shelves slouched under the weight of their burden. Boxes stacked everywhere, some with scrawled writing advertising the contents. It looked as if a family of six had moved in, then left without unpacking. No! Not that neat.

As her eyes became accustomed to the light, she could see oil lamps; old tins and ceramic cider jugs of various shapes and sizes; wagon wheels that looked like they'd responded to the proclamation, "Go West young man;" broken pieces of furniture that Mack intended to repair and refinish; bits of interesting looking wood; discarded tools awaiting restoration; parts for this and that, in case something broke down; several lawn mowers standing tall anticipating repair. Box after box of powdered milk and institutional sized cans of vegetables and meat. Alma was shocked at the amount of food Mack hoarded.

Did you never wonder what was piling up down here?

She knew the garage side was just as bad. But on this side, one corner had been cleared, recently painted and stood in stark contrast to the rest of the basement. A surge of panic sliced through Alma like a bolt of electricity. Time to get out of here, she thought. Alma stood and stretched, arched her back to relieve tired muscles. She turned to look for Petra only to bump into her.

"Let's see what's in these boxes," said Petra. She opened one. "Bottles. It's all bottles. This one, too."

Bolstered by Petra's presence, Alma made her way though a small passage between stacks. She took a box from the top. Opened it, focusing more on her breathing than the box, trying to stay calm, despite a growing anxiety. She heard Petra humming quietly. Alma watched her friend for a few minutes and tried to relax. *Nothing ruffles her. I wish I could be so easy-going, so confident.*

As Petra organized boxes of bottles, she quietly inventoried her find. Old bottles. Tall bottles and short, square, round and squiggly. Unusual colors too, lavender and blue. Listening to her friend's voice as if it were a radio in the background, Alma felt motivated to continue.

"There has to be hundreds of bottles down here, Alma. Too bad they were stuffed in boxes under layers of dust where no one could see them. Look at these! Old ink wells, they're unusual. Wow! Look at this one. Oh gross, my hands are filthy."

As Alma worked, throwing some things in a big black plastic bag, re-packing others, labeling, Petra's words drifted through her consciousness as if they were fragments of fragrance on a breeze that required no response.

"Hey! You're awful quiet. What're you doing over there?" Petra moved closer. "What's wrong, Alma? Memories?"

Alma squatted crouched in a corner, hemmed in by mounds of debris and windowless walls, her eyes not believing what they saw, as if she'd seen a ghost. "I've been sorting through boxes of tins." She sighted. "The kind that used to be filled with candy, cookies, fruit cakes. . . most of them so rusty and battered I've thrown them in the trash bag. I . . . um . . . ," Alma fought for control. "I opened this one because it . . . it was so pretty." She held a Christmas green tin up to the light. On its cover a serene winter scene with a horse-drawn sleigh carrying a young, smiling couple. Inside, a thick stack of five-hundred-dollar bills. "I . . . I . . . almost threw it out."

Petra gasped.

"All that scrimping, doing without . . . Why? . . . all that so he could hide . . . hoard his money?"

"Is there more, do you think? Let's get those tins out of the trash bag," Petra said, shaking the trash bag spastically creating a strange tin melody.

"I don't know. I don't want to know. I have to get some air. I have to breathe fresh air." Alma stood suddenly, bills falling to the floor. She heaved her way through the clutter, climbed up over the landing. She raced out of the garage and down the slope to the driveway. There probably is more. Hidden who knows where, she thought. It's possible I've burned some. Money going up in smoke. "Ha, Mack!" Her voice seemed to bounce off the trees. "How do you like that? Money going up in smoke."

As if in response, noisy mud wasps buzzed around, adding a new level to the nest they'd hung from the eaves over the garage. They dived at her as she stomped back and forth. An eddy of anger, not completely unfamiliar, rushed over the rapids of her discovery. She needed to run it off.

Long, with a gentle slope, the gravel driveway curved about a quarter of a mile toward the road. She crossed the road to the mailbox. But instead of getting the mail she continued to run, up Steep Hill Road and back. That wasn't quite enough to erase the image of sequestered money or block nagging questions from fully forming. "What was I?" She shouted to the wind. Another object salvaged and stored? Another acquisition, possessed, but hidden like beautiful bottles in a box? Hidden beneath the lives of my family? Another something to have on hand? "What am I Mack?" She ran up the hill and back again.

A post, made from the limb of a tree, held the oversized mailbox. Beyond the mailbox brush and grasses, trees and wildflowers grew free from the control of mowers and bailers. She pulled open the flap door, slammed it shut, intending to slam it a few more times, but the muted sound was unsatisfying. Hand trembling, she opened it again and reached in. Holding the bundle of mail in her hand, she saw a card with no return address and one envelope proclaiming her a winner.

"Trash, All trash," she said out loud. Ah! A letter from her daughter. Joy, a little spark of joy. She'd save Alicia's letter for later putting it in her pocket. Later, with a cup of tea. She turned and started toward the house again aware of how she'd look if someone saw her talking to herself, shouting, running the hill like a mad-woman.

Alma had neighbors, a couple about her own age to her right, strangers almost, though they'd lived there for twenty years. A new family down the road to her left. She could see neither house from where she stood. As she rounded the curve, she observed her house as if for the first time—a drab rectangle sliced into the side of a hill, the front and sides of the foundation underground. Brown shingles, dull brown wood siding with no grain or variation in texture. Her house. Her box?

"There you are. I've been looking all over for you," said Petra.

"I'm sorry, I needed to get out of there." Alma said, clamping down on her emotions, not wanting to think or feel anything and certainly not wanting to talk. But that old trick—turning off her thoughts and feelings, looking on the bright side— didn't work this time. "What do you think, Petra?" Alma gestured toward the house. "Is that my box? Did he pack me away just like he packed his junk?" Like his money, rendered useless in a rusty tin? She strode toward the garage, then back. "Is that why my Grace left home, hardly more than a baby? She bolted because she saw the lid closing on her, too?" Alma shouted at her friend, her voice echoing, neighbors forgotten. Petra, mouth open, eyes wide with amazement, was speechless for once.

"Shit!" Alma threw her hands in the air letting the breeze catch the mail. "When I find the rest, I'll burn it all, Mack, like it was scrap paper!" She grinned, nodding her head, heading toward the garage again, needing something to do with her hands. "Help me put another load in the washer, then we'll take that stuff to the tool shed. We are going to get rid of this garbage, all of it."

"I'll stay here," Petra lit a cigarette, "and try not to blow up the place." She looked over at the ignitable wheelbarrows. "Go on, you don't need me to help you. I need a break," she said without malevolence.

"I'll be right back," Alma called over her shoulder, trying to keep the tears out of her voice.

We lived in that foundation for two winters, she thought, slam, slam, slamming the lid of the washer a few times. Slam. *Two winters.* Slam. The sound was much more satisfying than the mailbox. You said we needed to save money and to pay off the loan we took, couldn't stand the thought of owing anything to anybody. Is that when you started hiding money, that first winter, when William was born?

"Nineteen degrees. Big snowstorm due tonight," Mack said. They stood on the cap of the foundation battered by the north wind, shoveling snow. It felt more like nineteen below to Alma. A black ski mask covered her face. Red and white circles outlined the mouth and eye openings. Vertical stripes defined her nose. Streams of breath became visible in the air and sculpted ice crystals around the red and black incision that formed the mouth. Her hands were covered with two layers of mittens. She wore a red wool hat over the mask and a heavy scarf around her neck pulled up to her mouth and tucked into her coat, a heavy down parka under which she'd put several layers of sweaters. The parka didn't close over her large belly. Long-johns and a pair of stretchy knit pants tucked into bulky snow boots that came to her knees. She stood with both hands pressed to the small of her back as she arched to ease the ache.

Mack worked without stopping. He was hatless and wore no gloves. A windbreaker topped a wool sweater. The more you wear, the more you sweat, he'd told her when she urged him to dress more warmly. The more you sweat, the colder you'll feel.

"We have to get this snow and ice off the roof. Can't let it build up. When it thaws, we might get water below."

The task was all but impossible. A thick layer of ice hid beneath a mantle of fresh snow. Alma swept the top layer off. Mack chopped at the ice. The air around them was crisp and clean. The brilliant sun belied the forecast of another snowstorm, but didn't melt a drop to make their job easier. Stillness blanketed their world: the quiet snow brings. The only sound was the crunching of ice underfoot and the scraping of shovels. And an occasional snap of a limb breaking.

Alma worked as long as she could. Finally she went below; she had to rest. Their baby was due any day and she'd already had two episodes of false labor. She stepped off the foundation, walked carefully, ice crunching beneath her feet, around the side where the garage doors were covered with tar paper, to the back. She opened the sliding glass door, welcomed by a surge of warmth. She peeled off layers, hung her coat on the hook next to the door and extracted her frozen feet from the boots. She stood by the wood stove and undressed completely. Mack is right, she thought. I am sweaty and cold. A hot shower is what I need.

The water thundered against the metal sides of the crude shower stall; the shower head, though, was the best they could buy. She adjusted it to massage and stepped into the steaming downpour. She let the water beat against her lower back to relax the spasms. Should have stopped sooner, she thought. She adjusted the water flow to a more steady stream and sudsed her hair with herbal shampoo. Rosemary and lavender, the fragrance soothed her. She lavished her skin with creamy body wash using a net scrubby she'd made. Her hands glided over her rounded stomach. The skin was stretched smooth and wetness made it glisten. Her belly button was completely popped out as if it were a weak spot in an inner tube. The baby moved beneath her hand. There you are, she thought. I've been worrying about you. You've been so still today. Did you get cold out there?" A kick, as if in response, raised a bulge on her belly. "I can't wait to meet you. I just know you are a boy, William. I hope you don't have red hair like mine. It looks funny on a boy. But take your time, little one. It's supposed to snow tonight. I'll build a snowman for you tomorrow and take its picture, so when I tell you about it, you can see what your first snowman looked like. We'll build one together someday.

She dressed quickly: A long green wool turtleneck sweater over a cotton shirt. She didn't want to itch. Pants were a problem. She cut the seam of her maternity pants then pinned looped-together rubber bands to the waist. Heavy cotton socks and wool slippers kept her feet warm. The floor, despite the braided rugs that covered it, was always cold. She looked around their bedroom. She'd hung strips of fabric over the unattractive, lifeless gray cinder block walls to add color and warmth. Soft blues, lavender, rose and green in the bedroom. Some were solid, some prints. Poles and rods, here and there, exhibited their clothes as if wall hangings, adding texture and insulation. She had strung white Christmas tree lights from the floor joists and timbers in every room. But here in their bedroom the lights were pale yellow to mimic the morning sun. A small window, high against the ceiling, admitted daylight. Before leaving the bedroom, she lit a candle on her night stand and another on a shelf. Mack had lectured her about wasting candles, but she enjoyed their fragrance and flickering light.

She trudged, baby weight weary, into the kitchen to start dinner, her favorite jazz radio station emitting music too peppy for her. Pots and pans hung about the stove looking like musical notes to be hummed while stirring. One undressed sliding glass door let in the brilliant snow-light. Shelves hewn from scrap lumber bore a jaunty display of dishes, cans, bottles and bags. A table and mismatched chairs—ladder-backs, cane-backs, high and low— described the dining area. They'd refinished them together, laughing and teasing each other as they tried to make them look like a set.

Alma reached into the refrigerator for the meatloaf she'd made earlier and a spasm grabbed her low back. Must have pulled something, she thought. She sat in a wooden rocker Petra had given them. The pain passed; she put the meatloaf in the oven. She scrubbed potatoes to bake. She cut a variety of fresh vegetables and put them in a double boiler to steam later, all the while trying to decide how she'd cover the insulation Mack put over the inside of the garage doors. Petra had suggested pasting the Sunday comics there. She was joking, but an idea was germinating. Wallpaper, maybe. She might persuade the wallpaper shop owner to give her some scraps. When she'd told Mack her idea, he'd laughed, "You expect him to *give* them away? Don't pay good money for leftover useless wallpaper. We're only going to be here for one winter. Just ignore the way it looks."

But she already had too much to ignore. Cold floors, dim lighting, make-shift everything. And a husband who seemed more involved with the mechanics of the house than the baby to come. She sat down in the family room area and picked up the afghan she was crocheting. Afghans were fast and easy to make. She got up, turned on the TV, hoping to catch the weather report. She could hear Mack still on the roof, his boots crunching on the icy snow, his steps heavy and pounding. She turned to look out the sliding glass door in the kitchen. The sky was gray.

The TV was another one of Mack's finds. He'd picked it up from the side of the road. He'd been willing to spend money to get it repaired. Televisions were more worthy than wallpaper, or lamps, or the washing machine she'd said she needed. Stop! She shouted inside herself. Bitch, bitch, bitch, is that all you do? Just ignore it. Be grateful for what you have, she said to herself. Your own house. It'll be finished next year this time. And it's nice and warm. Well, not the floor, but I can put my feet up.

"The weatherman said there is a blizzard on the way," she told Mack when he came in. "It's already snowing downstate. I saw it on the news. Five inches this morning."

"Yup. It's warmed up some out there. It's already snowing."

Alma got up to put a pot of coffee on. The baking meatloaf smelled delicious. She stopped short, put her hand to her back again. She glimpsed Mack watching her, but he lowered his gaze without a word. She stretched and felt better in a few minutes.

Alma went to bed as soon as she finished the dinner dishes, feeling unusually drained, her backache worse. Mack rubbed some Bengay on it. He'd filled the hot water bottle and brought it in. "Here, this will help the two of you to relax. That back's been bothering you all day."

"Must have pulled a muscle," Alma said. How could she possibly think he didn't care about the baby, she asked herself? "You're so sweet."

Mack had once suggested having the baby at home. He joked, saying he could deliver it himself. He'd had experience birthing cows when he worked on Reed's farm. Mr. Reed didn't call a vet. "'Tis a natural thing, boy," he'd said. "Nature does all the work. Never lost a cow yet. Only need a vet if something goes wrong. Sometimes you need an extra set of hands, though. That's you, kid. OK?"

"Heck, I was willing," Mack told Alma. "He paid me extra when I had to go there at night. Got so's I could tell when one was getting ready. I'd just stay the night. Mrs. Reed was a great cook."

"Well, forget that. I'm going to the hospital at the first twinge," she'd told him. And that's what she did. Twice. False alarms, both. She wasn't even dilated.

Alma awakened, startled by a loud thump on the roof. The wind was howling wildly around the foundation. Something fell on the roof. A piece of roofing paper must have come free. She could hear it flapping against the cinder block wall. She looked at the clock. Two A.M. Mack wasn't beside her. She got up to go to the bathroom. It was so dark she didn't see the blood stain on her underpants. Her back hurt again, another spasm, more intense, but it went away in a few moments. She shuffled out to the family room, Mack was reading. He quickly closed the book and tucked it beside him.

"How's the back?" he asked. "Better?"

"No. Would you put some more Bengay on it? Storm starting?"

"Been at it a while. Go back to bed. I'll fix the hot water bottle, too," he said.

She slept until four. Awakened with a gripping pain across her back. It built in intensity, demanded her attention. She moaned. It felt like her back was going to break. Mack was asleep beside her. She wondered if she could be in labor, but she had no pain in her belly at all. It felt tight, but didn't hurt. She had started to read *Childbirth Without Fear* early in her pregnancy. But it scared the daylights out of her and she didn't finish it. The doctor told her to time contractions and when they were five minutes apart, to call him. First babies aren't in a hurry, he'd said. Well, she'd done that twice. Felt pain in her low abdomen, timed them, called the doctor, went into the hospital. Got sent home. She didn't want to do that again. Especially since she'd pulled a muscle shoveling. That's what hurt.

The wind battered the house with such force she felt its impact. She stood up to go to the kitchen and look out the sliding glass door. A gush of water rushed from her and the pain struck again, building to such unbearable intensity she cried out. When the pain subsided, leaving as gradually as it had built up, she tried to sit on the bed but found she couldn't, she felt something between her legs. The baby's head? Her heart pounded harder then the wind that rammed their shelter.

"Mack," she screamed. "For God's sake, wake up."

He bolted out of bed. "You're having the baby," he said. This, not a question, Alma realized later.

"I think . . . my water broke. Oh God! . . . Another one's starting." More water gushed. "Help me lay down. Call the doctor. No. Don't leave me."

Mack lifted her onto the bed. "Okay. It's okay, Alma. Breathe. You're not breathing. The book said breathe, pant like a dog."

"Dog?" She glowered at him. She dug her fingernails into his arm. "Dog?" In a few moments the contraction subsided. "You read the book." He nodded.

Mack got the gooseneck lamp from his work bench. He pulled up her legs, "Help me," he said. "Bend your knees." He put the lamp on the bed, turned it on, its beam directed between her legs.

"Call the doctor. Get me to the hospital."

"Phone's been out for hours."

"Oh, God. Get me out of here, Mack."

"Can't. Car's buried. Hold still. Let me look."

"What do you see?"

"Moisture, some blood. Your body's opened slightly. The whole area's bulging."

"Another one. Here comes another pain. Help me, Mack. I can't stand it." She moaned, long, low and primal.

"Shh. Don't talk. Grab hold of the headboard and pull on it. Breathe."

She did as he said.

As the contraction built, he said, "You open wider when the pain comes. Something inside looks like black lines with two furrows going crosswise. What the heck?"

"What do you mean? What's wrong?"

"I didn't get this close a look before, at Reed's. Not sure." He sprang to his feet and paced beside the bed, his hands cupping his head.

"Not sure?" Alma shouted, raising on her elbows.

"Not sure about the breathing. Pant during the contraction or after?"

The contraction went away. Alma was sweating profusely. He wiped her face with the sheet.

"I'll get the book. And some water for you," he added.

"No, don't leave me."

"Have to. Need the flashlight. We could lose the lights."

"Candles. We have lots of candles, too. Light them all."

"Wood in the stove, too," he said. "And scissors on to boil. Mr. Reed always took precautions against infection."

He returned with a large flashlight that he put beside the goose neck lamp. "Candles."

"Be careful, Mack. Not too close to the walls. Here it comes again, another contraction."

A calm had swept through her. There was nothing to do but have this baby here in her own bed. "Get towels under me, Mack," she shouted before the pain got so bad she couldn't speak. Instinctively, she took a deep breath, held it and pushed down with all her might.

"The head. It's the head. It's coming." He gently stretched the lower part of her vagina as he'd seen Mr. Reed do. 'So's she won't tear,' he'd said.

The contraction abated. The head retreated a little. Another contraction.

The wind howled around their fortress in the hill. Whistling and whooshing then changing direction and slamming. She could see the Christmas lights above, twinkling like stars in the night. The fabric she'd hung on the walls was rippling, like a sea of muted color, responding to air from the baseboard heater. Her nightgown was drenched; the pillow damp and cold.

Without a reprieve, another contraction incarcerated her body. Pain seized her low back and cleaved her from any other reality. Alma clutched the headboard with both hands. When the contraction built to the peak of intensity, she sucked in a full breath and pushed with all her might. The lights went out.

"Where is the damned flashlight?" Panic filled his voice. He scrambled about, patting the sheets and the floor around the bed.

The room was dark as a cave: complete absence of light. Alma couldn't see her hand as she raised it to suppress a scream. The scream was silenced and her breath taken away by another contraction. Still holding the headboard, she moaned through the effort of pushing that was no longer under her control.

"Here it. . .Shit! God damn it, Alma, I told you to put new batteries in this." A loud crash sounded, as if he threw it across the room.

"Batteries . . . kitchen . . . ," she whispered when the pain subsided, "box . . . third shelf . . . by stove." She sighed with exhaustion. "Candles . . .there, bookshelf, matches. . ."

She knew he'd disapproved of her use of candles. "Not enough light for the price," he'd said. "Who needs to buy the smell of Soft Breeze? Step outside and take a breath of fresh air. Pure. And free."

She could hear him fumbling, swearing, books thudding to the floor and finally a dot of light emerged from the other side of the room.

"Too short, now that we *need* it," he accused. She could hear his careful strides toward the kitchen bumping into the chair, tripping over the wastebasket, swearing as he went. "Better be the right size."

"More candles . . . Look . . . Mack. No! Don't leave me."

The little dot of light moved farther and farther away, till there was none.

Alma knew she could put her hand right on those candles if she could get there. She inched her heels over to the side of the bed, raised up on her elbows. Another pain coiled around her, low in her pelvis, then slowly crept up, mounting in intensity as it rounded the mountain of her belly. A guttural, primal sound surrendered itself, one more in the collective voice of birth. She gripped the headboard with both hands, held her breath and pushed. Nothing existed except pain and the need to push.

Her body yielded. The baby, large, lumpy feeling, forcefully gushed from her.

"Mack, help me," she screamed, trying to sit, reaching for the baby.

The wind ceased its cry, creating a sudden silence. No light; no sound. Her hand touched the baby, smooth, slippery, wet: tummy, legs, feet. Neck? Face, she could feel the nose, she wiped it with her hand. Patting and shaking as she felt her way along the infant's body. A boy.

"Cry. You're supposed to cry." She shook the small body more vigorously. She slid her hands around the head, down its back, around to the front, panic escalating. "He's not crying," she shouted. "Come on little one, cry, move."

She felt his bottom. Tried to slap it like she'd seen in the movies. She found the feet again. She lifted the newborn in the air. The tiniest bit of light drifted unnoticed, through the high windows and glistened a speck on the cord coming from her body. She ran her hand along it. It's still inside me. The other direction.

"The neck, the cord," she screamed. "MACK!"

It felt tight, wrapped around the neck. So tight she couldn't tell which way to unwind it. She tried one way first. It felt no looser. She tried the other way. It did not slacken.

"Oh God, please help me, Oh God, Oh God, Oh God."

She lay the baby down between her legs. The bed was wet and cold. Frantically, she worked her fingers through coils that squished between her fingers. Warm, soft, slimy. She pulled. It stretched!

"Thank God," she wailed. "Baby, hold on, don't die," she said as she pulled one coil up past the face and over the head.

"I can fix it now, my little boy. Mommy's going to make it all better." She pulled another loop over his head.

The noose loosened. Relief flooded through her. Thank God, thank God. She freed another coil.

"Baby, wake up, wake up," she cried. She released the last coil. "You're free."

The wind screamed outside, joining her wails. She rubbed his body all over, shaking him. She grasped his feet, jerking him off the bed, held him up, and slapped his bottom again.

"Breathe."

The wind breathed loudly, whistled and whined. Tears steamed down Alma's face.

"I can't even see you. Don't die on mommy. We have a snowman to make. MACK!" she screamed, "I don't know what to do."

She put her finger in his mouth, it was full of slimy fluid. She cleared it out with one hand and held him up by his feet again with the other. Clearing, shaking.

A lusty cry rang out in the darkness.

Light suddenly seeped into the bedroom from the kitchen. Mack burst into the bedroom just as the baby wailed.

"Oh my God, Alma. It's here. You all right?" He rushed toward her. He took the infant from Alma. "Rest." He quickly dried its face with a towel. The absence of pain and the presence of Mack made Alma euphoric.

He put his son on Alma's chest. "Alma, put him to your breast. The book says that helps with the afterbirth." She did. William searched, then sucked without hesitation. Alma looked at her son. All cheesy white and bloody. His nose flat, his head pointed.

"Dark hair."

Mack looked. "He's got all his parts. Fingers, toes, everything."

William began bellowing again and they both rejoiced in the sound.

"I shoveled the car out, it wasn't as bad as I thought. Then, I drove it around the back to the kitchen, so the headlights would let us see better. See, I found the batteries," he said, turning on the flashlight.

Another contraction seized Alma and she cried out with the pain. "No more. No more." The afterbirth slipped out in the bed into the beam of light.

"You're bleeding. My God, Alma." He drove his hand into her jelly-like belly and kneaded vigorously.

"Stop! You're hurting me. What the hell are you doing?" She writhed in the bed, squirmed to get away from him.

"Hold still. The book said . . . I need to massage your womb. The book said, till it gets hard real hard." He kept rubbing, massaging. Alma tried to lie still.

"I can feel it Alma. It's getting hard. The bleeding is slowing."

"You get us to the hospital, Mack," she demanded through gritted teeth. Her face was twisted in pain, though he'd stopped kneading.

"What would Dr. Galvin have done that I didn't, except charge a delivery fee? I think we should wait. Till you stop bleeding. I can't massage you and drive, too. We need to cut . . ."

"Now, Mack. The hospital."

6

"You've been brooding for weeks, Alma. If you can't allow yourself to spend the money, and you can't burn it, then send it to Alicia. That would be a nice surprise for her. She said in her letter that her husband suspected he'd be laid-off soon. Do *something*. You can't just sit around moping, feeling sorry for your self." Petra parked herself, uninvited, in Alma's kitchen when her calls and messages went unanswered. "Get off your butt, girl. At least, let's move the flammable stuff away from the house," she persuaded. "Then we'll go out for lunch, or a movie, or both."

Alma knew Petra's concern was heartfelt, despite her harsh words. Alma liked that about her friend, though she didn't always agree with or like what she heard. But she always knew where she stood with Petra, no games, no gimmicks. Alma didn't quarrel with her friend's assessment.

The sun was muted by a dense cloud cover that refused to relent or rain. Neither did it offer a breeze to relieve the heat. Thunder rumbled in the distance as Alma and Petra pushed the wheelbarrows along the gravel path from the garage, up a gentle slope, past the front of the house, out back past the hen house, to the tool shed where they stowed the chemicals.

The tool shed was the only structure on the property that Mack didn't build or restore. It was metal and he'd salvaged it from an abandoned construction site.

"No. It's not stealing," Mack had said, looking offended she suggested it. "It was there. No one claimed it. So why shouldn't I?"

It was about seven feet by ten feet, no floor, just sides and a roof. In it he stored the ride-on lawn mower, the snow blower, the small tractor, the chain saw, various tools, and large containers of gas.

They brought sandwiches and iced tea with them, lunch that Petra made as she continued to pressure Alma. When they finished their chore, they picnicked in the shade under a tree. The women had been friends since high school. Alma imagined she knew what Petra must be thinking, but not saying: Hmm, no dryer or dishwasher there in the house, lots of cash in the basement, snow blower and tractor here in the tool shed. She told Petra this. "That's exactly what you're thinking, right?"

Petra nodded. "But I also think he needed that equipment. Look at the size of this lawn. You've got acres here. In the winter he'd put a plow on the tractor to clear the driveway. He needed the snow blower, too."

Alma, thought back to a particular snowstorm and the look on Mack's face, when she told him her water broke. "He knew, Petra. He knew that I had been in labor all day. Money is the reason he didn't tell me. I can't seem to explain that, or any of it. His behavior or mine. The money . . . I can't make that hurt go away. I can't find the good in it. I don't want to look for something to be grateful for. I've run out of ways to make excuses. I need to . . . I feel completely lost. My entire life . . . a pretense."

They walked across the lawn, past the piles of wood, logs precisely cut, and stacked. Held firmly in place. Alma stopped and stared at the stockpile as if it held the answers. She shook her head. She started to cry. "I'm not really feeling sorry for myself, Pete. I haven't got that far. I don't seem to be able to make sense . . . I feel like I woke up in a different life; I don't know where I am. In the day my mind wanders off to the craziest places. At night I dream the weirdest dreams."

Petra walked with her friend toward the trees, one arm braced across her shoulders. They were quiet for a few moments until words replaced the tears. "Sometimes we'd be snowed in for days, but the house was always cozy and warm until he . . . . At first, he chopped wood to have enough for the fireplace. He enjoyed that, making a fire. It gave him a sense of control over the cold."

"Uh-huh," said Petra. "You have lots of trees . . . every year he planted more."

Alma looked around; she loved this place. "Those trees are hemlocks," she said. "They never lose their leaves. Neither do the cedars. Soon the chestnuts and black walnuts will turn a brilliant yellow." Alma was calming now. "The apple trees are my favorite. The kids loved the pies and applesauce. I used to give apple butter to their teachers for Christmas."

Petra relaxed her hold on Alma and took a deep breath. "He could make anything grow, Al."

"My favorites are the evergreens. That Colorado blue spruce holds layers of snow. It's so beautiful."

Petra nodded. "You thought I was coming to see you on those snowy, winter days. Wrong. The trees and the pies, that's why I was there." They laughed.

"After a while, he had so many trees that he felt it was wasteful to spend money for oil. He found an old wood-burning stove, restored it, put it in our fireplace, and burned wood for fuel. Only thing was, the wood stove didn't heat the whole house. The bedrooms and the family room were cold. We'd freeze dressing and bathing."

"You were inventive," said Petra, grinning as if from some illicit pleasure.

"When I told him we needed more heat in the children's rooms, he bought sleeping bags. 'You never know,' he said. 'If we ever needed to sleep outdoors in winter, we could use these.' So I made afghans and quilts, moved the TV and the kid's beds into the living room, near the fireplace, for the winter. Since he didn't seem to mind the cold, I moved his favorite chair and reading lamp into the family room."

Petra nodded.

"Mack chopped wood relentlessly. The sound of the ax cracking in the air became aggravating, like a drippy faucet keeps you awake. 'What if we needed it?' he'd say. 'What if a bad storm knocked out the power for days, weeks?' He never had enough." Alma understood none of this was news to Petra. She was there, a witness. But Alma needed to say it all out loud today, not so much to complain, but to finally give voice to her hardship, to release smoldering torment long banked.

Petra didn't interrupt her friend.

"The wood piles, the enormous summer garden, the house he built with his own hands. If he couldn't keep the unthinkable disaster from happening, at least he'd be ready. But, he never seemed to feel ready. I should have seen it coming, Petra. The medical bills, his loss of control . . . I should have seen it coming. Mack was right. I am a friggin' Pollyanna."

"Stop," said Petra. "Stop it now. It's not your fault. You did everything you could do. It was him. It was his fault. What happened to Mack was his own fault."

"You're right," said Alma, crying. "But . . . but . . . It is . . . I should have made him stay in the hospital. I should have refused to drive him home after he signed himself out. I should have forced him to go back when he got worse. But I couldn't . . . ." She shoved Petra aside, knocking her off balance so that she turned her ankle and fell.

Arms flailing, screaming, "A friggin' Pollyanna, is that what I am, Mack?" Alma ran past the hen house toward the metal tool shed. She fell twice. Blood ran down her leg from her knee. Petra, hobbling on a painful ankle, was unable to overtake her.

The hen house was a rickety wooden structure that had been there when Alma and Mack bought the property. It was unsightly. The hot sun released the stink of chicken dung that still covered the floor.

Alma struggled to open the tool shed door. It was stuck. Petra was closing in. Alma kicked the tinny sounding door, banged it with her fists. "Open, goddamn it, open," pulling on the rusty hasp. Her voice sounded fierce, primal. "I know what I should have done. You're not the only one who can end it all." The door of the shed gave way, causing Alma to fall backwards. Petra caught up with her, grabbed her.

"Leave me alone, Pete," Alma shrieked. "Get away from me. I don't want to hurt you." Alma pulled herself free from her friend's grip, darting into the tool shed and came out wielding the chain saw. She pulled the starter cord. Its roar reverberated through the air, bouncing from tree to tree as if articulating Alma's anger. The sound empowered her. Wild eyed, she swung the saw around like it was a rolling pin. "Watch out, get away. I hope you're watching, Mack. Now I'm in control."

Petra was screaming, "Stop, put that down. No! Don't do that." Her words lost in the detonation of the murderous tool.

The chain saw stalled. In the quiet, Petra tried to reason with her friend.

"So I'm a friggin' Pollyanna, am I?" Alma shouted, hearing nothing. She yanked the starter cord again. "I'll show you, Mack MacCallum. You god-damned son of a bitch." She opened the hen house door, pulling it so hard the door came off its hinges. Inside she butchered the roosts, chopped them to little pieces. She flung the chain saw, slamming it into the wooden nesting shelves. The saw stalled; Alma restarted it. She massacred the feeding troughs. Smashed the windows. Outside again she attacked the frame with her weapon. "This fucking hen house. I hate it. I should have said, 'You take care of the fucking chickens, if you love them so much,' you fucking, self-righteous quitter."

Alma looked up to see Petra limping toward her, swinging Mack's ax. "Don't come near me, Pete! I'm going to chop this friggin' hen house to pieces."

"I'll help you!" mouthed Petra over the roar of the chain saw, as she swung the ax into the wall, knocking herself down but putting a hole in the side of the crumbling structure. She lifted the ax high and flung it into the rotten wooden structure again and again, until there was little left of the walls.

The roaring monster yielded to Alma's will as its teeth

devoured the heavier wood frame, leaving the hen house unrecognizable. Alma ran to the tool shed. "Call the fire department," she screamed as she returned with a gas can. She doused the remains of the hen house, igniting it when she heard the wail of the siren summoning the volunteer firemen. The two friends collapsed, physically exhausted. Alma felt like she was drunk, euphoric. They looked at each other, then at the blazing hen house and began to laugh—a rich full sound that filled the air, supplanting the roar of the chain saw.

"A burning permit, Alma, you're obliged to get a burning permit. Things so dry in the summer, that's why you need supervision for a burn. Mack woulda known that. Guess he didn't tell you. For papers, too, didn't he tell you he always got a permit?"

Big as a black bear, gentle as a lamb, his voice did not chastise. A big hard hat with an emblem on the front subdued an unruly shock of silver streaked black hair and shaded round, red cheeks and a clean shaven face moist with the effort of his work. His neck flushed with bashfulness he'd always struggled with. The other volunteer firemen had already left.

"Tuesday, you're lucky anyone was around on a Tuesday, Alma. Shouldn't be doing stuff like this by yourself."

"It was an accident, George. We were chopping the hen house down. I didn't know there was gas in there. Petra flicked a cigarette butt. We tried to put the fire out."

Petra's mouth dropped. Her eyes widened as her brows came together.

"It was kindling, dry wood—old, too. You didn't stand a chance. You gotta be careful, Alma, with no man around to take care of things like this."

He surveyed the remnants of last year's vegetable garden as if it gave testament to Alma's helplessness. The chicken wire fence sagging here and completely collapsed there, weeds celebrating freedom. A rake and shovel stationed sentry at the disjointed gate, rusting.

George Herlihy, high school football hero recast as fire-chief, scanned the property with a keen eye. Without a word, he ambled over to the house, and around it, twice, a little clumsy in his bulky boots.

"You blamed it on me," Petra said when George was out of hearing range. "It'll be all over town that I set your place afire," chagrin, amusement, and relief took turns on her face.

"It just slipped out. I got scared. I just blurted it out. Sorry, Pete. I didn't want to tell him we . . . I . . . did it intentionally."

"Do you think he suspects?"

"He waited till everyone left before he said anything."

"Doesn't he have to fill out a report?"

"George will take care of it, Pete. I know he will."

"How can you be so sure? Do you know something I don't?"

Alma avoided Petra's question. She felt heat rise to her cheeks. "I know. I just know." She walked toward the house, brushing ash from Petra's hair. "The whole time Mack was sick, I don't think he told anyone about his condition. George saw how sick Mack was. In fact, you and he are probably the only ones, beside the kids, who knew."

"I'm sure if he'd said anything you'd have heard it coming back at you down at McEvoy's, gossip headquarters."

When George disappeared into the garage, Alma and Petra followed him.

"Where does he think he's going? Nosey, huh?"

"He's okay. Be nice to him, Petra. He was about the only friend Mack had. He was here every week when Mack was sick. *Every* week, mostly in the afternoon. They didn't talk much, just sat around and watched TV. I'd fix them lunch or dinner sometimes."

She remembered how she'd fix a big pot of soup, hoping Mack would eat a little. George's face would light up when she put the steaming soup pot on the table with chunks of crusty homemade bread and a cake still in the oven. He'd finish off two or three big bowls and then be embarrassed when she'd insist he take some home too. She would always be grateful for George, his quiet friendship and unassuming mien. But she wasn't going to discuss that with Petra.

"Alma," George would say, "you make the best bean soup a man could hope for. Better'n my Maggie, though she wasn't much of a cook. Not much of a cook myself." George ate heartily and noisily. Mack couldn't get much down.

"I forgot you helped them when Maggie was sick, Alma."

"That was a long time ago."

"You and George were kind of close after Maggie died."

"He was devastated. Didn't know what to do with himself, no wife, no children. He always wanted a son." She avoided Petra's too direct gaze. "He plowed our driveway all that winter Mack was sick."

"You should have told me. I'd have hired him to do mine, too. He's kind of cute and lonesome, don't you think?"

"Neither of us asked him to do it, he just showed up snowstorm after snowstorm. Then he was back in spring with his mower. He wouldn't let us pay him. Just plowed and left not wanting even a thank you. Sometimes, I'd put a pot of stew in his truck, or bread and cookies I'd made."

The women found George in the garage inspecting Mack's tools. He held a pair of wire cutters in his hand. He put them down abruptly.

"What're you going to do with all this stuff, Alma?"

"I don't know, George. I'm just now starting to sort through it."

"Some of these tools would getcha a good price, Alma, if you were of a mind to sell them. A few weeks before Mack died, he asked me to take him downstairs. Remember that, Alma? He wanted to oil tools he thought might be getting rusty. He took good care of them."

"I have no idea what they're worth. Do you want those wire cutters?"

"No, Alma, wouldn't be right, I couldn't take 'em. You should sell 'em. Lots a folks 'round could use stuff like this." His eyes roamed from workbench, to shelves, to toolboxes, and pegboard walls decked with hanging tools. "You got a hardware store here, Alma. You better keep the garage door closed. Someone'll get in here, steal them on ya."

"Please, take the wire cutters. Mack would want you to have them." Feeling the lie, she added, "I'd like you to have them or anything else you want. Come on in for a while, I baked muffins this morning."

He seemed to consider the invitation. He took his hat off and tried to smooth his thick hair. First running his right hand over one side then his left hand over the other. Petra rolled her eyes heavenward, but said nothing. George shifted his weight from one foot to the other. Inspected the floor, then looked up at Alma, beaming.

"No thank you. Not today, Alma. Gotta be going. Petra, watch where you throw them butts, hear?"

Off he went, wire cutters in hand, boots crunching on the drive. He climbed into his battered, mud splattered Ford pickup. He dropped the tools as he tried to close the door and had to get out of the truck to retrieve them. He spun his wheels as he drove away, sending a cloud of dust and gravel flying.

They walked out of the garage, up to the front of the house, and went in without a word. Petra had this grin on her face that Alma ignored.

"Petra, put on a pot of water for tea while I unload the dryer."

Alma walked deliberately to the basement door and down the stairs more to avoid her nosey friend than anything else. The stench of mold, gas and chemicals still assailed her nose. She sneezed. She thought of George and began to imagine his big tender arms around her, warm, soft, safe. She didn't want to think about George that way, yet the thought released a need so strong it overwhelmed her. Wrong, she told herself, as she lifted the still warm clothes from the dryer and hugged them to herself. All wrong for George to think of her that way. It was Mack who was supposed to love her, not George. How long had it been since Mack held her? Years. "You're too soft," he'd tell her. "You've got to be strong." Right now, in the dank of the basement, she'd had enough of being strong. She wanted to be weak, to be held, cherished. She saw the way George had cherished Maggie. Alma knew George would cherish her. He already did.

How funny he looked, this big hulk of a man, carrying a scrawny bouquet of wild flowers, weeds really, into Maggie's sick room. He'd bend over, kiss her lightly on the forehead as if he were afraid she'd break. Then he'd sit on the edge of her bed, his bulky body tilting it so that she leaned toward him and he stroked her face, patted her hair. Come on, have a little drink," he'd say. "Doctor said you don't drink enough." Those chemotherapy days were agonizing. Alma helped with meals and laundry. Mack stayed away. Sickness seemed to disturb him, though he didn't say so. But that was a very long time ago.

Alma lingered in the image of George's big burly embrace. She forgot about the clutter, the money, the hen house, the blemish the old vegetable garden made on the overgrown grass. She allowed herself to be held, but only for a moment, the clothes in her arms painting her fantasy warm.

I've got to get rid of this stink, she thought as she piled the laundry on the dryer and made her way, without pausing for fear, to the far end of the basement. The cellar door hadn't been opened for years. If I could get this opened there'd be some cross-ventilation to clear the air. Mack always kept the doors and windows shut tight and locked. Even in the spring, when the weather warmed, he was reluctant to open the house. Alma would open windows, letting in the spring breeze. Later, she'd find them closed.

Should have brought a flashlight, she thought as she tripped over some pipes strewn on the floor. She picked herself up and noticed a tangle of bicycles. And a tricycle, red, rusted, Grace's. Alma smiled as peals of the child's laughter bounced through her mind. Then anxiety stabbed—Where was Grace? Was she safe? Did she need anything?

Alma shuddered as she brushed spider webs from her face. She maneuvered toward the cellar storm door. The narrow steps up were dark and airless. She pushed open the slanted wooden double doors stationed in the carpeted earth. They refused to budge at first, then gave way and suddenly she was in the sunlight. Fresh clean air scented with pine and alfalfa swept past her as if sucked into the dank basement. A bird, startled and confused by Alma's abrupt arrival, flew into the basement. It fluttered wildly around as if blessing all four corners, purging evil spirits and then flew out the garage door. Open, Alma thought, I will leave this open, till dark. I'll open it every day and soon it will smell just fine.

"Hey! What's going on down there? Tea's ready."

"Much better than a laundromat, much," Alma said as she put the clean laundry on the kitchen table. "Thanks for pushing me to do it, Petra."

"Don't mention it. I'll bring my dirty clothes over next time to keep you in practice. These muffins are good but they're different. What did you do?"

"Just used applesauce instead of oil." Alma sat at the table and sipped her tea. "It's been quite a day. Nothing like burning down a hen house to make a person feel alive."

Petra nodded.

"I found the kids' bikes down there, Pete. I didn't know Mack saved them. Grace's little red trike. I haven't heard from her for over a year. It's not right that a mother doesn't hear a word from her daughter."

"I'm sure she's fine. If something were amiss, you'd hear about it," said Petra.

Alma remembered again, peals of laughter when Grace clumsily struggled to ride her trike in the living room one Christmas day, almost new and shiny then. Mack actually bought it, at a garage sale. When they were older the kids raced along the gravel drive or zoomed out of control down the steep black-topped entry into the garage, usually stopping but sometimes crashing into a padded barrier. A few feet inside the garage door, Mack had stacked up piles of lumber and cement blocks, covered them over with newspapers and what looked like old gym mats. He tapped them securely and topped them with tarps.

"Once, he rode down that slope showing them how to pop-a-wheely."

Petra looked surprised.

"He had his moments. I have to remember those good times, Petra. I have to." Tears streamed down her cheeks. "I should have known."

"Stop," shouted Petra. "Don't start that again. Not today. Not after conquering the basement. Not after the hen house," she yelled. "It's *not* your fault. You did everything you could do."

"No, I should have suspected."

"It was him. It was his fault. It was Mack who didn't trust doctors and ignored his symptoms until it became an emergency. *He* did that. When surgery was suggested, he refused. *He* refused. 'I don't need an operation,' he told you. 'Those doctors are just out to make money.' *His* decision. Nothing could convince him otherwise: not you, Alma, not the kids, not the specialists he ran out of his hospital room, not even the pain," said Petra. "He was afraid the doctors would make some stupid mistake and he'd be an invalid. He's the one who stuck the gun in his mouth and pulled the trigger. He died on a freezing-cold winter day with enough food and wood for the whole town. You could not make him want to live. No one can make another person want to live."

Petra's cell phone startled both women. Annoyed at the interruption, she flipped it open. "Hello, this better be good," she said to the caller. Her eyes brightened as she listened, she blushed. Petra straightened her shirt as if making herself presentable. "Townhouses? Yes, I would like to see them. I like that area," she said into the phone.

She smiled as she listened, pushed a stray lock of hair into place. "Well, I don't know about dinner." She stood, petulantly, hand on one hip and walked into the living room. Alma could hear her giggle.

Alma cleared the table. She plunged the tea cups into warm bubbly-comforting water. She regained her composure. Petra's right. She is, and I just need to quit telling myself otherwise.

"Ahhh!," squealed Petra, running back into the kitchen some minutes later. "I've got a date. With the real estate salesman. A date, I haven't had a date in months."

"Petra, you sound like a teenager. Who is he?"

"I put my house on the market last week. I didn't tell you because I thought I'd change my mind. Anyway, Larry's the agent I listed it with. We took a few computer classes together at the community college in the spring. Hadn't seen him for a long time. He's tall and yum, very handsome," said Petra hardly taking a breath. "Come to my house quick, help me pick out something to wear. He's taking me to that new restaurant, you know, the one on the hilltop. Come on, I have two hours to get ready. I'll close the garage door. You lock up here."

"No locking, I want to leave the downstairs open."

"Okay, let's go. I'll meet you there."

Alma, caught up in Petra's excitement, impulsively agreed to go with her friend. Once at Petra's house, a fashion show began.

"Pete, you are so silly. Like that time you were going out with Larry McEvoy in high school. Remember?"

"I sure do. And it feels good now, too. Same Larry. Oh, those slow dances," Petra said, swirling around dancing with a dress as if it were a partner. "What about this outfit?" They'd already rejected three ensembles and had one glass of wine. Petra poured another.

"Larry McEvoy? You can't be serious. He's married."

"Hasn't been for a long time. She ran off with some unlucky fellow."

"No more for me, thanks, Pete. And you, you'll be drunk

before he gets here."

"How do I look, tell me, is this not it?"

"Depends. Are you going to hang out on the street in front of Duffy's Tavern? You could make a few bucks, or you could get busted for soliciting," Alma laughed.

"That bad?"

"That bad. You'll scare him away."

"If I remember Larry, he doesn't scare easily." Petra poured another glass of wine at the same time she climbed into a different outfit. She floated about the room as if she were on a runway, this time in a shocking pink sweater that hugged her body and shimmered as she moved. Black skirt, stockings, and spike heels completed the costume.

"Slinky. I've never seen you wear this stuff. When did you acquire this wardrobe?"

"Some time after you stopped having fun or maybe when I started having fun after my divorce. You haven't seen it because you won't come out with me on Friday nights."

"You're not going to a bar tonight. You have a date. How about this?" Alma pulled a lavender-on-lavender, silk dress she'd made for Petra from the closet. "Try this on. With these white sandals. The heel isn't quite so high, which is more than I can say for you." Alma put the wine away and rummaged in Petra's jewelry box. "This crystal necklace will go."

"I have earrings that match, they're in the other case," said Petra. She turned around. The silk dress swirled about her, and draped over her body in flattering folds. The low V in front showed off her cleavage without shouting.

"Sexy, but subtle. I like it," said Petra. "Now leave, get out. He'll be here any minute."

"I think I'll stay. See if his intentions are honorable."

"I hope they aren't. Go."

7

Alma drove home. It started to rain as the sun began its descent. The visibility was poor, not quite dark, but no longer daylight. Twilight. She hoped that the rain stopped before the fireworks tonight. She left Petra's fourth-of-July barbecue early, deciding she'd had enough fireworks lately. The headlights shone a narrow beam of light as she wound through the countryside, anxious to get home and not wanting to arrive to empty rooms too soon. Turning the wheel impulsively, squealing her tires, she took a side road that led up the mountain. Dark descended when she entered the narrow road, the oaks, maples, and pines absorbing what little light remained. The road wandered aimlessly, unlit except for a few feet immediately in front of her. She drove without purpose or thought. After many miles, she became aware that her detour had taken her far from home.

Petra. She's so full of fun and mischief. She has friends, goes to parties, has dates, Larry and before him Herb. Not that I want to go out on dates. Quite the contrary.

Suddenly a deer leaped onto the road ahead. Alma slammed on the brakes. The car screeched to a halt. Alma and the deer stared at each other for long moments. The animal in the car's spotlight was a full-grown male, taut, muscles alert, antlers amply developed. His large dark eyes shone in the headlights. He was the color of rich clover honey with white accents around his mouth.

You're alone, too, Alma spoke softly to the animal. He cocked his head and snorted. If I weren't alone, I wouldn't be here now enjoying your company. It's not so bad, being alone, is it? You go where you want, when you want, stay as long as you want, eat when you're hungry, even if it's not six o'clock. The deer seemed to nod.

So long did they inspect each other that the forest adopted the purr of the engine as its own. Silenced crickets shouted. Tree frogs sang to the accompaniment of locusts. Tree tops fluttered, bats probably. Crackling of twigs and rustling dry leaves announced the approach of another night creature. Alma and the deer listened, alert to the possibility of danger. The deer turned to face Alma. He raised his right front leg and struck his hoof loudly on the road, looking Alma in the eye. He lifted his head and brought it down quickly, sounding a loud snort and stamping both front hooves. A warning, Alma realized.

A doe and three fawns sauntered lazily into the road. They sniffed the larger deer in greeting. They responded to an unheard command and walked toward the edge of the road, the patriarch never taking his eyes off Alma. This is better than alone, his eyes flashed. So together were they, that each one moved the same leg at the same time. Each seemed to be fully aware of the presence of the other. The family disappeared into the trees, leaving Alma alone again.

This time she felt lonely. If I'd had that kind of a family, I'd want to turn time back.

The sound of William's cry supplanted the pain of the birth and the horror of trying to unwrap the cord from his neck. His lusty, loud wail pinked him and plunged her into euphoric joy.

She put him to her breast and he suckled without hesitation. Her body responded with cramps. The bleeding slowed. Mack watched as they slept. As soon as he heard the snow plows, he awakened Alma.

"They're clearing the roads. I'm going out to the road, see if I can catch them, ask if we can get to the hospital." Mack pulled on his boots and grabbed his jacket.

Sleep had refreshed Alma. She unwrapped William; he stirred but did not wake. Dried blood caked on his tiny face. She slid to the edge of the bed from the blanket in which she had swaddled him and put her feet on the floor. She was woozy but stood holding on to the bed. And felt the blood gush from her. She took the candle and made her way to the bathroom and cleaned herself as best she could. She wasn't bleeding as much as she thought.

The activity felt good; her strength was returning. Candles, she thought, we need light. I'll be careful, she said to the baby, we don't want to start a fire. She gathered and placed them here and there, feeling defiant as she lit them, all of them, every candle she could find. She dressed in sweat pants and a wool sweater, put on her rag socks and sneakers and checked William again. In the glow of the candlelight he looked like an angel. He curled into himself and slept peacefully. Alma went to the kitchen and put a pan of water on the stove to heat.

"Okay, we can go. The roads are passable. Not so much snow as I thought," Mack said, slamming the door behind him. "What are you doing up?"

"William needs to be bathed. I'm not letting anyone else give him his first bath. Put some more wood in the stove and pull the kitchen table close to the heat." The wood fire warmed the kitchen. William must be kept warm. She gave orders as she sat in a chair, her energy draining from her. "Bring him to me."

When Mack had the table ready for the bath, Alma unwrapped William.

"He's long," said Mack, "About twenty-two inches, I'd say."

William began to rouse. He opened his eyes, blinking. He startled when Alma touched him.

"Sorry, little one. You need a bath. Your first bath."

"He must weigh eight or nine pounds. Chunky, look at him."

"First your face, William." Alma dipped the wash cloth in the warm water. She'd saved some fabric just for this purpose. Soft, silky, smooth pieces that would lather nicely, dry soft.

"William? What kind of a name is that?"

"No soap today, not for your first bath." She wrung the cloth so there was the right amount of moistness. She touched the cloth to his face and gently wiped his eyes, first the right one. Dip the cloth again. Then the left. Starting from the center and moving to the outside.

"He needs a stronger name, that's why I never let anyone call me William."

She touched the warm cloth to his forehead, wiping away the blood. His head was cone shaped from the birth. No matter, he was beautiful.

"How about Strom?"

Alma rinsed out the cloth again and smoothed it along his cheeks and chin. A fine chin, she thought. Strong and determined, you must be, my little man. She turned him to one side and washed the back of his head.

"My father, he didn't want to be called William, either. He preferred Mack, too."

"Now your arm. Let me straighten it. You don't have to be so curled up any more. Your fingers are all there. So tiny, all five of them. Look at you. Your nails need to be trimmed already."

The white cheesy film on his skin did not wash off and Alma didn't try to get it off. Just the blood.

"Get me some fresh water, Mack." Alma dried the baby's arm and covered him while they waited for Mack.

She wondered how long the power would be out. Mack had turned the car headlights off to conserve the battery. The room was dark except for candle light. Mack lit two kerosene lanterns, but Alma turned them off. Too smelly.

The candle light made the kitchen feel cozy, welcoming. Just right for a baby boy. This will be a loving home, we'll be a family. A happy family, I will make it so. William moved his arms and legs, jerky movements in response to his mother's touch. Alma was overwhelmed with the strength of the love she felt for this little stranger. So complete and unconditional.

She imagined William, at about a year-old, playing in the kitchen, while she cooked dinner. She'd put the pots and pans in a low cabinet. They'd have cabinets by then. He'd get into the pot and pan cabinet and close himself in, play peek-a-boo. He'd rattle and bang and toss all the pots and pans on the floor. She'd sit on the floor with him in her lap and kiss his fingers if he caught them in the cupboard door. She'd show him how to put the measuring spoons in the pot and how to take them out.

A knock startled them. Headlights silhouetted the figure at the door.

"What the . . . "

The sliding glass door opened without invitation and George walked in, bundled head to toe.

"I was on duty tonight, the whole town crew was called out. The roads need to be cleared and salted before morning. They radioed me, Mack. Said you needed to get Alma to the hospital. Follow my truck. We'll get you up the hill. There should be no problem once you're out on the highway."

Alma had forgotten that. All these years, she never once remembered he'd been there. George had escorted them, with his big town snowplow, all the way to the hospital that night. Why did she recall it now, on this dark road? What in the world am I doing here anyway? Be on your way, she told herself. Your family is grown. To be a little part of their lives will have to be enough. William and Alicia kept in touch at least. Who knew where Grace was? No amount of wishing will change what was. She drove home.

The rain stopped by the time she got home. The air smelled fresh and fragrant with some night blooming plant. The moon lit the driveway. Alma went into the garage. She walked all the way to the other side, to close the cellar doors.

I shouldn't have left it open this late, she thought. Some skunk could get in here. I'd surely not like that smell, either. She pulled the door shut, bolted it and went looking for the trike she'd seen. It was dark and she fumbled around trying to find the trike. I'll give it to the Kelley's. Their four-year-old will love it.

She smelled him first. An unfamiliar and unpleasant

scent. Wild and gamy. Something's in the basement, she thought. She held still, listened. No sound. A movement across from where she stood. She could see across to the garage side. The moon lit the drive and the garage entry. But this side was dark. She was midway between the cellar storm door and the stairs toward the front of the house.

Oh God! What am I going to do? Think, Alma, think. There are guns down here, her mind raced, mentally searching. I don't know where, but they are here somewhere. The ammunition stored in a separate place. Mack hid them. If I could find a gun, that would be enough to scare off an intruder. I could shout and scream. That might intimidate him.

Crouched down to hide herself, she felt at a disadvantage, small, defenseless, cowering. She stood up again. It's not like he doesn't know I'm here, she thought. He probably watched me come in. I could shout, "I have a gun. Get out or I'll shoot." Maybe he'd leave. He can get out easier than I. That's what I'll do. Her hand trembled as she picked up a piece of pipe. She held it to her shoulder like it was a shotgun. Her heart raced. She held her breath so she could hear better.

I'll have to say it like I mean it. He must hear shoot to kill in my voice. She practiced it in her head. Commanding, threatening. She stood taller, tried to feel powerful. I'll shoot you as sure as look at you, she practiced. You're a dead man.

She opened her mouth to speak those murderous words. Then she saw eyes flash red at the same time she heard the growl, low, guttural, a preamble to a roar. Her heart leaped. Pounded in her throat. She sensed rather than felt its hot, putrid breath on her neck. Quiet filled the space between them for a moment as both creatures sized up the situation.

She carefully searched the shadows. What is that? She looked in the direction the sound had come from. She couldn't see it. It was big, at least it sounded big. The glowing eyes were taller than hers. It could be smaller, but on top of a pile of stuff. There'd been reports of bobcats.

A stack of boxes near the washing machine crashed to the floor. Glass shattered. Another roar. She could hear the thing moving around. Then she saw it. It *was* big. A brown bear stood on its hind legs and bellowed for her to leave.

But I can't leave. I would if I could. I am too far from either exit. I'd have to move closer to the animal if I tried to get up the stairs. Did I lock the upper basement door?

Alma inched toward the stairs. Maybe I can get underneath them, keep the stairs between me and the bear. If I can get there, I'll be safer, maybe even get to the garage side and out. The bear will have as much trouble navigating the clutter as I will. At least I was down here today. I know where to find the passage through the junk to the driveway. I can find that before he figures a way out. As soon as she moved, the bear closed in, growling, stepping on top of the clutter or flinging it to one side. Not trying to find his way around it.

A clap of thunder distracted the animal. In that moment Alma, shot through the clutter and positioned herself under the stairs. She threw the pipe she still clutched across the room. It struck the washing machine. She could see the animal better from this angle. It turned toward the sound and took a few steps in that direction, away from Alma. Then as if realizing he'd been tricked, he turned toward Alma again, more enraged. The bear came closer.

Frantic now, Alma tried to barricade herself under the stairs, heaping boxes on either side of her, stuffing them between the steps. There weren't enough boxes. The bear growled as he shot his paw through the space between the steps, pushing protective boxes away, reaching for Alma. She could feel his breath on her face, hot and pungent. She managed to back away from her attacker, where the stairs became higher. He couldn't reach her.

Don't panic, don't panic, she told her panic-filled self. Oh, God. The potatoes and apples. I stored the baskets of potatoes and apples down here. Mack told me not to because they'd attract predators, bears. I didn't believe him, but while he was alive, I never stored food down here.

"Get out, get out," she shouted. "Get out of my house. Go away, you bastard," she screamed. She stood tall, made herself big and shouted. She was tempted to throw the thing in her hand. She thought better of it, but looked at it as if it were her last hope. It was an air horn. The sound was deafening, thunderous and it stopped that bear right there. Loud as loud could be, she blasted it over and over as she bolted through the obstacle course to the driveway, up the path, into her house. She slammed the front door and locked it. She turned around and leaned her back up against the door to steady herself. Her knees buckled and she slid to the floor. Silence. Blessed silence!

The phone, she thought, get help.

"Animal control," she said out loud, but she couldn't hear herself speak. With a trembling finger, she dialed the number that Mack had taped to the phone, holding the headset to her ear, but she couldn't hear the ring. She looked at the headset, shook it, jiggled the receiver and dialed again. She heard nothing. Then she realized it wasn't the phone. She shouted her address into the phone. At least it felt like shouting.

"I have a bear in the basement. Please help me. I'm deaf, I can't hear if you are speaking to me," she sobbed into the mouthpiece. She wasn't sure if she'd told a real person or an answering machine. She dialed 911. They'll answer for sure, she thought.

The volunteer fire department was dispatched to Alma's house for the second time that summer. George. And the local vet often called on to subdue wayward wild animals, were with them. They found the bewildered bear standing in the driveway. From the window, Alma watched beams of light bounce and shift as if exotic fireflies chased the bear into a wooded area. She knew it would be sedated and tagged, then relocated.

Hours later, past midnight, George knocked at her door.

"Alma," he called softly, "are you awake?"

She heard his voice as if through cotton plugged ears, distant, muffled, like he was speaking through a tube. She sat, curled up, in the chair closest to the front door, rather than her favorite La-Z-Boy. The TV flashed bright colors, now light, now dark, but Alma would not have been able to say what program was on. Must have dozed off, she thought, not sure if she heard George's voice, or the TV, or if she hovered on the edge of one of her wild dreams, until he knocked again. She jumped to her feet alert to danger, knocking the candle off the side table.

"Are you OK, Alma?"

She let him in.

"Jittery, I guess, and exhausted, George. I need to sleep, but I can't go to bed. I wasn't sure if the doors downstairs were still open and I was afraid to go down to check."

"That's why I came back, Alma. I couldn't remember either. I didn't want to be making noise, closing your doors, without telling you what I was doing."

Alma thought she could still smell the bear in the basement when she opened the hallway door. As she followed George down the stairs, he chatted on about how the bear was subdued. She didn't listen to the details, instead she scanned the basement suspiciously. She stayed close to George, grasping the back of his shirt, as he maneuvered the cellar storm doors shut, then wove his way toward the garage.

"This is what attracted him, Alma." George juggled the baskets of apples and potatoes. "They've started to spoil. That smells pretty good to a bear. I'll get rid of them for you." He hauled them out to his truck, closing the garage door behind him. "I'll meet you upstairs."

I'll go with you, were words that came to her mind but were contained there by her stubbornness. And shame. She felt like a little girl who knew better, but was still frightened of the monster in the closet. The garage door rattled in its track. Too late now. Alone in the basement, armed with a flashlight, Alma began to shake. Her imagination conjured up the bear's saliva drenched teeth. What was that? She directed the beam toward the sound. She stood, unable to move, looking around as if she were in a house of horrors. Shadows crept about as she moved the flashlight, rising in the corners, tall as the ceiling, then hiding, then slithering out from behind a stack of boxes. She dashed for the stairs, took them two at a time, slammed the door shut behind her, rammed the bolt in place.

"What happened, Alma?" George said as he let himself in the front door. "You're all pale... you look scared."

Alma was happy to see this man she'd known for so many years. He had a way of showing up when she needed him. She resisted the impulse to rush toward him, longing for the safety of strong arms. Except for the emblem identifying him as a town employee, his navy T-shirt could have been one he wore in high school, looking as if it shrank, sleeves rolled up though there was no longer a cigarette pack pocketed there. He'd quit smoking when Maggie was diagnosed with cancer, saying he felt responsible for her disease. His jeans showed signs of the struggle with the bear: remnants of caked mud on his knees, briars clung to the frayed hem of one leg. Dark hair spronged from a navy cap with an emblem that matched his shirt. When he wasn't working, he wore jeans and a T-shirt without the emblem and a rumpled, tan fisherman's hat with flies hooked onto the band.

"I'm kind of shaky. I heard something down there... got thinking that bear might have family."

"You're all locked up downstairs. You won't see no more bears down there tonight, Alma. I'll check the doors and windows up here." His heavy boots clomped down the hall. "They're building that hotel up there on the mountain, you know," he said from the bedroom. "All that land they cleared. We could see more bears around." He returned to the kitchen. "All locked up."

"George, I baked cookies this morning. Stay, have some."

"It's kinda late, Alma. You're tired. You don't need to

give me cookies," his eyes looking around her but not at her.

Ice cold milk swirled into the glass Alma set next to the plate of chocolate chip cookies.

"I didn't come here for cookies, Alma. Just wanted to make sure you were OK. Haven't seen much of you, 'cept when I come here to do your lawn." George lowered himself into the kitchen chair which seemed too small for him. "You don't come into town much anymore. Thought I'd be seeing more of you after Mack passed on." He broke a cookie in half and dunked it into the milk, just like he did in high school when they sat in his mother's kitchen. Alma knew that if he'd been in the basement with her earlier, he'd have wrestled that bear if he had to.

"It's been more than a year, George. Even so, this summer's more difficult than last. I'm sitting here in my own kitchen, but it's not my kitchen like it used to be. It's a kitchen below which a bear nearly attacked me."

"You're just unsettled, Alma. It was a fluke, the bear. You'll be OK."

"I *am* unsettled. This is the kitchen of a woman who didn't know there were thousands of dollars in the basement. That woman can't be me. I'm a stranger in a familiar place. I'm like that collection of bottles on the window sill there. Set in place, moved about, at someone else's will, but belonging in another kitchen, a kitchen that wasn't real." She told George about finding the money. "Thousands of dollars, George, thousands."

He listened intently, half a dripping cookie in hand. "That's not right, Alma. A man shouldn't keep his wife and family like that. Little Gracie could have used that money for college. That's what the big fight was about, right? Her going to college?"

Alma nodded. "Partly. He wouldn't pay for it."

"She was a good girl, Grace was. Headstrong, Alma, like Mack, and a tomboy, not a girly girl like her sister. We never had no children, Maggie and me, but Grace was like my own." George smiled, as if he were remembering how he taught her to fish, and set traps for rabbits. Grace called him George, not Mr. Herlihy, not Uncle George as Alma suggested. "He didn't treat you right, Alma, or his children. I didn't like him much." He made eye contact, a rare gesture, as if he were making sure she got the message beneath his words.

"Will you stay? I still have the jitters."

His eyebrows arched in surprise, then knitted together as Alma finished.

"I'll put sheets on William's bed."

"It wouldn't look right, Alma, but I don't want to leave you alone, neither."

"Who's to know, George?"

George automatically reached for the phone when it rang the next morning; it was on the wall right next to him, as he waited for breakfast. Alma scrambled eggs with bacon and sausage.

"Hello? She's right here, hold on. Oh. OK, I'll tell her. Bye." Forehead furrowed, he relayed the message. "McEvoy. There's a package at the post-office for you. Sorry, Alma, I ... the phone, I just grabbed it, without thinking."

"I'm glad you stayed. I wouldn't have slept as well alone."

"But McEvoy, of all people to call, Alma."

"I know," she rolled her eyes knowing that everyone down at the post office would be talking about her and George. "Here's your eggs." She made her voice sound calm and unconcerned. Inside she wanted to call McEvoy and explain about the bear, that George slept in William's bed, alone.

He picked up the phone when it rang again, but passed it to Alma saying, "Here, you answer it."

"Who was that?" Petra asked. "George?"

Alma told her about the bear in the basement, leaving out the fact that it happened last night.

8

Petra was in Alma's kitchen, weeks later, washing the dinner dishes. Alma had made Chicken Paprikash and for dessert, fresh Georgia peach pie. Alma looked out the window above her sink. Twilight seeped into the earth. She dried her hands and went out on the back porch. Petra followed.

"You don't *have* to go with me, Alma. I think you might have fun, meet a few new people. Some old friends, too."

"Soon the chestnuts and black walnuts will turn a brilliant yellow."

"Leaves changing color? That's more than a month away. Are you changing the subject? It wasn't that long ago that you were feeling boxed in. Come on. Just for an hour."

"All right, Petra," she answered impulsively, "I'll go, for one hour, but I'm taking my own car. And, I don't want you to play match-maker. I'm just going because you seem to have fun when you go. I'm curious, but don't make a big deal out of it."

"Hello! It is a big deal. This is your first time."

"I've been there before. For dinner."

"Not on singles night, you haven't. Now. Let's see." Petra was in Alma's closet so fast it seemed like she beamed in. "You need to wear something black and low cut."

"See this?" Alma pulled out a pink tailored cotton blouse with a button down collar. "This is it. But, I will wear black. These slacks. This is as slinky as I get."

"Well, at least borrow my black spike heels."

"These loafers are perfect. Do you want me to make a complete fool out of myself walking around on those stilts? Don't push it, Petra. I have no great expectations for tonight, except to feel out of place and uncomfortable."

Alma opened the door to Patsy's Pizza Pub and squeezed herself into the crowd. She waited for Petra to slide past her and lead the way. She didn't. The air smelled like beer and pizza, cigarette smoke and too much cologne. Punctuated by sudden bursts of laughter, many voices blended, hummed, rising, falling, cluttering the atmosphere, invading her comfort zone.

The bar was a large rectangle enclosing glasses and bottles of all shapes and sizes and two muscled men in black t-shirts mixing and pouring. It filled the center of the room. Alma knew entrances to several dining rooms were at the back and the side of the room to her right though she couldn't see them.

People jammed around the bar. Men and women sat on stools. Behind the stools there was scarcely enough room to cruise around the bar. Red lips smiled plastic smiles. Bodies pressed together as they flowed along through tight spaces like pond lilies floating with the current, each vying for the best spot, some pushing ahead of others. Music blasted, harsh, discordant.

"Music's great, don't you think?" This from a man about her own age wearing a polo shirt, jeans and a broad smile on his tanned face.

Startled that someone spoke to her, someone she didn't know, Alma said, "It's not my kind of music." What is he thinking, she wondered? Does he envision buying me a few drinks then taking me home? If I speak to him would I be encouraging his fantasy? Because fantasy is all it would be. I have no intention of going home with anyone. She noticed that Petra wasn't behind her. Where is she? Alma looked around the crowded room.

"What kind of music *do* you like?"

"Um, I don't . . . I can't think of who . . ." She fidgeted with her purse. Examined the floor, his shoes, scuffed work boots. "Your shoe's untied." What a dumb thing to say, she thought.

"Well, I hope they play something you like." He turned to another woman and said, "Music's great, don't you think?"

A little Sinatra, Barry White, or Al Green, she could have said. And Ella, Ella Fitzgerald. She knew this was true but where or when had she listened to this music? How did she know she enjoyed this? She didn't own a stereo or a CD player. Just an old radio that didn't work well anymore.

One hour. One hour, I can make it through one hour. I *will* stay for one hour. I promised Petra. She disappeared as soon as we got here. Some friend. I ought to leave now. Alma gritted her teeth and pushed her way through to the bar. Standing between two seated people, a man to her left and a woman to her right, Alma signaled the bartender who didn't notice her. Alma raised her hand again and waved weakly, feeling like a shy first grader asking to be excused to go to the bathroom.

"Hey, Steve. When you get a minute," he gestured with his thumb, toward Alma. The bartender responded instantly to the man beside her whose moustache, flecked with grey, smiled at her. He had brown hair with silver streaks at the temples. His sense of humor was revealed in the deep laugh lines around his face. He reminded her of tweed, rich, soft, textured tweed.

"White wine, please?" Herbal iced tea, that's what I really want, but Petra suggested white wine. She should be here to help, Alma thought, looking over her shoulder at the sea of faces. Walking off, leaving me like this . . ..

"What do you want, Doll? Got all kinds. Chablis? Chardonnay? Pinot Grigio?" The bar-tender rattled off an inventory of white wines. He had a shaved head and the shoulders of a weight lifter. His black eyes impervious to her discomfort.

"Um." Her face felt hot. What was that last one? Dumb, dumb, dumb, she thought.

"It's a dry Italian wine. What do you like? Dry ? Fruity? Sweet?" His voice edgy. "While she's making up her mind, what'll you have?" He turned his attention to the man next to Alma.

"Corona, with a slice of lime," he said decisively. He

looked at Alma. "Can I buy you a Chardonnay?" He didn't wait for an answer. "Chardonnay for the lady, Kendall Jackson, Vintners Reserve."

"How about me, honey? Gonna buy me one?" slid a syrupy voice from her right. Alma turned in amazement. The woman leaned in over the bar to make sure her words reached the Corona man. The low cut of her dress revealed her deep cleavage, which spilled over the confines of a black harness beneath the dress. Her blond hair with its dark roots dusted the bar. She held up a long stemmed glass and gazed at the chartreuse liquid it contained as if it were a rare jewel. "I was here first, you know," she hissed, one eyebrow arched over a glazed eye.

Alma looked at the glass of wine that suddenly banged in front of her, then up at the Corona man who was looking directly at her. Eye contact. Hazel met green. Moisture gathered between her breasts. She fumbled in her purse, which was too large with too many compartments and held too much junk, and had eaten her wallet. The purse on the bar to her right was small, black with sequins. She wrestled three dollars out and onto the bar and snatched the glass of wine. She steered herself through the crowd away from the bar.

Forty-five minutes to go. If I find that Petra, I'll . . . .

"Hey, where're you going?" The Corona man put his hand lightly on her shoulder but withdrew it quickly. He was as tall as Alma. "A little conversation would be nice." He fidgeted with the collar on his burgundy, button down shirt. He brushed his hair with his hand then shoved that hand in the pocket of his khaki slacks. He held the bottle of Corona, into which he'd squeezed the slice of lime, in the other. He shifted his weight and looked away for a moment. Change jingled in his pocket. "I just bought you the best wine they stock here."

"Thanks. I didn't know what to order. I've never ordered a glass of wine at a bar before." Alma felt guilty for only a moment. She said, "But, *I* paid for it."

"Three dollars? That doesn't cover half." He rolled his

eyes to the ceiling and sighed. He looked like he wished he hadn't spoken those words. "Just trying to be friendly."

He's as nervous as I am, Alma realized.

He was looking at her again. Mack seldom looked directly at her. A smile grew on Corona man's face, a grimace on Alma's. He smelled like tweed, earthy, she thought, feeling alarmed at her reaction. The crowd had pushed them too close together. Her purse felt like a satchel on her shoulder. She looked around for Petra, but his was the only friendly face. Alma took a gulp of the wine then shoved the glass into his chest. "Here's your half of the wine." Some sloshed onto her hand and his shirt. She shouldered her way into one of the small dining rooms.

A large table was filled with cheese, crackers, veggies and dips, fruit and snacks of all kinds. The pizza smelled fresh and looked hot and inviting. She wasn't hungry but she needed something to do. She carried a full plate to an empty table in a corner.

I'll do a long run tomorrow, she thought.

"Can I get you something to drink?" Another black-T-shirted server approached her with an order pad in hand.

"Kendal Jackson Chardonnay," she said knowingly.

"So, you liked the wine," said a familiar voice. "Can I join you?" Without waiting for a reply, Corona man sat opposite Alma. "Hold on! Before you chuck another glass of wine at me, I just want to say something. Then I'll leave you alone."

Alma said nothing. There was a big wet oval on his shirt. She noticed he wore no wedding band and neither was there a stripe of pale skin where a ring had been, like the man with the untied boots. She took a bite of the pizza without tasting it. She looked at her watch. Half an hour left.

"I'm sorry," he said, looking directly at Alma. "I'm nervous. I didn't mean to bring up the price of the wine. I didn't know what to say, you know? I was desperate for words and those are the ones that came out, unfortunately."

"It *was* good wine." It was a relief to have someone to talk to. Sitting at the table alone made her feel lonely in the crowd of revelers. His presence made her feel like part of the group and less like the kid chosen last for the ball team.

"I was nervous, too. I didn't know what to order. All those different wines. If I'd said iced tea, I'd probably have gotten laughed out of here."

"I don't think there is iced tea at the bar," he laughed.

Both looked around the room. As Alma's eyes searched for Petra she glanced at Corona man, then looked away.

"I don't usually come here," he injected into the awkward silence. "It is my first time at a singles thing. I was hoping you'd stay at the bar and make the lady in black disappear."

"Me too. I mean, it's my first time too, and my last. As soon as I find my friend, I'm leaving."

"Do you need a ride?" Immediately he looked like he wished he hadn't asked.

"No," Alma answered quickly. "I have my own car."

"My sister talked me into it. Coming here. She lives in Stony Ridge. I'm new in town. But, I don't think it's for me either. That lady drinking the green thing was scary."

Alma laughed for the first time that evening. "It was my friend. She kind of dragged me here. Then she vanished—deserted me." She pushed the plate of food toward him.

"No, I'll leave you alone. Thanks. I promised myself I'd stay for a little while," he looked at his watch. "Only 22 minutes to go."

Alma laughed again. "I'm counting the minutes too." He has a gentle face.

The waiter brought her wine. "What would you like to drink, sir?"

Corona man looked at Alma and asked, with his eyes, if it was all right. Alma nodded.

"Another Corona." Then to Alma, "I won't stay long. I'll be able to tell my sister I stayed over an hour. My name's Tony." He extended his hand. It felt large and muscular in hers. He had a firm, confident grip. His hands were soft and warm. She enjoyed the touch.

"I'm Alma MacCallum," she said out loud, but in her head she was having a different conversation. I'm sorry. He said I'm sorry. Mack would have never said that. He'd never admit he was nervous or uncomfortable. And he would not have asked if it was okay to sit at the table. He would have considered it his right to do so. Of course, he wouldn't have come here in the first place, but if he had...

They talked for a while and Alma found herself relaxing and enjoying herself. Tony was an attentive man. He listened to her. Responded. Looked at her as if she were interesting.

"A bear in your basement? I didn't know there were bears here."

"Not usually. But this summer, there have been several bear sightings. They have an acute sense of smell. I left the doors to the basement and garage open. He probably got a whiff of the apples and potatoes I had stored in an open crate."

He can't possibly enjoy hearing about the kinds of trees on my property and how I staved off a bear in the basement. He's being kind, Alma thought.

He was an architect, he said. He'd been hired to design a hotel being built in town. He'd been married, but his wife died of breast cancer about two years after they wed. No children, which he regretted.

His hobby was pottery. He enjoyed getting his hands into the clay and shaping it on a wheel, creating something that did not exist before.

"You know what I'd really like to do?"

Alma shook her head. When he smiled, the skin around his eyes crinkled. Alma no longer noticed the harsh music or the cacophony of voices.

"I'd like to open a pottery shop. Give lessons, teach the use of the wheel, sell greenware. People could make their own sets of dishes, or bowls. Or they could glaze ready-made pottery, compose their own designs."

The time drifted well past their self-imposed deadlines.

When he left, he shook her hand.

"I had a good time after all. Thanks for rescuing me from the green drinking dragon. Maybe I'll see you around." He didn't look back.

He didn't ask for my phone number, Alma thought. She was both disappointed and relieved. She wandered through the dining rooms in search of Petra and spotted her with a group of laughing men and women standing around a buffet table. Alma was hurt. Why hadn't Petra included her in this happy group?

"Hey! There you are," said Petra as Alma approached. "I was looking for you. Then I noticed you were talking to that good looking guy at the bar. I figured you were doing all right on your own." Turning to the group, she introduced Alma. "I want you all to meet my best friend, Alma. I was telling you about her."

Murmurs of admiration over her defeat of the bear and stories of experiences worse than her own, made her feel less awkward. They laughed when she told them about the lady in black asserting her territorial rights. But she didn't want to get involved in a conversation. She just wanted to tell Petra she was leaving.

"You should stay," said Duke, one of the group she'd been introduced to. He was a tall man, even Alma had to look up at him. He was brown: brown hair, brown eyes, brown shirt with a stiff collar, brown tie that clutched his neck. He carried his head high with his chin tilted up slightly. Despite the warmth of late August, he wore a blazer, brown. He held an unlit pipe in his right hand. He affected a professorial air: educated, refined and above it all.

"You need to face your fears, m'lady. Just what is it you are afraid of, Alma?"

"I . . . um . . . . I'm not . . . What?"

"Denial is your worst enemy. You know what denial is, Alma? It's a defensive mechanism, a refusal to recognize the existence of an unpleasant reality," he recited. "Especially the significance of one's own behavior, like your refusal to face your fears."

He turned to the woman next to him, as if he were taking a bow. She gazed up at him with adoring eyes. He preened, smoothing his hair which was parted low on the right side and swept over a bald crown to the left. He tamped the empty bowl of his pipe.

Alma looked to Petra for help. Petra rolled her eyes upward and looked toward the exit. Several people drifted away from the group. Those who didn't leave gave there-he-goes-again-looks to each other and began talking among themselves. Petra stayed with her.

"But, Alma, there is hope for you," he put the pipe in his mouth and grasped it between his teeth as he continued. "Cultural Relativism says there are no *absolutely* correct standards of behavior against which varying cultural and personal behavioral patterns can be measured." The words sluiced between his teeth and the pipe. He looked down past the crook of his nose at her as if she too must be enthralled with his wisdom.

"In that case, Duke, you won't be offended by my exiting behavior when I leave you to expound further on Cultural Relativism . . . without me. I'm going home. See you tomorrow Petra?"

"Well," he called after her, "come to the Sheepskin Singles meeting in Poughkeepsie."

Alma rushed out of the dining room without looking back.

"On Thursday night. Marriott Hotel." He followed her. "We have invigorating discussions I'm sure you would enjoy. A very intellectual crowd." He projected his voice to bridge the growing space between them. "Seven o'clock. In the lobby."

Alma was in the parking lot. Right, she thought, just what I need, an intellectual crowd. The drive home was peaceful.

Alma unlocked her front door, shut it behind her, and dropped wearily into the embrace an overstuffed chair. She breathed in the quiet of her living room. Roses from her garden fragranced the silence. A soft breeze from the open windows caressed her face. She took a deep breath and breathed it out noisily. Ahh! No bears in the basement. No pedantic pop psychologist at her elbow. No discordant music. But, she rose and went over to the fireplace. There is that ugly wood burning stove still in my fireplace.

She walked slowly from room to room. Familiarity greeted her in the bedrooms, in the kitchen, in the hallway. She passed the basement door and she knew she could go down there to do the laundry any time she pleased. See, she told herself. She faced her fears. No more ghosts there.

She opened the windows and the night music wandered in. Tonight, for the first time since Mack died, she felt completely at home. She sat in her chair again, appreciating her aloneness. Soaking in it as if it were a warm, fragrant bath.

Alma woke up at two a.m. still in the chair, a little chilly and very hungry. An omelet. That's what I feel like eating. She bustled around the kitchen being careful not to make too much noise. She grated some sharp cheddar cheese while bacon fried in the pan. Fresh orange juice, she thought. Better not, the juicer's too noisy. That was one gadget Mack had approved of. Cheaper than buying juice, he'd told her. The kettle signaled her tea water was ready. She rushed to silence its whistle, when she stopped herself.

Why in the world are you trying to be quiet, she asked herself? Habit. No one's sleeping. There's no one to complain about the kettle's whistle or the pans clanging, or the silverware chinking. I can make as much noise as I please.

She turned on the radio. A static-y Ella Fitzgerald crooned softly to the bacon sizzle. Night Train.

I used to listen to that while I was making the kids' school clothes. I wonder if I can trade in the sewing machine for a CD player. A little louder. She turned it up, but the reception was so bad she turned it off. That's why I haven't listened to it for so long. Why haven't I bought a new one, she wondered?

Denial, the refusal to accept . . . These words floated into her mind. She shooed them away.

She sliced some crusty rye bread, and toasted it. The caraway smelled good; she inhaled the bouquet as creamy butter melted into the bread. She sat down and ate her mushroom, bacon, cheese omelet, hot and fresh. No interruptions. Hot food. A unique experience for Alma. She hadn't appreciated her hot meals since Mack died, or even noticed. She ate slowly and savored every bite. Sipped her orange spice tea in the quiet of her kitchen. Alone. I haven't noticed how good alone feels, she thought. I need to make some changes around here. That Duke guy. What a jerk.

9

Weeks later, Alma awakened lazily. She pulled the covers over her head to shut out the brightness. Brightness? She sat up. She glanced at the clock. Ten! The phone rang.

"Hello," she tried to say. But no sound came out. She cleared her throat. "Hello."

"You sound half asleep."

"Petra, I haven't seen you since Patsy's. I'm kinda mad at you," she said languidly, yawning.

"How many times do I have to apologize? Get over it and get to the good stuff—you and that good looking guy with the mustache?"

"I don't even know his last name. I'll never see him again. And there will be no more singles nights for me. Where have you been?"

"I had to go out of town on business. And, Larry and I have been spending a lot of time together. A lot of time. There won't be anymore singles nights for me either. For a while."

"Sounds serious."

"Who knows? What about the junk in the basement? Have you decided what to do with it?"

"Been working on a dress for Jessie Delano."

"Whoa, now that's a lot of fabric."

"You're cruel."

"Have you finished my dress?"

"I might get around to it." Alma stretched and yawned. "George is going to help me price the tools. I guess I'll have a garage sale. Sonya from the antique shop is going to look at some of the other things. She'll know what's valuable."

"Have you found any more money?"

"I haven't looked. I have thrown some things out. I

burned more papers. I haven't opened any boxes."

"How much was in the tin you found?"

"About ten thousand."

"Ten thousand! Unbelievable! Do you think there's more?"

"Maybe. I don't know. I hope not. We could have done so much for the kids with that money. I don't want there to be any more money."

"What are you going to do with it? The ten grand?"

"Right now it's in my freezer. I'm afraid to put it in the bank. There might be tax complications. And I don't want to ask anyone. I don't want anyone to know Mack hid money from us."

"I'll ask at work."

"I've been thinking . . . Petra, want to go shopping?" Alma jumped out of bed. "I'm going to buy a CD player and a dishwasher. Then I'm going to hire someone to get that ugly wood burning stove out of the fireplace. I want a real fire this winter. Maybe I'll even buy that computer you've been telling me I need."

"Hey, there's some great Labor Day sales going on, even though Labor Day is over. I bet George would help you with the stove. Get up you lazy woman. Sleeping half the day away when there's shopping to be done."

"And let's stop at the record store in the mall. I want to buy some CD's."

"I'm not so sure I want to go shopping," Alma said when Petra picked her up. "You know I'm not a shopper," she said, rinsing the last of her breakfast dishes.

The women redefined middle age— both in jeans and pink tops. Alma's faded jeans hung loose and relaxed on her long, athletic legs. She wore the same blouse she'd worn to Patsy's Pizza Pub. Petra's dark blue jeans clung to her curves. A sheer blouse with silver threads that caught the sun shimmered over a skintight tank top.

"What happened to change your mind, Al? An hour ago you were hot to buy a dishwasher. What's going on?"

"Nothing's going on, not really. I'm thinking I don't need a dishwasher. I mean, it's just me. I don't have that many dishes. It's foolish. I mean, what a waste," she said pointing to the drain board. It held one cereal bowl, a teacup, a juice glass, and two water glasses. "Why should I buy a dishwasher just to buy a dishwasher?"

"There are times you could use one, girl. If Alicia visits with her kids. Or Grace. You might find yourself cooking a big Thanksgiving dinner. You'd be glad to plop all those dishes in, push the button and play with your grandkids instead of soap suds to the elbows for a half hour."

"Grace doesn't even call; she won't visit. Neither can Alicia. To fly from Texas with two kids, they don't have that kind of money."

"Okay, nix the dishwasher. Let's go to Wal-Mart. I have some shopping to do. We can check out CD players. You're still up for that, right?"

"I suppose so. I'll drive so I can leave when I've had enough. You could spend the whole day shopping." A caustic edge crept into Alma's tone.

"Did you sleep okay last night?"

Alma gave her a look of exasperation.

They drove in silence.

"Maybe I'll buy a new purse," said Alma as she pulled into the shopping center, parked, and walked toward Wal-Mart, her long-legged strides challenging Petra to keep up. Alma heaved her large brown-so-it-won't-show-the-dirt purse with many compartments onto her shoulder. No sequins, she thought.

"Slow down, Alma, this isn't a race."

"I want to get this over with."

"You should buy a Coach bag at the Mall, you can afford it. They are expensive but they last for years and never go out of style."

"Right, you know what a slave to fashion I am."

"You're touchy today, Lady A.."

Alma stopped short next to a van with ladders lashed to the roof and red flagged two-by-fours protruding from the back window.

"Duke said..."

A car horn blasted, startling both women. They leaped out of the way as a car zoomed by, the driver barely tall enough to peer over the steering wheel.

"Parking lots," said Petra, "traffic's crazier than on the Thruway."

"Duke said..."

The sound of shopping carts being collected and wheeled along unnerved Alma. She turned in the direction of the sound and gasped.

She seized Petra by the arm and turned sharply to the left, like a fugitive on the run. She dragged her friend between the van and a Mercedes.

"What're you doing?"

"Shh! Be quiet." Alma rushed across two parking rows pulling Petra along. She stopped and tugged Petra behind a U-Haul truck.

"Don't shush me. Are you nuts? You'll get us killed running around the parking lot like that."

Alma pointed. Petra saw a man getting into an SUV three rows over.

"Huh? Who is he? The Boston Strangler?"

"Tony. I saw him at Patsy's."

"Patsy's? Oh! Right. You were sitting at the table with him."

"I don't want him to see me."

"You *are* nuts. Just say hello and walk on by. Don't endanger *my* life, just to avoid someone you don't want to see," Petra shouted angrily.

Alma glared at Petra. "That's it. I'm going home."

"Alma! You're jumpier than my cat. Settle down. Let's get a glass of iced tea. Then we'll leave." Petra looked across to the empty space where Tony's car had been. "He's gone. Let's go." She led Alma by the sleeve to a small café, next to Wal-Mart. They sat at a corner table.

"Your drinks are on the way," the backwards-baseball-capped teen shouted from behind the counter. He didn't bother to come over to the table to take their order. "Iced tea, right?"

Petra nodded assent.

"No! I want hot tea. Decaf green tea." Alma felt tears pushing for release.

"What are you crying about?" The usual demand had gone out of her tone.

"I'm *not* crying." Alma wiped her hand across her wet face. She was irritated as hell with Petra. Her life seemed so simple. "That kid is the best example I've ever seen of fresh-mouthed-high-school-drop-out-arrogance."

"He's just young, Al. I bet he goes to school on the second shift."

"This table is dirty. He should clean all the tables, look at them—every one dirty from the breakfast crowd. But, no. He's standing there chewing his gum and blowing bubbles."

"He's fixing your tea, Alma. What's bothering you?" Gentle understanding shaded her voice.

Both women were silent when the teen, all arms and legs, came over and set their drinks in front of them sloshing tea on the napkins.

"This table's dirty," he said. "I'm sorry." He turned and went back to the counter. "I'll get a rag and clean it. You know the owner? He had a heart attack here this morning. Paramedics took him to the hospital. He turned blue and stopped breathing. I tried to give him CPR. Another customer called 911 while I was doing it. Then she helped me. I don't know if I did it right. We learned it in school." He wiped the table with a clean, Clorox-smelling cloth. "I hope he's going to be all right. I'm worried about him. I'm the only one here, so I can't go over to the hospital. I hope I did the right thing."

"Good for you. You're a hero. You probably saved his life," said Petra.

Oh God, thought Alma. Picking on this poor kid. What is wrong with me. She couldn't look at him.

"Yeah, maybe," he chomped on his gum furiously, "if I did it right. It's been a long time since I learned." He disappeared into a back room, still talking.

"Not everyone would be willing to give CPR," said Petra. Alma nodded her head. She was crying now.

"We're going to sit here until you tell me what's wrong. You are hardly ever this cranky."

"It's just me. I think I'm going crazy. Lately, I'm up one week and down the next. Great in the morning, depressed by evening. I don't even know Tony and I overreact about nothing."

"For a year you did nothing, No grieving, hardly any tears. Look on the bright side, look on the bright side, look on the bright side. You were like a broken record. This crazy mood swingy time is normal. It's about time."

"Denial is your worst enemy." That's what Duke said. "I remember every word. He said 'Denial is your worst enemy. You know what denial is, Alma?'" She repeated in a mocking tone. He said that to me. I don't even know what it means but I can't get his words out of my head. How would he know anyway?"

Alma rummaged through her purse and extracted a crumpled used tissue. "I have got to get a new purse," she said as she patted her face. "I carry this big ugly purse loaded with everything and I don't even have a tissue. Where is that Coach store?"

Petra spoke not a word.

The sound of dishes and pots and pans banged and clanged from the back room and competed with the low tones of a jazzy tune on a distant radio. The café, empty except for them, witnessed Alma's struggle.

She twisted the tissue. She sipped her tea. She looked around the café blinking her eyes to stem the flow of tears. Small etchings filled the wall beside their table. Alma inspected each one—A doorway with a grapevine arched over it, a cat on a cushion, a girl on a swing. On every table, cheap glass vases propped up limp carnations. A fan whirled above them.

A fly buzzed Alma's hair and landed on the table. She swished it away with her ragged tissue, but it returned.

Another sip of tea. Alma scrutinized the counter. Seven stools stood silently by.

The twisted tissue crumbled. She put the remnants into her purse and found another to mop the constant stream that flowed over her red cheeks. She blew her nose. Swallowed. Cleared her throat.

"Did you have another flashback?"

Alma shook her head. "I saw . . ." She put her hand in a stop gesture. She wasn't ready for words.

Petra nodded her assurance. She'd wait.

An angry sounding car horn blared from the parking lot, repeating its cuss word several times. The phone in the back rang once. The baseball-capped teen's voice could be heard but no words could be discerned.

"All right!" the teen shouted. He leaped into the dining room, "he's going to be all right. That was the paramedics. Mr. Fernandez is going to be all right." He danced around the café. "The EMT said I saved his life. See, the lady didn't know how to do it. I told her what to do. Then we did it together. You were right," he thanked Petra with his eyes. "Are you going to be here for a few minutes? I want to go over to the dry cleaners to tell them Mr. Fernandez is okay."

"Sure," said Alma.

The boy ran out without acknowledging Alma's response.

She took a deep breath. "When I saw Tony in the parking lot, my purse was heavy with Mack's money, and I'd been talking myself out of spending it. Doesn't feel right, spending it. Doesn't feel like I should. And at the same time, I wanted to spend it all just to get even. Spend his damn money, every cent on nonsense. Stuff I don't need, just want—like the dishwasher. Call the appliance store, have them deliver, install, do the plumbing, for a dishwasher I don't need. Be extravagant. But, here I am walking into Wal-Mart for god's sake, not Lord & Taylor, but Wal-Mart. And I'm saying to myself, you don't need a CD player. The wood stove's not so bad. You don't mind washing dishes. At least you have a washer and dryer now. The money getting heavier every minute.

"But when I saw Tony, the heaviness shifted from this god-damned ugly purse to inside of me. Leftover feelings, leftover love, that nobody wants, heavy in my chest. Sort of like my freezer. Every time I make too much for me to eat, I wrap up the leftovers and put them in the freezer. You know what my freezer looks like."

Petra nodded. "It's stuffed."

"So there's the freezer, full, things falling out as if it were wanting to give some of its fullness to me. But, I keep stuffing it fuller and slamming the door."

Petra nodded. "You only put the good feelings away?"

Alma shook her head. "I put everything away that disrupted the peace. That became the most important thing, peace. I put hate in there too. I'm ashamed to say it. I hated him, Mack, . . . sometimes. Me, the one who says look on the bright side. Me, the one who says there's always something to be grateful for. I have little packages of hate stored up. But I didn't know it till now."

"Are you saying that the denial stuff Duke spouted applies to you?"

"I don't know. Why did I let him get away with making us live like paupers? Why is it that I don't know if I loved him, but today I know I hated him? And you know what else? When he was sick and so nasty to me, I wanted him to die. I'd imagine how peaceful I'd be without him." She blew her nose. "I'm not even the person I thought I was."

"I'm here to tell you that it is only you who are surprised you're not perfect," Petra laughed. "You did the best you could. Better than me. You kept your family together. None of them got in trouble. Well, except for the time William got caught growing pot in the garden. Remember how Mack interceded for him with the Justice of the Peace, negotiated a punishment. Remember?"

Alma smiled, "That was genius. They call it community service now. William had to get up at four in the morning to clean out the cow barn for old man Reed. He was sick or something. Did it for six months. Nothing went on William's record. Mack was kind, didn't raise his voice, didn't put William down. He drove William over to Reed's farm, every morning. Picked him up at seven thirty and brought him home to shower and get ready for school.

"I never once heard Mack complain, either. He even sat with him the first few mornings when the sight and smell of cow shit and ammonia fumes made William sick to his stomach. There they'd sit, William on the floor, head in the toilet. Mack on the edge of the tub, rubbing his son's back. I haven't thought about that for a long time."

"Did you hate him then?"

"No, I loved him for that, Petra."

"I guess there is always something to be grateful for," said Petra.

Alma was quiet as she re-ran the father-son cinema in her head.

"And always something to drive you to look for those moments, sometimes in desperation."

"Like today. Thank you, Pete."

They spent hours in Wal-Mart. Alma examined every CD player in the store. She studied every last CD in the jazz section. Even Petra, who lived to shop, found the experience too intense and left for a while to do some shopping of her own. When she returned, Alma hadn't paid for her purchases.

She stood at the counter, her brows scrunched together looking at the pile of merchandise she'd placed there: a CD radio cassette-recorder with a six CD changer system and speakers for every room in the house, six CDs, a Walkman, and two cassette tapes.

"Come on, Alma, get me out of here. Let's go to the mall. There's a place with a hundred times as many CDs."

"I don't know, Petra, this is too much money."

"OK, you really don't need a CD player. You have that nice old radio. Static's good. Here. Here's an FM antenna. Lots cheaper. Let's put Ella and Duke back, too. Get the antenna."

Alma looked at her friend in disbelief. "You know who you sound like, Petra?"

"No, who?" Petra feigned ignorance.

"You *know* who. I'll take these," she gestured toward the CD player and the CDs. She pushed the speakers, the Walkman and tapes aside. Looked up apologetically at Petra. She needed encouragement. Petra obliged.

"Unacceptable. She'll take it all," Petra said to the sales person.

"That's going to be at least eleven hundred four dollars and thirty one cents, Petra. I can't spend that much."

"How much did you bring?"

"All of it."

Petra's eyes widened, her mouth opened and her breath caught in her throat. "All of it?"

Alma opened her purse. There, in her purse, was this thick, moist looking freezer-wrapped package, one end opened for easy access.

"And why is it that you can't spend eleven hundred dollars?"

"It's just too much to spend all at one time."

"Now, who do *you* sound like? Buy all of it."

"I'll buy only three of the speakers," she said more to Petra than to the sales person.

"Good. I want to copy your Barry White tape. Larry is coming over tonight. A little mood music will help. Not that he needs any music to put him in the mood."

Petra opened her package. Alma looked in. Then, confused, reached in and pulled out a box. "Trojans? What are . . . ? Oh my god, Petra. Condoms?" She shoved them back into the bag and looked around hoping no one saw her. "You bought condoms? You need that many? Ten?"

"Shh! Don't announce it to the world."

The sales person finished bagging the purchases and gave Alma her change, the corners of his mouth straining to remain serious, nonplused. Alma looked away quickly, realizing he saw the condoms.

Petra giggled. "Let's get to the mall."

"We'd better get the dishwasher next," said Alma. "At least look. Then the mall and the travel agent."

"You are going to drag me around all day. Okay, I'm ready. You know, George would do the plumbing for you. That would cost you only a meal."

"No, not George," Alma said, raising her voice.

"Have you two already gotten it on?"

The sales man asked if he could help carry the packages to the car. They'd both forgotten about him standing there. Alma wondered if he offered to help so he'd hear the rest of the story. Petra's not getting any more out of me, she thought, the heat in her face rising.

Montgomery Ward's going out of business sale had no customers more eager than Alma and Petra. Feeling lighter, brighter, Alma sported the earphones attached to her new Walkman. Her step bounced ever so slightly, to Stan Getz's tunes. When she let herself for a fleeting moment, she even felt a little like the Girl From Ipanema. Free and lovely, Alma went walking through the parking lot, toward Montgomery Ward.

By the time they reached the entry, she was feeling heady, her shoulders bounced out the rhythm while her hips swayed and her feet strutted to the tempo. When they pushed open the heavy doors, a teen wearing a brightly colored knit cap over his braided hair, jigged to a lively tune being pumped into his ears by a Walkman like Alma's. He danced around her gesturing with his hand until she hesitantly high-fived him.

Alma didn't buy a dishwasher, but she did discover she could purchase one that was portable and didn't require any plumbing. The stop at the travel agency was more fruitful. She bought travel vouchers for Alicia and her family. A practical gift. She didn't buy any tickets for herself.

"I thought we'd never get here," said Petra, as the entered the air-conditioned mall. The air smelled like roasting nuts and Gloria Jean's coffee beans.

"I want to go to the Coach store you were telling me

about. And there," she pointed to Baby Gap. "I'll get some things for Alicia's kids. I'd get something for Grace too, but I don't know where to mail them."

"We can stop in Gap. You could buy something for yourself."

"We'll see."

10

A warm late September day soon after, her new purse bouncing on her hip, Alma jogged to McEvoy's post office to mail a package to her daughter. She'd send the gifts to Alicia and her family: clothes for her children, toys, travel vouchers, and dinner for two gift certificates for the Cheesecake Factory. She knew Alicia loved to eat out but didn't because she couldn't afford it.

As she jogged past trees still wearing their summer finest, Alma remembered a September morning long ago when these same trees had changed their leaves due to an early cold snap. She remembered that day the way some people remember the day Kennedy was shot. She'd returned from McEvoy's with William in a homemade sling. She bought milk for him, feed for the chickens and a newspaper. She'd never bought a newspaper there before that day. September 25, 1968, twenty-seven years ago.

The sun, still low in the sky, beamed across her kitchen sink flashing diamonds in the dishpan filled with water. She had saved the not-too-dirty dish water. Their shallow well was nearly dry after a summer of drought. Mack pigeonholed her request to dig a new well before the ground froze. Sometimes it's necessary to make sacrifices, he'd told her. The well has served our needs so far, he'd said. It will rain soon. Then we'll be glad we didn't waste our money because of a little inconvenience.

To do the dishes and bathe herself and the baby, she hauled water from the stream that ran along their land. Mack bathed in the stream. She boiled the water for drinking. Even though he was too young, she'd switched William to whole milk. She didn't want to make formula with either the stream or the well water. William, so good-natured and amenable, took to the change without noticing.

When she returned home, she'd transferred the sleeping William from the sling to his crib. She gazed at her son's face, angelic in sleep. Amazed at her own capacity to love so completely, without limit, she stroked his soft cheek and hoped that he wouldn't grow to hate her for what she was about to do.

Alma made a cup of peppermint tea to ease her nervous stomach, queasy with anticipation. She sat at the kitchen table, crafted by Mack from a large spool that once held cable for the phone lines. If she could find a job, she'd leave him. Feeling like she did when she told a lie, she opened the newspaper to the classifieds. Employment.

I'll get a job.

Alma, have you lost your mind? What are you thinking?

Something I can do at home would be perfect. I can live simply. She tried to ignore the inner voice, always critical lately.

But you are living simply already, she argued with herself. *Why leave? What would improve?*

I'd have my freedom, she argued back. I feel ruled over. Trapped in the small world of this house, this garden, his kingdom.

You have everything you need. He makes a good salary. Better than anything you'll get.

He parcels out enough for the grocery store. If I want a haircut, I have to save a dollar here and there until I have enough.

You're leaving over a haircut? You don't think you'll be getting haircuts on the money you'll be making, do you?

She skipped over the Professional, Management, and Financial sections. Discouragement slid between the lines.

He doesn't beat you. He's building a big house for you.

Maybe in the office/clerical section. I took typing in high school. She went down the listings, her right index finger stopping here and there. Not this one. I don't know shorthand. Fast paced office. No, sounds exhausting, she thought.

He loves you. Lots of women would give anything for the security you have.

Security? Every week there's some new disaster he's preparing for. Now we're stockpiling wood just in case oil becomes too expensive or a blizzard shuts down the power. Whichever comes first. A wave of nausea swirled within her for a moment.

This one: Law Firm—typing/billing clerk. Min 75 wpm. Call Mrs. Torres. Seventy five words a minute. I was never that fast, but I could learn. I could take a night class at the high school. Her shoulders sank. That won't work, she thought, remembering the evening she went to the Laundromat. She came home to find William sobbing in his crib, the dinner dishes piled in the sink and a dirty diaper spilling its foul contents on the bathroom floor.

At least he changed it. He goes to work every day to earn money for you and William. Doesn't that show you how much he loves you?

That's about him and his fears. Not about loving me. Not about loving William. I live in the shadow of his fears. I am tense and tired all the time. Today my stomach is rolling with anxiety.

You'd better get to the applesauce before the apples go bad. The green beans are ready to freeze for the winter. You don't have time for this foolishness.

Here's one. Seamstress/tailor—lg dry cleaner. Exp. Work in shop or at home. Perfect. She reached for the phone with a trembling hand and arranged an interview later that day. She packed William in his sling again and brought samples of her sewing.

"Mrs. Stodder?" Alma's stomach clenched nervously as she entered the shop.

The woman nodded and extended her hand. "You must be Alma."

"Yes ma'am, I'm Alma MacCallum," she placed her bundle of samples on the counter and took the older woman's hand.

"What a beautiful baby you have there," she said as Alma adjusted his position in the sling. "How old?" William smiled a smile that brightened his whole face and Mrs. Stopper's.

"This is William. He's seven months."

"Can I hold him?" Mrs. Stodder held out her arms.

"I have experience, Mrs. Stodder, not working in a shop, but I've been sewing for years." Alma lifted William from the sling and placed him in the woman's arms. "I've made all my own clothes since high school. I even design my own patterns. I made my mother's clothes, too."

"Your mother," she looked down and away, nodding. "Yes, I remember your mother, mmm. Yes, well, come. Let's talk my in office, Alma."

She gathered her samples and followed Mrs. Stodder to the back of the shop through long narrow aisles between racks of plastic wrapped garments that fluttered and rustled as they passed. There were no windows. The only ventilation came from the sliding glass doors that spanned the front and a small door in the back. Even with the sliders fully opened the shop was hot. The further back they went the hotter it became; heat and chemical fumes swirled around them.

I can't work here, Alma thought. Maybe I should leave now. These fumes can't be good for William.

"I have an air conditioner in the sewing room, which is my office," Mrs. Stodder said as if she read Alma's thoughts. "When you drop off finished garments, you can use the back entrance. Goes right into the sewing room." Her office was cool, the air smelled clean. "See, this is much better. Now, let me see what you have there," she said shifting William to the other hip.

Alma sifted through her samples and selected the tweed sport coat she'd made for Mack. While Mrs. Stodder examined that, Alma shook out dresses she'd made for herself and placed them over the back of the chairs. She arranged the other garments on a table.

"Here, let me take William. You'll be able to see that

jacket better."

"Where do you find time to do this kind of sewing with the baby and that big garden?"

How does she know about the garden, Alma wondered? But only for a moment. Everyone in this town knew everyone else's business. "I sew in the winter. I won't be doing the garden anymore. I'll have more than enough time to sew."

"You're going to let the garden go?"

"Look at this dress I made for my wedding. Notice the sheer dress over a silk lining and the bead work on the bodice. I'm working on this one for my friend, and this one," she handed a lavender linen dress to Mrs. Stodder." No need to be telling her my business.

"Beautiful work. The job is yours if you want it. It doesn't pay much. You get whatever the customer gives me. Five for a hem, seven for a zipper replacement and so on. Not enough to make a living on. I don't make anything on the alterations unless you work here. Then I take ten percent."

Not enough to make a living on, thought Alma. Her heart sank.

"You were hoping to make more."

"Well, . . . um."

Mrs. Stodder took a slip of paper and jotted a phone number. "Call Joan Nash. She's a dressmaker in Kingston. She used to work here, but now she has her own business. She makes garments for wealthy women from the city. She told me the other day she has too many clients. She's looking for help. That's a job you could make a living at, even establish a business of your own some day."

Alma thanked her. A business of her own. She hadn't hoped for that much, but she knew it was possible, in time. She packed William into his sling, rolled up her samples, her stomach swirling nausea despite the hope she felt. But hope sometimes makes a mockery of us all.

Alma named her second child Grace because she'd

prayed for the grace to accept the change in her plans. Grace to deal with Mack's rigid, fanatic ways, when she realized she was pregnant for the second time.

Leaving Mack was out of the question, with another baby on the way. She didn't go to church, but she prayed daily for strength and perseverance. She was raised to believe that birth control was wrong, and she just couldn't shake that notion. The nuns committed themselves to saving her soul and keeping her from living the life of sin her mother had led. She'd heard them say so, once when they didn't know she was listening. They'd taught her that the husband was boss, her place was to please him, that birth control was wrong and that God answered prayers. Grace was what she asked for.

McEvoy's hadn't changed much in the last twenty-seven years. When she entered McEvoy's today with the package for Alicia, Frieda Baker, town gossip, was chatting with a group of women near the hardware section of the multipurpose store. Her husband, Clyde, was standing around with an impatient look on his face, the slimy end of a cigar in his mouth, foul clouds rose, defiling the air.

"Heard you had a fire up there, then got attacked by a bear," said Frieda.

"Yes." She knows everything, Alma thought as she accelerated toward the exit. She'd mailed her package and hoped she'd get out before Frieda noticed her. No luck.

"You're up there all alone now that Mack's dead. Over a year now, isn't it? Not good for a woman to live by herself. No man to protect her. Besides, it doesn't look right. If you get what I mean." A knowing look overtook Mrs. Baker's pinched face, her eyebrows raising Groucho Marx style.

Boxes of produce filled the aisle near the entrance. Mr. McEvoy stacked bright orange peaches next to red and yellow Delicious apples. The store smelled like Mrs. McEvoy's famous chocolate chip cookies, cigar smoke, and old fish.

"No, Mrs. Baker. I *don't* get what you mean." Alma

turned and faced her dead on, eye to eye.

"Well," her face looked startled, caught off-guard. "It's just that you're alone. You went to Patsy's Pub that time. Some folks are saying you bring men home with you now you're alone."

Patsy's Pub was in Roseville, two towns over. But Frieda's far-reaching, tongue-wagging connections knew no boundaries.

"Besides," Frieda added hastily, spewing her cigarette exhaust-fume breath in the faux-sympathy that was her trademark, "You've got that long driveway to shovel. Gonna be a rough winter. And that lawn of yours, it's huge. You can't be getting on Mack's tractor to mow it."

"It's *my* tractor, Mrs. Baker. And I do get on that tractor to mow the lawn and plough the driveway."

A hushed silence replaced the chatter of voices. No *ka-ching* of the cash register. No *zing* of the slicer because Rita, referred to by everyone, except the McEvoys, as their old maid daughter, stopped slicing cold cuts for Hildy Stodder, the dry cleaner. The talk about the new hotel being built in town stopped mid-sentence. No pings as dried beans hit the tinny scoop on the scale. Giggles, coughs and ahems suspended. If audible, eardrum vibrations would have filled the silence with a roar.

"Consider this, Mrs. Baker. I don't have to marry a man to get the lawn mowed. I can hire someone to do it. Then, Mrs. Baker, I don't have to put up with his snoring, or his dirty underwear on the floor. Or his stinking cigar."

Frieda was impervious to the reproach. "I hear George Herlihy's been up to your place a lot lately. Hiring him?"

Alma tried to think of a barbed retort, but instead she put her earphones in place and turned up the sound on the Walkman. She turned a glowering glance back at Frieda through narrowed eyes and without looking, reached for the door to escape. The door opened on its own.

Her momentum hurled her into a tan blockade that let out a sound on impact. "Umph" said the escaping air as the impediment to her progress leaned forward and grasped her shoulders. She looked up not knowing what hit her. For an instant, the opposing forces of the collision held them in a unexpected embrace. There she stood face to face with Tony, Corona Man, as Barry White's sexy tones filled her head. She felt the warmth of his breath on her cheek, smelled mint as surprise opened his mouth.

11

"Hey!" he said, "Sorry." He released her. "Oh, hi. Remember me from Patsy's a couple of weeks ago? Tony."

"Hello." Alma groaned and glanced sideways at Frieda who had an I-knew-it-all-along smirk on her face. Alma rushed outside. Tony followed her. Frieda followed Tony.

Alma landed flat on her face, her foot tangled in a sign proclaiming the last outdoor concert of the season was being held Saturday night a month ago. She banged into a flimsy newspaper stand which in turn crashed against the storefront window announcing to the world what a klutz she was. A crowd gathered. Everyone who was inside was now outside. All seemed to be nodding: klutz.

"I'm fine. I can get myself up."

What an idiot I am, she thought. Could I just once look like a sane person? How much more humiliation can you heap upon yourself? She shook off Tony's assistance.

"I *will* get up by my-*self*, thank you."

Good grief, is this any way to make an impression? Who says I want to make an impression? Suddenly Alma became aware again of Barry White's crooning tones in her left ear and in her right nostril. Yanking the ear phones off, she tried to stand. Her knee ached. There was an enlarging red area tinting the edges of the hole on the right knee in her tights.

She tried to stand but her foot was still caught in the sign. When she moved, the newspaper stand came down on top of her. Her ankle throbbed. Damn, damn.

"*I* can do it," she growled at Tony, who still insisted on helping her up.

"Every once in a while a person needs another's help," Tony whispered. He moved the newspaper stand.

"Call 911," shouted Hildy.

"No, the rescue squad. It'll take too long for 911 to get here from Roseville," shouted someone else.

"NO!" shouted Alma. Leave me be. I can get up." She accepted Tony's help. Better him than the rescue squad.

"Don't put your weight on it," Tony suggested.

She did. A sharp pain shot from her ankle to her knee.

Mr. McEvoy came rushing out with the straight-backed chair Clyde Baker had been using as a foot rest.

Arms floundering, trying to grab something to support herself, Alma couldn't seat herself without fear of falling again.

Tony lowered her onto the chair and raised her foot gently. He put it on a second chair that seemed to appear out of nowhere.

Klutz, klutz, klutz.

A crow in a nearby tree agreed. Caw, caw, caw.

"This needs an x-ray," said Tony.

"No x-ray. No rescue squad. I'll be fine. Give me a few minutes, then I'll go home."

She tried to stand. The blue on her ankle, which pressed too tightly against her shoe, was not her sock.

"Where's your car? You can drive, if we get you to your car. You don't have a clutch, do you," he asked?

"I don't have the car. I ran."

"Running! At her age. She's no kid, you know," Frieda mumbled loudly. "I'll drive you home," she offered, the same smirk still on her face.

Alma could picture Frieda rummaging through her house once she got there, while Alma sat helpless on a chair. Frieda would be sure to go into the bedrooms, down to the basement, snoop in the medicine cabinet. Probably, run her finger over the furniture inspecting for dust. "My, dear. You must dust three times a week," she'd say, tut-tutting her tongue against the roof of her mouth.

"No, I'm fine. Really."

Rita was wrapping an ice pack around Alma's ankle.

"Do you have ice at home? I'll check when we get there," said Frieda.

See, already, she's planning to see what I have in my refrigerator. Probably looking for beer and wine that I give the men I bring home. Alma groaned aloud.

"Hurts that bad?" asked Tony.

"No. Yes. I mean that's not . . . Never mind," said Alma gesturing with a furtive sideways glance in Frieda's direction.

Tony leaned in close. "Who do you want to bring you home?" he asked quietly. "Me or Frieda?" The sleeve of his tan T-shirt brushed against Alma's arm. Soft cotton comfort. His jeans wrapped tightly around him as he squatted beside her. The prong of the brass buckle pulled against the hole in his brown leather belt. Alma studied his brown moccasins. She was aware of the tweedy smell of him. Earthy mixed with leather. She looked up. Hazel to green, sparks flew.

"Maybe we should bring her inside," said Mr. McEvoy. "Then we can put the heating pad on."

"No don't move her," said Clyde Baker. "Get a hot water bottle."

"Take her shoe off."

"Ice, you put ice on for the first twenty-four hours."

"Forty-eight," said Rita.

"No, leave her shoe on. It will keep the swelling down."

"My car?" Tony slid his hand in his pocket and pulled out keys. He looked directly at her.

Alma nodded. She avoided his eyes.

Tony rose slightly. He pulled her arm across his shoulders and put his arm around Alma's waist. He lifted her to standing.

She felt his breath on her neck, warm, minty. His mustache had been trimmed.

Tony whispered. "Don't put any weight on it, Alma. My car is around the back. We'll be there before they object." The two hobbled along for a few steps. Small pebbles rolled under her foot and she stumbled. In one fluid movement, Tony slid his free arm under her knees and swept Alma up as if she were a delicate, long ball gown.

"No, no. That's all wrong," shouted Frieda.

Tony and Alma both jumped at her loud, grumpy tone.

"You're supposed to alternate. First ice for twenty minutes then heat for twenty."

Tony picked up his pace. "How're we doing? We're almost there," he whispered. "A few more steps and we'll be out of sight." They were about to turn the corner of the building when Frieda shouted again.

"Hey! Where you going? I'm going to drive her home. My car's over here."

"We're going in my car, Mrs. Baker, more room." He didn't stop for explanations.

He lifted her onto the back seat. She scooted over to the other side with her good foot and her bottom. A least her ankle was more comfortable on his plush back seat than it had been on the wooden chair. The ice pack had fallen off somewhere. She noticed her elbow was bleeding and tried not to get blood on the leather seat. Leather, it smells good. She nestled her face into the back of the seat and inhaled. Mack would have said leather was frivolous, a waste. Now that she thought about it, he did say that about Petra's car.

"I'll come too. It's not proper," Alma heard Frieda say as Tony shut her in his Suburban.

"No. No need, Mrs. Baker." She realized no one could hear her. "I'm always bringing strange men home."

Tony opened the car door in time to hear the last sentence.

"What?"

They were driving up the hill toward Alma's. Maples and pines bowing in the breeze before them. An empty school bus passed them going in the opposite direction. She shrank back from the window when she saw her neighbor walk by. Then she noticed he didn't need directions.

They turned into the inclined drive to the front of her house. Alma was shocked to see George on his huge ride-on mower down near the tree line. He didn't seem to see them pull up.

Tony's car will be gone soon, thought Alma, and George might not notice I'm home. Carefully, she opened the car door and swung herself around. As soon as she lowered her foot, it began to throb.

"Let me help you," said Tony as he slipped his arms around her shoulders and under her legs. He carried her to the door.

"Keys?"

"It's not locked."

"Aren't you concerned? Your yardman's here."

"He's a friend. Not the yardman. I can tell you're from the city."

Alma turned the doorknob; Tony pushed the door with his foot.

"Where do you want me to put you?"

"Um, in the kitchen, I guess."

"Don't you think you'd be better off in that lounger? You could put your foot up."

"You're right." She grabbed hold of the arm of the chair, happy to be able to help that much at least. "Thanks for your help; I'm fine now."

"Do you have an Ace bandage? I'll wrap it for you. Ice too, you'd better keep this iced for a while."

"No, That's okay. I don't want to hold you up. Thanks so much for your help." Alma could hear the mower getting closer.

"If it were wrapped, you might be able to put some weight on it. You're going to need to get around. Are you alone here?"

"No. Yes, but my son lives in the area. He might stop by."

My son lives in the area. Right, if you consider about 150 miles away in the area. I'm alone here with this man I don't know. And I'm practically helpless.

"I'm not Jack the Ripper," he said as if he could read her thoughts. "Do you have a first aid kit?"

Alma started to laugh and once she started to laugh she couldn't stop. Tony looked at her in dismay.

"What's funny?"

"It's just that Petra called you the Boston Strangler," she forced out between chuckles.

Tony furrowed his brows and cocked his head slightly. "What? Who's Petra? Boston Strangler?"

"She didn't exactly call *you* the Boston Strangler. Oh! She ... Long story. You had to be there."

While she told him an altered version about seeing him in the parking lot, she watched his brows knit together. His eyes narrowed, looked to the ceiling as if searching for understanding, then back at Alma. No matter how she tried to tell the story, it was obvious she'd been trying to avoid him.

"Look, if you want me to wrap your foot, I will. Otherwise, I'll be on my way."

"The Ace bandage is in the bathroom closet. Go down the hall, there ... That's right. First door on the right." She raised her voice. "Open the closet by the tub. Can you hear me?"

"Yeah, The closet door's open."

"The Ace bandage is in a box, third shelf from the top on the right side."

"Oh shit."

"What happened?"

"I knocked over the stack of toilet paper. What are there? Fifty rolls here?"

"My husband, Mack, taught me to be thrifty." The words spilled out in a voice mixed with laughter and derision. She was shocked at the flippant way she spoke of Mack. Shocked that she spoke his name aloud to this man with hazel eyes. This man who smelled of tweed, the earth and fresh mint.

"You're married?"

Alma hadn't mentioned Mack when they were sitting together that night in Patsy's Pizza Pub. He'd told her a little about his wife and her illness. That after her death he hadn't been interested in dating. She wasn't going to reveal anything about herself then. But, today the words slipped out, spoke themselves.

"No."

Tony looked puzzled. He'd returned to the living room with the rolling desk chair from the bedroom and the ice pack. "You can get around on this. You're going to have to get to the bathroom sooner or later."

"He's dead."

"I'm sorry to hear that. I know how difficult it is to lose a spouse."

Tony got down on one knee in the I'm-about-to-propose posture. He gently placed her foot on his raised knee and began to unlace her shoe. Shades of blue and purple spilled over the top of her low-cut sneaker. He removed the laces, one eyelet at a time, so as not to cause pain. He opened the mouth of the shoe wide as possible and eased it off her foot. A gentle, but distinct, stinky feet scent wafted into the space between them.

"Not exactly what I'd call putting your best foot forward," said Alma in a tight little laugh. God, she thought, he's probably gagging. "Sorry."

"Hey, feet are feet. Yours, mine, everyone's. Your foot needs an x-ray. With all the small bones in the foot, an x-ray is the only way to be sure none are broken."

He's kind. Mack would never give an inch to ease another's discomfort. He'd let silence potentiate the pangs of unease.

"You seem to know a lot about bones and ankles."

"I was a med school drop out. Couldn't stand to see people suffer, despite my desire to heal. So, I decided to create beauty. Beautiful buildings, beautiful pottery. Not nearly as noble, but satisfying."

He was lightly palpating her bones. His finger tips moved from her lower leg to her ankle, to her toes and back again.

It was an oddly sensual moment, for Alma. Mack had been dead over a year. How long before that had it been since he touched her. Years. Many years. She hadn't missed being touched. Hadn't missed it at all. Until this moment.

Another ache joined the painful ankle. Alma glanced at Tony to find him looking directly at her. She yielded, permitted the eye contact, allowed him to see into her.

A crashing sound intruded upon the moment as the front door slammed against the wall and startled them. George stood in the doorway, rifle in hand.

12

George placed his rifle casually under his arm, but Alma knew George was anything but casual when it came to the gun he always carried in his truck.

Tony carefully lowered Alma's foot to the floor. He rose to a squat, then to standing. He backed up a few steps. His brows drew together making a furrowed question mark on his forehead. Tony stood silent, alert, ready. He seemed to be sizing George up. Tony was tall, muscular, but George was the Hulk. The moment held few options for Tony other than silence. He looked at Alma. Alma glanced over at the fireplace where Mack's rifles hung above the mantle.

A family photo on the mantelpiece bore witness to this charade. In fading colors, William and Alicia flanked the scarecrows they'd made for the garden. Their laughing faces revealed the fun they'd had dressing them. One scarecrow wore Mack's undershorts and threatened pilfering rabbits and chipmunks with a cardboard rifle. The other was clothed in Alma's old nightgown, hair in rollers. Grace posed on top of a huge pumpkin, her face alight with a great smile, uncharacteristic for her, as if she were a bright patch of color in the black and white picture.

A black and white wedding portrait, aged to a natural sepia tone, stood silently by as the happy couple gazed at Mack's retirement photograph. He was forced to have that photo taken. It, too, was black and white. He was wearing a dark suit, white shirt and dark tie. His last job, in the company he'd worked so long for as a machinist, required the formal attire for a desk job he hated. He looked directly at the camera as if daring the film to capture anything of him beyond the superficial image of his features. Mack stared out from the frame, his face expressionless except for those challenging eyes.

From Alma's line of sight, they formed a trio. Tony, Mack, George. George, focused on Tony. Tony's eyes moved between Alma and George. And Mack looked confrontational.

"Sorry, Alma. I didn't mean to let the door slam into the wall like that. The wind caught it. I thought someone broke in. The strange car in front, and all."

For a few seconds Alma was stunned. But seconds can enclose years. Past converged with present, memories mingled with this moment's reality. George in high school, hunting, teaching Alma to shoot his rifle, weaving his presence through her life since then. Tony arousing in her feelings she'd denied. Mack hammering rifle racks above the mantel over her objections, a deer carcass waiting to be skinned, expecting too much and nothing and everything. Tony was today with no yesterdays.

Alma felt exhausted and disheartened. A hollow feeling grew in her chest. George had pillaged that moment between her and Tony, a moment she'd never be able to retrieve. She wondered what Tony was thinking. Had he noticed the longing she'd felt, a longing she was reluctant to admit? Where did that come from anyway? Alma, you're a grown woman. A grandmother, for God's sake. She took a deep breath, smoothed her hair, and planted a smile on her face and an evenness that she didn't feel in her voice.

"George, I'd like you to meet Tony, uh. . . ." She blushed.

"O'Sullivan," Tony extended his hand to George.

"Oh," George gave a quick, obligatory shake while keeping as much distance between them as possible.

"Tony's the architect for the new hotel."

"Oh."

"He drove me home after I twisted my ankle. That's all that's happening, George." Guilty? Did she feel guilty? Had she betrayed George somehow?

"Get that gun out of my house, George." She adjusted her body in the La-Z-Boy so that she sat up taller.

George looked bewildered at the force of her statement.

"I thought someone broke in. Mack always..."

"And take Mack's with you. I do not want guns in my house. When we find the guns Mack hid downstairs, they'll go too."

George walked over to the mantel, without taking his eyes off Tony, except for a closer look at Alma's foot. "You shouldn't walk on that, Alma." He reached for Mack's rifles. Not looking at her, he said, "Mack wanted these here for your protection."

"I don't need protection. I appreciate your concern, both of you. I'm fine. I can handle things now that I'm home."

"But what if you... Alma, you might need..."

"No guns, George."

He put his rifle on the mantel.

"Let me finish wrapping your foot, then I'll put some ice on it and go," Tony said.

George lowered Mack's guns.

"I can wrap it myself, thanks, Tony." She bent her knee and forced her throbbing ankle up onto her lap despite the pain in her knee. The ace bandage, partially wrapped around her instep, fell and rolled along the floor.

Shit, she said inside herself.

Tony and George both scrambled toward it. Tony grabbed it; George muttered something unintelligible. Tony looked like he was trying desperately to keep the corners of his mouth from rising toward his laughing eyes as he rewound the wayward bandage around itself.

"George. The guns." *Petra, not me, should be in this predicament.*

"I'll get the ice pack." George, now clutching three guns, started toward the bathroom and glared at Tony with an *I-know-where-where-the-ice-pack-is* look.

"The guns, George." Alma narrowed her eyes and pointed to the door. "Get them out of here. All I need is for someone to be shot accidentally."

Alma heard George's truck door open and slam shut. Then he rushed through her living room headed down the hall for the bathroom. "I'll get the ice pack."

"I've got it." Tony was already clunking ice cubes into the ice pack.

Tony pulled over a kitchen chair, sat, placed Alma's foot on his knee. He wound the elastic bandage skillfully around the injured ankle as they both explained to George how she fell.

Alma felt convicted of some sin or other; she didn't know what one. Frieda Baker's accusation of bringing strange men home now that she was a widow rang in her head.

"I'll stay and keep her company, Tony. You can go on."

"I'll call Petra if I need something. You both can get on with your day. Right now, I need a nap." She popped the La-Z-Boy's leg rest into position, careful not to let it jolt her foot and pushed with her good foot to recline. The chair's soft overstuffed fullness embraced and comforted her. She sighed as she began to relax.

"She's out of town. Remember, Alma? She and Larry went to Cape Cod. I'd better stay, in case you need anything," George said, giving Tony a triumphant look. We've known each other a long time, was the message beneath his words. You're not part of our history, said the look on his face.

Alma noticed George's jaw muscles were working the side of his face. His hands were rigid in his pockets.

"My phone's right here." She picked up the portable phone and waved it in the air as if to prove something. "The wheely chair's within reach." She extended her arm to show she could reach it. "Now, I'm going to take a nap. Thank you both. Tony, George." A good-bye-and-leave-me-be tone etched her voice.

"Okay, I'm sure you can manage," said Tony. "I left my card on the kitchen table. Call if you need anything." He closed the door quietly, tires crunched on the gravel driveway.

"I'll take you down to my place, Alma. You shouldn't be alone. How will you . . ."

"No!"

"But, Alma . . ."

"George, please. I'll call you next week. We'll sort through Mack's tools and try to figure out how much to sell them for."

"Okay, Alma, but . . ."

"Before you go, see if you can find some pain killers. I may have thrown them out. Look. Tylox or something like that. They're in the bathroom, in the closet, with Mack's medicines. You remember?"

He got her a glass of water and handed her two pills. "Directions say one or two every four hours."

Alma took one pill. She took the second pill after George left, reluctant to admit the extent of her pain. She put her head back on the lounger. That was like a bad slapstick comedy routine, she thought. She hated the idea of her being disabled. The whole day was a black comedy, only it wasn't funny. George was especially ridiculous. What the heck was he thinking? Bursting in here like the lead man on a S.W.A.T. team. When's the last time we had in an intruder around here? Then she remembered the bear and that he'd spent the night. She grimaced at the memory. And before that, there was the hen house fire.

He's just protective. When his wife was dying, he was attentive and thoughtful, anticipating her needs. His way was different from Mack's. Had it been Alma who was sick, Mack would have said, "Get up. Get out of the bed. Fight back. Survive. Work will make you strong. Don't give in." Maybe not in those words, but that's what he'd say with his body, his attitude. George, on the other hand, wanted Maggie to stay in her room, in bed. Alma thought he'd taken good care of her. She remembered one day in particular toward the end of Maggie's illness.

Maggie's room was darkened by drawn shades. The odor of sickness strong, like a spring bouquet left too long in its vase. All the windows in the house were shut. "I don't want her to catch cold," he'd said.

Alma offered to spend the day with Maggie, so George could go to work for a few hours, then do the grocery shopping. She brought some homemade chicken soup for Maggie, pureed so it could be easily swallowed.

"Want me to heat some soup, Maggie?"

"George just made me eat a soft-boiled egg, but it's like a rock in my stomach now."

"You've got to eat, Maggie. Keep up your strength." He put a glass of water to her mouth, wiggling the straw between her lips. "This will help your stomach. Take some."

Alma was touched by the tenderness he showed.

"I'll be back soon. Don't exert yourself, Maggie," he said as he kissed his wife. He lingered in the kiss, full on the mouth. "Sleep, rest. Be sure to ask Alma to help you to the bathroom." He motioned Alma to come with him as he left the room. "She wants to get up by herself, Alma, and she shouldn't do that."

Alma went back to Maggie's room when George left.

"Please. Please, pull the shade up and open the window."

"George is afraid you'll catch cold."

"I need to see the sun. I have to feel spring on my face, on my arms. This will be my last spring. Please, Alma." Maggie lifted herself onto her elbows, then inched her rail-thin legs over the side of the bed. She sat unsteadily on the edge of the bed, looking toward the window.

"Maggie, you don't know that."

"I need to get out of this bed."

Alma fidgeted around the window, pulling up the shade, adjusting it to the right level, opening the window a crack, propping Maggie with pillows. She straightened the sheets, placed the bed tray with the glass of water within Maggie's reach.

"Here, have a sip of water."

"George doesn't like it either when I say things like that. But it's true, I'm dying. George is just trying to protect me, but you don't need to."

Alma was startled to hear Maggie speak so bluntly.

She'd always been very meek, rarely offering her opinion.

"What I'd like to do is get into real clothes and go out in the garden."

Maggie's eyes pleaded. Alma couldn't resist. They spent two hours outside. Maggie trimmed the spent blossoms from the Azaleas. She cut roses for her room. They enjoyed the sun and the soft spring breeze. A fawn and its mother shyly left the wooded area that bordered the back of the yard and cautiously approached the apple tree. The women silently admired their grace and beauty. Maggie soaked in everything: the delicate shape of the irises, the scent of the apple blossoms, the antics of two cavorting blue jays. She followed the journey of a black ladybug with orange spots as it climbed her index finger, crossed the back of her hand, explored the valley between the bones in her arm before it flew off.

Neither of them mentioned the outing to George when he returned. He commented about the roses as he removed them from her night table. He was very careful about these tiny details that affected her well-being, Alma thought.

"You don't need these right here to get your allergies going, Maggie. I'll put them in the living room. Alma, you probably didn't know she has hay fever this time of year."

Alma was relieved when George finally left her alone with her throbbing ankle, though his departure left her in a hollow silence, remembering the depth of his grief after Maggie's death. Poor Maggie. I was wrong. He smothered her. That was more than ten years ago, but each time she saw him lately, she struggled to subdue the memory of that day when her attempts to console him led her in an unexpected direction.

From the La-Z-Boy, she could hear the rustle of the trees. A soft breeze entered the living room window, carrying with it the scent of freshly cut grass. A dog barked in the distance; the special bark of a hound that had treed a squirrel. She could hear the last of the cardinals. Soon some would flee the winter chill.

Alma felt like she had come through a chilling winter already. She fidgeted in the chair. I wish I could run, just run up that hill again or scrub the floors, anything. Too many feelings. Angry at Mack, but worse, angry at me. Mack was mean when he said it, but there was some truth there. I am a Pollyanna and I hate the idea that I've lived like that. But it was so much easier, a way to hide from myself. Hide my feelings. Hide memories best forgotten. Like that time with George, after Maggie died. Pain—a prickly, pinching feeling—persisted, her ankle aching despite the pain pills.

George, Poor George, that's what she called him in her mind. A brute of a man who seemed so strong sometimes and so needy at other times. He was so distraught, after Maggie died, drained of all sense of meaning or reason to live. I couldn't bear the sight of his red swollen eyes, his slumped-shoulders sitting in her bedroom, windows closed, shades drawn, phone off the hook. His wife died and he had loved her, cherished her. I could empathize with him. I felt as if I'd lost my love, too. And I was needing to be cherished, like he cherished Maggie, I wanted to comfort as I needed to be comforted. George had no one, no children to gather round and console him. He'd always wanted children—a son.

Drowsy memories ebbed and flowed. As she remembered, Alma felt a heaviness around her, like a winter wool blanket on a summer day, itchy, dense, disturbing, burdensome. She'd pulled it closer, this protective cloak she had donned to shield herself from Mack, from feeling disappointment, hurt, and, later, to hide the betrayal of her wedding promise. She'd peeked out from it for a time, with George, but today its weight felt like it had become part of her, stuck to her skin, weighing her down. She yawned. She wanted to throw it off, get rid of it. Take the risk of living without it. Would she feel cold, naked? Naked and ashamed.

Naked felt free when she was with George. She'd tried to convince herself that it wasn't about the sex. She was comforting him. She owed him at least that, to console him, though why she thought she owed him anything was vague in her mind.

It grew out of the comforting. Well, that's how it started. But pain pills dissolved her denial. It *was* about being naked, about being touched, about revealing herself. It was about the heights of pleasure she'd reached and satisfying the cravings for more. She'd guided his hands to increase her delight. She used her mouth, licked his most sensitive places. She'd never been that free with Mack. He'd been efficient with her, if not tender or sensual. She thought the lack of desire that grew between them was her fault. That she'd had too many babies to feel again the pleasure of their first year together.

But George, George was a lover. This big hulk of a man with unruly hair and a clean-shaven shy smile, knew how to touch. His callused hands turned to silk, his lips pulled her to passion, his tongue made her willing, adventuresome. He touched her from head to toe, his tongue in her ear, his fingers like feathers on her neck and the curve of her waist, his hands cupping her breasts, his mouth caressing them, his lips lightly brushing the fine golden hair that grew in a line from her navel to the more dense growth below. Penetrating and withdrawing, penetrating again but only after engaging her most erotic spot. Skin to skin, they came together and it took her breath away.

For months they met secretly, always at his place. Each time, she promised herself, would be the last time. It was like having a box of chocolates. Just one more piece, then I'll close the box. Her burden of guilt became heavier with each passing month until Mack almost caught them. He dropped in on George to offer to cut back the apple trees. He rarely offered to help anyone. Perhaps she had misjudged his capacity for giving comfort as badly as she had her own. Why on this day of all days? Mack knew Alma had brought a casserole to George. Did Mack know about the affair? Had someone seen her calling too often on George? Alma quickly grabbed her clothes, and scooted down to the basement. She dressed and let herself out the basement door into the garden. She came back into the house disguised with an armload of vegetables. After that, she refused George. Her shame put an end to the affair, extinguished desire, made sex with Mack unbearable. So great was her shame, she didn't tell Petra, couldn't say the words out loud.

Throughout the years, George seemed to show up in the midst of Alma's need. He'd been there the day Mack died. The memory triggered a flashback. She saw blood spattered on the walls and ceiling, on her clothes and hands, pooled on the floor. Mack's body, face down, in the corner, the gun still clutched in his hand. She heard Alicia behind her, screaming, screaming, sirens screaming. Images and sounds swirled and smudged together. She relived the whole scene, in disjointed fragments.

Alicia had been visiting. They'd come home with groceries and the broth Mack requested. She called for Mack. No answer. The basement door stood open like a proclamation plastered to the wall. Fear pierced her like an arrow slices into its target.

"Bring the rest of the bags in, Alicia, please." But, Alicia, not noted for obedience, followed her downstairs. Newspapers had fallen from the stairs to the floor below. Further down she nearly tripped on old paint cans that were tipped on their sides in the middle of the step. It was dark; she could smell the blood before she saw it. She stood frozen, aware of Alicia's footsteps bolting loudly back up the stairs. Suddenly the lights blazed on. For a minute Alma was blinded by the brightness. Instinctively she knew where he was, though there was so much junk, she couldn't see him. First she saw the blood. His body was still warm as she tried to rouse him; blood covered her hands, soaked into her skirt and splattered onto her shirt.

That's when the screaming started—Alicia, not Alma. It was the screaming that was the most terrifying part. She screamed one long continuous scream until her breath was exhausted. Then, still screaming, Alicia clomped up the steps, her footfalls pounding on the floor overhead as she crossed the room and shouted, "Operator! Help, Father's hurt." She'd never called him Dad or Daddy, or Papa.

Wails of the siren replaced Alicia's screaming. Alma remembered the sights, sounds, smells. But she couldn't recall her feelings. Paralyzed, she'd felt nothing but the holding of her breath and complete disbelief. Like a bright light can cloak images, shock had eclipsed her feelings. George was there. He'd been on duty at the fire house. He responded to Alicia's call for help. Alma remembered his strong arms holding her, helping her up the stairs.

Did she know what she'd find when she'd seen the basement door open? Had she suspected he was planning this? He'd been so calm those last few days, sending her out for a lumbar support pillow one day, ace bandages for his swollen legs the next day. He'd refused to wear them the week before. Threw them in the trash in a fit of anger. Was he trying to get her out of the house? Did his requests raise some suspicion in her mind? Suspicion she'd refused to acknowledge? He'd wanted a certain brand of vegetable broth on that day. All items had to be purchased in the city forty five minutes away. Previously, he hadn't wanted her to leave him alone. But, days before he did it, he'd sent her on these long trips. Had she secretly known what he was planning? If she'd known, why did she give him the opportunity? Why didn't she stop him?

She was haunted by her questions. The house was haunted by his deeds, his fears, superstitions, obsessions, his miserliness, the absence of her children. They'd left home young, their anger at Mack drove them out of the house as soon as they were old enough to get jobs. Grandchildren would never play in her living room. There'd be no more bicycle riding in the driveway. Only William lived nearby. The girls were scattered across the country. Since the funeral, William visited rarely. Mack's death . . . his suicide . . . was his ultimate betrayal. His everlasting rejection of the children who could never satisfy him.

Why didn't he grasp onto the possibility he'd recover? Why didn't he give the treatments a chance? He'd never be completely well, but wasn't living worth anything to him? Wasn't his family? Mack couldn't tolerate imperfection. He wouldn't follow the diet, or take the prescribed medications. He mourned the loss of his ability to eat his favorite foods, the loss of his strength, his independence. Focused on the illness; he ignored the progress he'd made and the possibility of reasonable health in the future.

The strain of these memories, and the self doubt they left in their wake, exhausted her. Alma closed her eyes. If only I'd come home as he was going down the stairs. I could have stopped him. She opened her eyes. There was that photograph, Mack's eyes challenging her. The frame looked as if it had been stretched diagonally. It teetered on the edge of the mantel. The photo seemed distorted: the black blacker, the white glaring, the greys gone, edges blurred as if looking through a smudged lens. A dreamy, surreal feeling replaced the heaviness.

She drifted outside of herself. She was on the basement stairs behind Mack. They were steeper than usual with a weird torque, as if the upper level had shifted. They stretched out before her, misshapen, without end. The railing Mack had put up after William's fall swayed, though it was solidly secured to the steps. The beam of light from the flashlight in his hand radiated out, its edges smeary. So dark for a snowy afternoon. No light from the windows. There was a sharp odor of mildew and rotting apples. The steps were so far apart that Mack stumbled several times on his way down.

"Mack, don't go down there." Her voice, sounding like she was speaking through a tunnel, drifted off into the distant darkness as if the lack of light was absorbing her words. Mack did not respond. She said it again, louder, but it didn't sound louder. Still, no response.

Alma stepped down. As she did, she grasped the railing but didn't feel her hand as her fingers curled around the support. She felt like she had no body, as if her movements were liquid waves in the heavy air. The cluttered stairway took her deeper and deeper.

I have to stop him.

Mack, stop. Don't do this.

No response. He stumbled again, knocking a stack of newspapers off the step. He sat to catch his breath, his face in his hands, supporting its weight with his elbows on his thighs.

His thoughts drifted from him as if he were whispering them aloud. "I'm back to hunger. Back to being locked up."

Alma was watching, listening, unable to make her presence known to Mack.

Then another voice, Mack's father. How Alma knew this she couldn't explain; she'd never met the man. But it was Paw sure enough. Then an image projected into the darkness like a miniature drive-in-movie. An old man, a young boy, maybe seven, in a dark, wooded area.

"'Fraidy-cat. Fraidy-cat. Fraidy-cat." Or was it Mack's voice?

"I can't fight any more," a wisp of a voice, neither child nor man, hung limp in the air.

He struggled to his feet, knocked over some paint cans.

"Stop Mack. Don't do this. You're not alone. I will help you. We'll get your strength back."

When he reached the last step and had regained his breath, he weaved his way through the boxes and piles of junk to the far corner and sat.

He'd been there before, getting ready! He'd cleared a space near the workbench. A pad of paper occupied the bench top and two pencils, one yellow, the other green. She could see the tight, tiny scrawl of his handwriting wandering askew across the top page. A small lamp glowed on a photo of Alma and the children. His favorite tools, freshly oiled against rust, were lined up on the shelves of the workbench: screw-drivers, hammers, a chisel, a small hand saw, his new power drill plugged in, fully charged. He'd placed a small stool in the clearing next to the workbench. He sat without moving for a time. His thoughts were silent now. He reached into a box on the lower shelf and pulled out a small gun. He examined it closely, turning it over in his shaking hand.

"Where did you get that gun? How long have you been planning this? I won't let you do it." She didn't take the gun from him; it was just there in *her* hand as if of its own volition. Alma felt its weight and coolness, but it was more imagined than real. It was smooth and textured at the same time. It fit Alma's hand perfectly, not too big, not too small. She turned the gun over, examining it closely. The handle was white, mother-of-pearl with an insignia on it. The chamber where the bullets went was small. There were bullets, she knew that, but how many? Had he spun that chamber, gambling? No, that was not Mack's style. She had never held a pistol before, but this gun felt familiar. Again her thoughts floated about as if they were part of a conversation. She grasped the handle and curled her finger around the trigger.

I wonder how it would feel, she thought, to put this to my head. She did that, the gun in her right hand, pressed against her. I could pull the trigger. Just a little squeeze and it would be done. What would it feel like? Maybe there wouldn't be any pain at all. It would be all over before pain could express itself. She shifted the gun to her ear, then back to her temple. She noticed her feelings had evaporated. She stood there with the gun to her head thinking and comprehending nothing but the presence of the object in her hand.

She looked over at Mack. He was motionless, still holding the gun. Alma was holding the same gun, too. No, it was different. What was he thinking, she wondered? Alma tried to remove the gun from his hand. Her action had no impact, as if she hadn't touched him. Her attempt to wrestle the gun from his hand was somehow short-circuited.

Alma released Mack's hand. She was aware of a presence helping her let go. She looked up to sense, rather than see a dim glow. It was as if Alma were looking in a murky mirror and seeing something both known and unknown.

Calmly, Alma looked at Mack. She put her gun down. Yes, I did suspect you'd do this, but I dismissed the idea. I refused to believe it could happen. I was not thinking rationally, I told myself, it was my imagination. I was just too afraid to talk about it, as if talking would give you the idea. Alma moved closer to Mack.

Alma watched as he seemed to calculate angles to ensure success. She could see his thoughts now, his struggle, his determination, his indecision.

13

An explosion ripped through Alma's head and tore her from that image. She was sweating, gasping for breath, confused to find herself sitting in the La-Z-Boy, in her living room, wrapped in an afghan that had been draped over the arm of the chair. The room had darkened with the passage of the afternoon. A chilly breeze drifted through the windows. The intruding noise sounded again. This time she recognized it as the phone. She grabbed the portable next to her, wanting to quiet the thing more than answer it. Dead, it didn't respond to her shaky hello. Damn! The kitchen phone. She lowered her foot to the floor, groggy and clumsy, but the phone stopped ringing before she could maneuver herself onto the wheely chair.

She leaned back into the La-Z-Boy but didn't raise the foot rest. Her ankle throbbed. She was aware of her bladder's need to be emptied but didn't want to move. She wiped the drool from her mouth with her shirt sleeve. Despite being damp with sweat, she pulled the afghan closer, up to her chin. She needed its insulation. She slept.

When she finally roused herself, she eased off the La-Z-Boy. The wheely chair was not easy to steer. It was determined to go in whichever direction was opposite her urging, crashing Alma into the wall like a canoe steered by an inexperienced paddler bangs from one edge of a narrow channel to the other. She parked the stubborn chair in the hall outside the bathroom door sill, hopping on one foot to get herself in and out, grasping the towel rack and sink. Of course, the minute she got herself situated on the toilet, somebody banged on the door, ringing the bell at the same time. Who in the world could that be, she wondered, knowing it must be a stranger. No one she knew would bother knocking. She lurched down the hallway on that disobedient chair, struggling with her clothes, not wanting to get caught with her pants down, before she called out.

"Come in, come in. Stop making such a racket."

The door opened. "Alma?"

"Stay where you are!" she ordered, checking to see that she was decent.

She emerged from the hallway to see Tony standing there with a pizza held high on the flat of his hand. She was glad to see him and she was hungry. The smell of the pizza brought moisture to her mouth.

"Patsy's finest," he said. "I called. No one answered."

"That was you? I tried to answer. It was dead. The portable needs to be charged."

"I see that chair was helpful. Shall I close some of these windows?" he asked, making shivering sounds.

Alma nodded. "Thank you." She lopsidedly pushed her way back to the La-Z-Boy, still feeling groggy. Tony refrained from helping her, choosing instead to walk through the house closing windows against the cold night air. She pulled the afghan over her lap. "You must have to manage all kinds of details when you design a building."

"Hungry?" he asked when he'd secured the last window.

The aroma of tomatoes, cheese, spices made Alma's stomach growl. Tony seemed at ease finding plates and glasses for the iced tea. They ate in a comfortable silence for a few minutes.

It was so fresh on her mind and she needed to put it in words, her own words, that she told him about her dream. He listened, asked no questions, offered no advice, no platitudes. Not once did he say, "Time will make it better." He allowed long silences.

"I wondered what it felt like so I put the gun to my head, like I was killing myself." She lingered on that thought, like I was killing myself. Like I was killing myself. Like I have been killing myself.

"Are you okay?"

Alma nodded. "I know it wasn't my fault." She let go of

the thought that she'd been killing herself. "I mean, I knew that but I didn't, not really."

"Something about the dream convinced you?"

"I don't know. Let's not talk about it just now."

"I have to ask you something, it may be personal."

Alma was too satisfied with a full stomach to be alarmed.

"When I went into the bedroom, there was this thing, shaped like a body, standing in the middle of the room. It looked like something you'd put in a window to give the impression you weren't alone. Only it didn't have a head, but it was wearing a hat anyway. A little spooky, if you ask me."

Alma laughed. "That's a dress form. It's adjustable to the size of the garment you're making. I'm working on a dress for Petra. She was trying to make up her mind about the hat."

She remembered her long ago dreams of starting her own dressmaking business. She did work for Mrs. Stodder, the seamstress, on and off over the years. Alterations mostly. She had a few customers of her own, too, though she didn't earn much. Grateful friends paid her in freshly killed chicken, eggs still warm from the nest, milk from their cows. Mack approved of that, especially after she'd sold their chickens.

"I guess you could call it a hobby, like your pottery. I've made wedding dresses—my own in fact, toddler outfits for my kids and grandchildren, jackets, curtains. I design my own patterns. I'm particularly good with hard-to-fit figures. You know, bust or hips too big or too small. There is always some sewing project or other underway." She sat up sharply. The afghan became too confining; she threw it aside. It fell to the floor.

"Wait one second! Why would I buy a computer? Petra says I need a computer. I need a sewing machine with all the latest gadgets. William's bedroom, that's where I'll put it. On a big work table." Alma transferred herself to the desk chair, wheeled over the afghan and down the hall to

William's room. She still called it William's room even though he hadn't slept in it for years, except for a few nights after Mack died. Tony followed.

"Slow down. I'm not getting this. Computer? Sewing machine?"

She told him how she'd fantasized about leaving Mack, living independently, supporting herself and her son with her own dressmaking business. She'd envisioned wealthy women besieging her with business. Having to hire a secretary, an assistant. She'd work only with the finest fabrics. She visualized her own studio with floor to ceiling windows, padded cutting tables on which the even the most delicate silk would be safe. The studio would be set at the edge of a forested lot so she could see the trees and wildlife and yet have plenty of natural light.

"A dream. Just a dream. But at least I can get the sewing machine that matches the dream. Maybe put bigger windows in here," she said looking at the narrow windows set high to eliminate the need for drapes but which made the space look more like a bunker than a bedroom.

"It could work. I can see the studio you describe right here on your property. You have the space, you have the trees. An A-frame would be perfect." He opened a napkin. With a pen he pulled out of his pocket he sketched his vision. "It could be done."

Alma could see it. The A-frame, facing southeast, two sides completely glass. The rear, open to the forest and stream below. He drew stone steps leading down to the stream. Just a trickle wandered over dryness trying to remember its ancient path, but in the spring, if she listened carefully, from her kitchen, Alma could hear the waters bounce over the rocks and boulders.

She moved to another life, no longer in the kitchen but in the studio's backyard. She walked barefoot to the forest that was her joy. A quiet enfolded her, the kind of silence that only a forest offered, a kind of insulation from the artifice of the rest of the world. Alma breathed deeply. She felt her shoulders descend a few notches and her jaw ease.

She inhaled the musky forest air, cool, damp, sensual, alive with pine fragrance. Her toes sank into a cushion of pine needles and fallen leaves. Sunlight drifted through the tree tops in patches of bright. Birds chirped, squirrels scampered, and worries faded away. She walked a few more yards and looked back at her studio. Gratitude welled within her. This is genuine, this feeling. It's real, not the usual fake face I put on to pretend that everything's wonderful. This is me, my real self. Grateful, genuinely grateful for what's right here, not for a substitute—a stand-in for what could be —but for what's real. She moved toward the structure. I wonder what it looks like inside. As she approached the back door, "Alma," Tony's voice called her back to her kitchen.

"You could put a salt lick here for the deer." Tony sketched as he spoke. "They'd be sheltered by these trees," his pen creating them, "and the evergreens. And some bird houses hanging in the trees or placed on tall posts. Nope, no. The squirrels. They'd be after the bird seed. Ah. We could build a squirrel feeding station. Squirrels like dried corn cobs. Put it far enough from the birds, there maybe. Mmmm. Let's put some baffles on the bird houses. Like that. No more squirrel problem..."

"How'd you do this so fast, come up with this design?"

"You could do the same if someone asked for a dress suitable for a particular occasion."

Alma nodded. "No guarantee she'd like it, though."

"There never are. Guarantees." He continued with his pen shading here and there bringing the scene to life. "This is what my pottery studio will look like. Larger. I'd live in it."

"Live there?"

"Right, right," half listening as he fashioned a new world.

It could be done. What an extraordinary idea. "I really had only thought of it as a dream, but it could be done, you say."

"Easily. Easily. Right over there on that rise." He

pointed out the window. Even though it was dark, they both knew exactly the place. "If you started now, it could be finished before winter, if we can get the kind of thermal windows you'd need."

"I could live in it, too?"

"Can you imagine yourself living there?"

"I'd tear down this house and live in a studio." Alma's thoughts found their way to the outside.

"Tear it down?" Tony stood up. "Why? Why would you want to do that?" Tony wandered around the kitchen. "This is a wonderful old house. Quirky to be sure, but so full of life, of stories. That huge window in the living room and the warehouse type windows in the bedrooms. Unusual, really unusual." He went to the back door. "Look at the finger-shaped impressions here on the door jamb. Years of hands grabbing on as they swing through this passage, in and out of your kitchen." He rubbed his hand on the worn door jam as if it were a fine work of art. "See that baseboard there, that big ding in it? Look, the cupboard door, here, it's all out of alignment. Which one of your kids pulled up on it to reach an upper shelf? Or did it get slammed too hard, too often?" He walked into the living room, over to the fireplace, his hand rubbing his forehead where furrows appeared. "Here, here. What about the chunk broken off this piece of slate?" He looked at Alma. "These are all stories about your life. Not all of them happy, sure. But, would you really want to tear it down? Build the studio on the other side of the stream and you wouldn't even see the big house."

"William. He'd get so mad at Mack he'd slam that cupboard door over and over. Mack would have gone stomping off in the woods and William went to that cupboard. Slam, slam, slam until the steam had gone out of him. I let him do it, too. Then my Grace, she used the same door. Except she couldn't get rid of her anger so easily. She slammed out the front door one day."

"I'm sorry. Perhaps I shouldn't have brought it up. And I'm sorry that your children had such bad feelings they needed to slam doors."

Alma looked at the clock. "Do you realize it's after midnight?"

Tony picked up the dirty plates and looked around the room. "No dishwasher? You could rent this place, but you'd need a dishwasher."

"Just leave those dishes. I'll get them in the morning." Alma lowered her injured ankle from the chair it was resting on. "You know, it feels better."

Tony filled the ice bag with fresh ice. "This will be good for a few hours. Try to keep it iced tomorrow too." He pulled the wheely chair to within Alma's reach. Consider an x-ray. I'd better be on my way. I had fun tonight. Thanks for sharing my pizza."

On his way out, he noticed the porcelain doorknob. "This is beautiful. You'll have to put it in your new place."

"You sound as if it already exists."

"It does."

14

"I had the most marvelous weekend and then the worst week at work." Petra came in the front door like a gust of wind being chased by a tornado. She flung her purse on the kitchen table. "Larry and I drove through the Hudson Valley. We joined the tourist leaf-peepers. Gorgeous fall leaves this year. We stayed in the nicest bed and breakfast, an old, old stone house."

Alma washed lingerie in the kitchen sink. She turned carefully, leaning against the sink, resting her nearly healed ankle. But before she could greet her friend, Petra laughed.

"Good God, Alma. Do you still have that old lady nightgown? You have to get rid of that rag. Aren't you afraid to be seen in that old thing?"

Alma squeezed the water out of the nightgown and rolled it in a towel. "My soft, comfy nightgown? We've been through breast feeding, tomato canning, kid-throw-up, and even weed pulling." Handing the limp, wet, garment to Petra, she said, "Here, put this over the chair on the porch while I rinse the sink."

Petra took it in two fingers as if it were slimy.

"It's like my second skin. Why would I trade it for some itchy, uncomfortable need-to-be-washed-a million-times-to-be-cozy nightgown? It might fall apart before it ripened. This nightgown has withstood the test of time. And just who is going to see me in it, Pete?"

"You never know. Life is full of surprises. See?"

Squealing, Petra jumped up and down. She thrust her left hand out, waving it about, rotating her wrist and wiggling her fingers.

The diamond was huge, but not as large as Petra's tear-filled eyes.

" Oh my God! Petra! When did this happen?" She sat at

the table pulling Petra to her for a hug. "Congratulations."

"It's too soon, I know you're going to say that. You've only been dating for a few months, right? That's what you're thinking. But, we dated in high school and then again a few years later. Last weekend. It happened last weekend. We had a fabulous time. The sex was great, but the talking was better. Did you ever hear me say anything like that before, that talking was better than sex? Now I'm not saying the sex wasn't good, but we were really honest with each other. I think it was the first time I was honest with myself . . . about my ex-rat-fink spouse. It wasn't all his fault. Did you ever hear me say that before?

"We talked about our marriages and divorces, how both of us hurt and were hurt by the person we married. We analyzed what went wrong and why. We helped each other gain perspective, you know? Both marriages were put on the table and autopsied."

Petra went on without taking a breath. She and Larry had talked about who they'd dated, who they'd had sex with, who they'd rejected and why, the state of their health, Larry has a colon problem, Petra has had STDs.

Alma rolled her eyes. Do I need to hear this?

"The bottom line is, I want to get married, he's not perfect, but he's the best one so far. You know how long I've been looking. And, look at this ring. Isn't it gorgeous? Larry has his own real estate business, good health insurance, security, *and* he's hot. The thing is, Alma, we know each other, there's no secrets in this small town. Larry's been in and out of my life since high school. Sorta like you and George."

"George. Right." Oh, if you only knew. Alma was tempted to tell Petra about George but he was coming over soon to finish sorting through Mack's tools and price them. She knew Petra wouldn't be able to keep a straight face with George once she heard about the, she shuddered, affair. The word made it sound sordid. I surely don't need her to be playing cupid. "Have you set a date for the wedding? Are you going to *have* a wedding?"

"I don't know about a wedding. I don't want one, but Larry says now that he's finally found his soul-mate, that's what he calls me," she giggled, "he wants to make a big deal about it. I don't know, we'll see.

"But the ring, the ring, let me tell you about the ring. Larry had been planning this, he had the ring with him the whole weekend. It was the most unromantic proposal possible. We were driving back on the Thruway and he says, 'Get that package on the back seat, will you?' It was one of those paper shopping bags with the twisted paper handles on it, from the pet store. That's the only glitch, Al, Larry has this slobbery basset hound. You know how I feel about dog slobber." Petra grimaced. Alma laughed.

Alma took some cookies out of the tin hoping George didn't come early. She sat and rested her foot on a chair.

Petra spoke with her whole body. Her arms waved about. They were in her hair. Her eyebrows raised and lowered to punctuate the feelings that showed all over her face. She was up and down, all over the kitchen.

"Under the newspaper there was a big box wrapped up in pink paper and a silver bow. 'It's for you, open it,' he says.

"Well, I thought it was some souvenir or something, we didn't spend *all* our time in bed or talking. Anyway, the package. I opened it. There was another box inside, different wrapping paper. I opened that one and there was a silk scarf.

"'Careful,' he says, as I pulled the scarf out. I felt something hit my foot. 'Shit,' he says.

"We had to pull over. Here we are on the Thruway, on a Sunday night with all the city-folks driving like maniacs to get back from their weekend in the country. It was dark, he couldn't find the flashlight at first." Petra laughed. She twisted the ring on her finger.

" I saw it first. I didn't realize what it was, though. It sat in the leaves and dust under the front seat. There we are, all scrunched over, me looking under the front seat, Larry in the back seat, when we find it.

"'Will you marry me?' 'Okay,' I say. That was it. There we are on the shoulder of the road, crying, laughing. No soft music, no candlelight, just the whoosh of cars and the disco-like effect of the headlights."

Petra took a deep breath. "Then, this week I'm thinking, was he that sure I'd say yes? Do I look that desperate that he was so sure I'd say yes? Bought the ring, wrapped it and all. Am I that easy? What would he have done if I'd said no? I'm cranking and crabbing at everyone at work. He's out of town on business. I want to scream at him when he calls, but I don't."

Petra searched for a tissue in her purse, pulled out a crumpled used white scrap of tissue and blew her nose and dabbed her eyes.

"Are you scared?" Alma poured tea in Petra's cup.

Petra nodded again. "Scared to death."

"Do you think you're that easy?"

Petra raised the cup to her lips. Then put it down without sipping. "Do you?"

"I'll tell you what I think after you answer. Honestly. Be honest with yourself, Petra."

Alma drank her tea; Petra stirred hers. The refrigerator motor began to hum. Ice cubes clunked into the bin.

"You got a new refrigerator! An icemaker! Wow, when did you get that?"

"It came yesterday. Don't change the subject. Do you think you're easy?"

"No. Yes, sometimes. I mean I'm easy when it comes to sex."

"So, you'll sleep with anyone, any time." Alma pointed her finger at Petra.

"Well, no. I'm not a slut," Petra's voice raised an octave. I won't sleep with just anyone. But, I'm not the virginal type, like you. You've only slept with Mack. I've . . . um . . . Let's just say I've stopped counting."

"And you want to get married so bad that you'd say yes to the first person who asked? Larry just so happened to be that person."

"No. No, you know that's not true. I've turned down some offers."

"How come? Why did you turn down offers if you're so desperate to get married? If I remember correctly, one guy was rather well off, owned two homes, a summer home in the Islands, I think."

"He wasn't interested in me so much as he was in having another possession, a reason to buy another house."

"Do you think you're that easy?"

"Well . . . Not in that way, no."

"Remember how you went about getting the job you have now? You knew what you wanted. You weren't willing to settle for anything less. Remember?"

"Yeah. Took me a year of looking. I was shooting for the moon. Pretty picky, wasn't I?"

"Tell me this. When you finally found the right job, did you ask yourself if they hired you because you looked so desperate for a job?"

Petra rolled her eyes, sighed loudly. "Alma!" Sighing again, "God! That's totally different and you know it." Petra shook her head. She looked at Alma. "Well, it *is* different."

Alma examined the tablecloth, smoothed it. She crumpled the empty Equal packets.

"I suppose in some ways it's the same. I know what I want, what I'm willing to compromise on, what I won't settle for. In that way, it's the same. I knew the right job when I saw it and I went after it."

Alma rearranged the cookies on the plate. She offered them to Petra.

"But, still, it is different, finding the job I wanted and finding the man I want. There's no slobbery basset hound involved." She laughed, twisted the ring on her finger, held it to the light. "Beautiful, isn't it. We'll take it slow. Did you make those cookies for George?"

"No. No more cookies for George. They're for us."

The fire whistle sounded, loud and penetrating at the same time the smell of smoke drifted in.

"I guess I won't see George after all." She put the

cookies in a container and put on the lid with a loud snap. "Probably someone burning leaves started a brush fire." Alma went over to the sink and washed her hands. "Want a sandwich?"

"I get the feeling you're relieved. What's up? Is there something you're not telling me? A lover's quarrel, perhaps?"

Alma gave Petra an exasperated look.

"Why don't you give him a chance, Alma? He's definitely interested in more than friendship. Is it because he was Mack's friend, too?"

"Sort of."

"Do you feel guilty about letting another man take Mack's place?"

"I'm not ready."

"What's wrong with George? He's such a sweet guy."

"He'd be like Mack. Controlling, confining. Maybe not miserly, not in the same way Mack was. I don't want to belong to anyone."

"Tell me more."

Alma wrung her hands. She gathered cookie crumbs into a small pile. She examined her fingernails and pushed back her cuticles. "He wants me to sell Mack's tools and the rest of the junk in the basement. We've been pricing items, marking them. I gave some things to the church for the white elephant sale. Sonya, you know her—she owns the antique store. Sonya said they were worth several hundred dollars each. George objected to me giving them away, said I should get as much money as I can and save it."

"That seems reasonable to me."

"I suppose it should seem reasonable to me too, but..."

Drumming her fingers on the table, Petra's voice sounded sharp. "We've been over this a million times. I'm guilty, I'm guilty, I'm guilty. That's your sad song, stuck in a groove."

"Petra, I let it happen. I sanctioned Mack's warped mind-set by not confronting him. He was right to call me a Pollyanna. I am a plastic Pollyanna, putting on the oh-let's-make-the-best-of-it mask as a cover up."

"Al, stop it. Why do you keep blaming yourself? We've been through this over and over. You're not responsible for Mack, for the way he was. You are not to blame for his death. He is."

"No, damn it. Petra, we haven't been through it, *not even once*. I know I'm not responsible for what he did. I know it. Okay? But, damn it, I *am* responsible for the way I was. You're not helping when you stop me every time I try to talk it through. If I'm ever going to be free of him, I need to take an honest look at my part in it all. That's *different* from blaming myself." Alma readjusted her foot on the kitchen chair. "Remember Duke? The man at Patsy's Pizza Pub? Remember what he said about denial?"

"That jerk? He thinks he's the guru of mental health. Don't listen to that pseudo-psychology mumbo-jumbo. He is a postal worker, not a shrink."

"Maybe so, but he made me think. You know, it's almost more painful to keep secrets from myself than it is to honestly admit I was wrong. At the time, I did the best I could do, raising those kids, mediating Mack's moods and fanatic ideas. It is in looking back that I can see it could have been different."

"What? What could you have done?"

"I'm not sure. I buried myself so deep, I can't put my finger on what exactly I'd do different. It's like I was asleep, like I walked through my life asleep. I just feel like I could have been different."

Petra crumpled the Equal bags, then smoothed them out.

"The money. I could have insisted on sharing control of the money. Not that there was anything I wanted to buy. Well, maybe a dryer. I paid the bills. But I never knew how much money Mack made until he died. I didn't know how much I wanted a dryer until now. I just wasn't aware of it."

"Just how would that change things?"

"I would have known what we could afford, how much we were spending. When Mack started using wood to heat the house instead of oil, I'd have known what we *were* able to afford. It was okay to supplement the oil heat with the wood fire to keep the cost of oil low but Mack made it seem like we couldn't afford to use the furnace at all. The sad thing is, I did know. Deep down I knew that was unreasonable, but I put that knowing to sleep too. I didn't challenge it."

"Do you think you could have changed Mack?"

"No."

"You always took the high road, Alma. You put the best spin on things, grateful for the small stuff, searching for the bright side."

"That's what I'm talking about, Petra. I did that because I was afraid to fight with him, to say, 'No, Mack. If you still need to live in a shack in the woods to prove yourself, then go do it, but I am not going to live like this.' "

"It's over, Alma. What good does it do to drag up old grievances?"

"Just as much good as it did for you and Larry to dig up the dirt from the past. It cleared things up for you to move on."

Petra arranged Equal bags in three straight lines. "Then we cremated it, buried it again."

"I'm still letting him do it to me, Pete. I still hear his voice. Even just sitting down to read, I think, I should be gardening, or painting, or scrubbing the floors. To buy that refrigerator? I called. I saw the ad in the paper. I said deliver it ASAP, I'll pay cash if you deliver it today. Do you know how many times I picked up the phone to cancel the order?"

Petra nodded.

"I'd hear Mack's voice in my head. 'I have the part to fix it. It's in the basement. Call the repair man and show him where the refrigerator parts are.' Isn't that ridiculous?"

"Is there a box of refrigerator parts?"

"I don't know. There might be. That's not the point. The point is that I still struggle to subdue his voice so I can hear my voice. He's still doing it to me. I'm still letting him." Ice cubes clunked into the bin. "That's it. *My* voice. That's what I'd do different. I'd let my voice out. I'd have something to say."

"Hear that? Fresh ice. You may have heard his voice, but you had the last word. You need to practice."

The phone rang.

"Hello?" There was a long pause. "Hello, who is this?" Alma heard a distressed voice she didn't recognize. "Hello?"

"Mom," was all the distraught voice could manage.

Alma forced soothing into her voice, "Calm down, calm down. Tell me what's wrong?" She wasn't sure which daughter it was.

Petra mimed a who-is-it? gesture.

Alma ignored it, saying softly into the phone, "Quiet down, take a deep breath, settle yourself." She recognized Grace's voice.

Petra stood, arms extended, palms up, and said out loud this time, "Who is it? What's wrong, for God's sake?"

Grace, Alma mouthed, shushing Petra with her hand before she placed it over her free ear.

"Who?" Petra refused to be shushed.

"Grace, honey. Tell me what's wrong."

"Mom . . ." Alma could hear a baby crying and a cat howling. A car horn blasted.

"Are you driving?" Please don't be calling me while you're driving, Alma prayed.

"Yes. I almost had an accident. This big tractor-trailer . . . I was trying to quiet the baby. The driver blasted the horn . . . I looked up . . . " She sounded as if she'd been running. "It . . . I had veered over into its lane. It was coming right at me."

"Are you hurt?" The baby cried in gasps now. And another child-like squeal. *Two* children? She didn't hear Grace's husband's voice trying to soothe it.

"No. Scared the shit out of me."

"Where's Cliff?"

"Home. I've left him . . . we're on our way . . . to you."

Grace's voice sounded calmer but edged with emotion.

"Please pull off the road. I won't talk to you while you're driving. Pull off and call me back." Alma put the phone down.

"What is going on, Alma? That was Grace and you hung up on her?"

"Yes, I hung up. I was afraid she have an accident. She's on her way here."

"She's driving here? From California?"

"Says she's left Cliff." Alma stood and paced the floor, limping. "She's running away from home just like when she was a little girl. She used to run away to the hen house. Running away, that's not going to solve anything."

"Again?"

"Again? What do you mean, Petra?"

"What do *you* mean running away won't solve anything? You want her to stay there and face her problems? Or pretend she's facing them, pretend everything's okay? Put on her happy face and make it work? You want your daughter to follow your example? From what you've been telling me, you ran away too. Except you didn't need a car."

"You knew she's left Cliff before?" Anger flared in Alma's voice. "She's had another baby?"

"Michaela."

"God. Damn it, Petra!" Alma slammed her fist into the table.

The phone rang. It was Sonya with information about a chair Mack had refinished.

15

You would not have believed it was she. She looked so forlorn I could hardly believe I wasn't dreaming. You have dreams all the time, really weird ones and you tell me about them. Me, I never dream, but I thought I was having one of your crazy dreams, Alma. I was sound asleep when I heard the doorbell, sure I'd dreamed the ring. Then the knock, real soft, weak. No, more like someone whose arms are so full there's no strength left, not a muscle that isn't already strained with holding the load. Really, when I looked out the peep hole, I thought, This can't be real. How can I describe this? To me, even after all this time, the details are still so vivid.

A person, I couldn't tell who, drenched by the rain, soaked through, a shape outlined by moonlight. The face in shadow. Long hair, dark in its wetness, drooped toward slumped shoulders as if the wetness were heavy. Its clothing stuck tight to some places and sagged in others. Too short to be my ex, who I'd recently ex-ed again after a brief fling—I told you about that—ended in a black eye, for him, I ducked, he didn't—I didn't tell you that part. A sack of something slung over its shoulder. Definitely not Santa.

What a dumb ass you are, I said to myself, you should be calling 911 instead of gaping at a potential Jack the Ripper. Which I would have done, had I not heard something that made me want to open the door so urgently I couldn't turn the damn doorknob.

"Aunt Petra, it's me."

"Grace, for God's sake." I fumbled with the door, frantically. "What are you . . . Is your mother okay?" Now that was a dumb question. I'd begun to imagine she'd run miles from home to get help for you or her sister or someone. But she would have picked up the phone or driven.

She did drive, you know, and had her license. I taught her how. Mack wouldn't let her take Driver's Ed. That was the first *big* secret Grace and I shared. And, maybe someday I'll tell you all this for real instead of running it through my head again and again. Now that she's on the phone, coming here, now that I've given it away, I guess I'll have to. I wasn't trying to deceive you or anything like that. I didn't tell you because if Mack found out then you'd be in the clear. It'd be all my fault, mine and Grace's. It's just that she told me some kid at school was letting her use his car, teaching her to drive and I thought that was dangerous and since she was already doing it, I decided, well for her safety, I'd teach her. I didn't let her use my car—much—but there are more important things I want to tell you. About that night and what happened after.

I pulled her into my house by her soggy sleeve and tried to get those wet clothes off her at the same time I drilled her. "What happened? Tell me. What are you doing here? You're making a puddle in the entryway. What time is it, jeez, two. Your curfew is ten. What are you doing out so late? Did someone hurt you?" You know me, Alma, I spit out the questions one after the other as I pulled that swampy jacket off her.

That's when I noticed she was crying, just standing there like a limp shirt on the line, dripping wet from the rain *and* tears; then suddenly she became energized.

"No. No! Stop it." She shrugged away from me. "I won't stay, not until you promise you won't call my mother. If you don't promise, I'm out of here." She pulled that jacket back over her shoulder.

"Okay, okay. I promise, I promise." I ran for a towel and my terry robe. She shivered violently and cried loudly. Not the great Sarah Bernhardt tears of her childhood, but the deep, primal moans of a fatally wounded animal. That's what it sounded like to me—still does.

That's when I began to think she'd been raped, Alma. I knew she'd been seeing someone. Brought him home, you told me. God knows why she'd pull a stunt like that. She had to know Mack would freak. I met the guy once, in the drugstore. I thought she'd given him money. He was too old for her, but I'd never say that to Grace. She's the kind of kid who has to decide that for herself. Instead, we had a talk about birth control. Not at the drugstore, of course. I knew you hadn't, didn't think it was appropriate, like giving her permission. That was stupid. Besides, you said, she was a good girl and all that crap. I could see the rebellion in her, could see her having sex just because you expected the opposite. So I had the birds and bees and the STDs talk with her. Even bought condoms for her. I knew you'd be totally horrified by this. You would have told me to mind my own business. Maybe not, you seemed so beaten down then. But anyway, I thought she'd been raped and I wanted to help her. I was ready to swear to anything.

"You swear. You swear?"

"I swear, Grace. Tell me what happened." She was too smart for that, so she made sure I wouldn't tell.

"If you tell my mother or father, I'll kill myself. That's it."

And that was it. How do you evaluate that threat? Would she? Wouldn't she? She shook and sobbed, unable to speak. This, the kid who never cried, my godchild, my favorite of all your kids. I just had to shut up and hold her, and she let me do that, again, so unlike her, but only after I promised, word of honor promise, the kind of promise you know you'll never break, a pull-my-nails-out-but-you-won't-get-a-word-out-of-me promise. I love her. I love you. What else could I do?

"She was there. She was naked."

"Whoa, back up, Grace. Who was naked?"

She paced around the room, hands over her eyes, bumping into things and me right behind her wanting to hold her, wanting to save my LLadrós, expensive gifts, not my taste but still who wants to see them crash to the floor.

"Miranda, that slut, and so was he. After she climbed off of him, I could see he was naked too." Grace was in the kitchen now.

"Slut, slut, slut," she said over and over.

Every time she said the word she opened and slammed a cupboard door. I'd only seen William do that. Every time she slammed, the plates and cups and glasses rattled and clanged. She brought her fury back into the living room, down the hall and back stabbing her legs into the carpet, cussing, oh Alma, such foul language, words I knew she knew the meaning of. And maybe she didn't. They were just words she could dump all the rage into and jettison it outside of herself. This is where I decided she might just be capable of killing herself. You have to know, right now, before I go on, I'm not sorry for any of this. Especially after Mack.

Between the curse words, fragments of what happened splattered forth. Not that I could make sense of it. It's my money, why should I buy sneakers for the whole family. Married, I wanted to get married? My essence lit his soul? Crap. He lit his soul with pills, pills and liquor. My essence, ha! Muse, ha! More like a fool. Unfolded my beauty. How could I have fallen for that crap? I believed him. He pretended he loved me so he could steal from me. And they invited me to get in bed with them. To get naked too and get it on with them. She screamed down the hallway, then slumped in a pile on the carpet and whispered hoarsely, tears gushing, I almost did just so I wouldn't loose him, so I could prove I was better than that slut.

Alma, it was days before I got the whole story. Days. That's what you're mad about. That I know something about Grace that you don't. But it doesn't end there. Your sleep-walking-burrowing-your-head-in-peace-keeping-sand days are over, my friend.

The phone, it must be Grace.

16

Alma picked the phone up immediately, before it's ring was complete. "Are you parked in a safe place?"

A breathy, "Yes, Mom," followed an exasperated sigh that echoed a familiar tone. The image of her long lost, mistreated daughter who was neither willful nor selfish, not belligerent or stubborn, burst like a rainbow soap bubble. Alma's gut wrenched and her hand gripped the phone more tightly.

"Where are you?" Alma sat in the kitchen with her foot planted on the seat of another chair. Petra listened.

"Utah." Traffic sounds wrapped around her response.

Where? Where? Petra asked with wild gestures?

"Utah," glancing at Petra. "Are you all right?"

Alma could hear the cat screeching and Aaron saying "No, No, Titty." A horn sounded and drowned out the conversation for a moment.

"No. I just almost got creamed by that tractor-trailer."

"It's shorter to go back if you're not okay to drive."

"I will *not* go back. If you don't want me there, I'll go somewhere else."

"I want you here in one piece, Grace. I'm just concerned for your safety." Alma reached for the salt shaker, picked it up and dropped it, knocking over her tea cup. A sepia toned stain spread in a circle on the table cloth around the tea cup.

"Tell her you love her." Petra whispered. She was now on her feet, pacing the floor, her fingers combing her hair.

"I love you, Gracie."

"Aren't you even going to ask me what happened?" petulance emphasized her words. "Between Cliff and me, I mean?"

"When you get here. We'll talk about that when you get

here." Alma mopped the spilt tea with shredding paper napkins. "When do you think that'll be?"

Petra asked the same question with her expression.

"I'll be there next week. I'm not sure how long it will take. I could run into snow in Nebraska and Iowa. No! Aaron, don't unzip the cat carrier." Aaron screamed his protest. "I have to stop every few hours or he goes ballistic. I have to sleep."

"Where?"

"Where? You mean sleep? We . . ." Music blasted. "No, no, Aaron. Don't touch." The pulsating beat stopped. "We're at a rest stop. I have to let him run around for a little while."

"Where do you sleep?"

"Pull over. On the side of the road or a parking lot or rest stop."

"Grace, don't do that, pull over and sleep in the car. Stay in a motel, even if it is only for a few hours. You need a good night's sleep."

"I know that, Mom," her voice breathy, ire colored her tone. "I'm a big girl. Remember?"

"Consider a motel."

"I don't have much money, food is more important." Aaron screamed again. "Gotta go."

"Wait. Please. I'll make a reservation for you, my credit card. Call me when you check in."

"I don't know."

"If he gets a comfortable night's sleep, Aaron might be more manageable. And the baby . . .," Alma shot a fierce look at Petra, "the baby too."

"How would I get in touch with you anyway? You might be out or something when I'm ready to stop?"

"I'll be home."

"I can't stand the idea of you waiting around by the phone."

"I'll borrow Petra's cell phone."

Petra's body language said, What? Are you nuts? Then, she leaned toward the phone, "Yeah, Grace, she can borrow my phone."

"I . . . um . . ." Then Michaela started crying again. Aaron apparently found the volume control again. "I'll pay you back, every cent." Grace shouted over baby screeches and a new blast of Rap music. Petra shouted the phone number.

"Damn," said Alma after she put the phone down, forgetting for a minute to question Petra. "I forgot to ask for her cell phone number. God what else could happen?" She took a deep breath and shook her head. "I haven't heard from her since . . .when? . . I'd better child-proof the house. Aaron's what? Two-and-a-half?" Alma was on her feet, and now it was she who paced the floor and wrung her hands.

"Grace can do that when she gets here. When will she be here? Do you still have a crib? Do you need two cribs?"

"Two cribs? Petra, how could you keep that from me? How did you find out? When?"

The front door slammed and in walked George. "Small brush-fire, Alma. You probably heard the siren. That's why I'm late. Hey, Petra."

"Hi." Petra eyed Alma.

Alma groaned inwardly, not sure she wanted George in on this but not sure she could wait for Petra's answer.

"George, no tools today." No hellos, how are yous, have some cookies. "Grace is coming to visit. Would you go downstairs? I think I have a couple of cribs. Would you look? I actually need both of them.

"Gracie?" His face lit up. "When does her plane get in, Alma? Gosh, Gracie. Hey, we'll go fishing. The little guy, I'll teach him."

"She's driving with the children and a cat."

"With her husband, right, Alma?"

"No, just Grace and the kids."

"That's dangerous, Alma. All the way from California. There's long stretches that are desolate. She could have an accident, or something. There'd be no one to help."

"She's unstoppable, George."

"She coming for a vacation?"

"I need your help, George. Would you find the cribs?" That'll keep him out of the kitchen for a while, she thought, shooting another angry look at Petra.

"Come on, Georgie Porgy," Petra taunted, glancing sideways at Alma, as she took him by the hand. "Talk about dangerous. You're about to enter the twilight zone, Georgie Porgy Puddin' an' Pie."

"Shut up, Petra."

When they emerged with two unassembled cribs, all the nuts and bolts and parts neatly secured to them, and a cradle, Petra grabbed her purse.

"I gotta get going, have an appointment, I'll pick up sheets and stuff for the cribs, leave them at your door tonight after my date with Larry, on the way home. Out of town for a few days. Sales convention. By Georgie Porgy." The door slammed behind her.

"She's a pain. She sure got outta here in a hurry." George began the assembly, asking all sorts of questions about Grace, making plans.

"I don't know anything," Alma said throwing her hands in the air.

"She's got a new baby, right? Girl, right, Alma?"

"How do you know? How does everybody know about the baby but me?"

"Petra told me. I mean . . . uh . . . when we were down there . . . uh . . . we brought up *two* cribs, right? and that there cradle. Hey, you been working, cleaning up some more down there, Alma. Not storing apples and potatoes, I see." He laughed and patted her on the shoulder.

Alma searched his face but decided to drop it.

"Petra and I brought some things to the antique shop. Sonya agreed to sell them on consignment. And we returned some stuff to the dump."

"There's still lots of valuable stuff there, glad you're selling it. The snow blower and tractor in the garage. All them tools and glass things. Too easy for someone to steal, Alma."

"George! They've been there for years and nothing has been stolen."

"You're a woman alone, Alma. Word gets around. You gotta get locks, lock it up. Lock up the garage."

"I'll get to it. I want to get rid of all that junk. Clear the basement entirely. Maybe Grace will help, too."

They built the first crib in silence, except for a few cuss words George muttered when parts didn't fit together without extreme encouragement with a hammer.

"Time makes changes, Alma. Wood swells and metal corrodes. Maggie's gone, Mack's gone. Everything changes. You and me, we change. No sense in us being alone anymore, Alma."

"Did you know Petra's getting married? Larry. Do you remember Larry?"

"Sure I do. I seen him the other day. See what I mean, Alma? They don't want to be alone either. That's what we should do."

"George." She put her hand on his face and shook her head.

"Alma, that new mattress I got? I got it 'cause I was thinking you and me would get together. Making that thing, I wrestle with them sheets. First off, getting them on and off the clothes line ain't easy. Getting them on the bed is harder. I get one corner on and it pops off when I pull the other corner."

"George..."

"Then in the morning, Alma, them sheets are all rumpled and twisted, corners off and I gotta do it all over again. For what reason? And why do they need to go on the line anyway? Isn't the dryer good enough?"

Alma started to speak. George put up his hand, set the screw driver down, got off his knees and looked away.

"When I don't do the sheets like she done, I feel bad, like..."

Alma shook his shoulder. "Look at me. Maggie, God rest her soul, wouldn't mind if you...."

"Stop, Alma. I hate it when folks automatically attach

that to her. Maggie wasn't much into God and she wasn't much for rest, especially in bed. You don't get it. I'm not talking 'bout sheets, Alma."

"We've known each other a long time. We've been good friends." Alma hoped that didn't sound as hollow as she felt saying it. She looked away, unable to look at him.

"We were more than friends. Did you forget that, Alma? *I* didn't forget that. Lately that's all I do is remember. Me being alone, you being alone don't make sense, Alma."

"I haven't forgotten. That was a special time for me too." Her heart seized with the memory of his touch. But it was guilt that gripped her, a nonspecific, accusing sense of guilt. I should be saying "I love you too, George." But I don't. I can't. I won't.

"When Mack died, I thought, maybe you and me, we'd get together after a reasonable amount of time." He looked uncomfortable, shifting his weight, putting his hands in his pockets, then taking them out.

Alma held her body stiffly in an effort to disguise her discomfort. Inside her shoes, her toes curled and uncurled. This feels like high school, like I'm trying to dodge the question of whether I want to go out with him. But he's asking for more than a date and I owe him, I owe him.

"I know you'd take care of me, George. You're doing that already. It's just that time changes things, just like you said. Right now, I need to be alone. And I need your help and friendship too. You have a special place in my heart, George. Always will." This is true, she told herself. It is. Then why do I feel like it's a lie? "We helped each other through tough times. You're still helping me. Who else would set up these cribs without me even asking?"

George's face looked as if he'd slammed his thumb with the hammer. "You sound like Saint Alma the Pure. 'A special time for me too. . . .you have a special place in my heart.' We fucked, you and me." His voice was filled with passion but not anger, his face a map of anguish. "Maybe in your sainthood you're telling yourself that it was only because you felt sorry for Poor Georgie. But you kept coming back for more, Alma. I didn't come to you, Alma, 'cause you were married, but I figured you needed me as much as I needed you. Still, too." He moved close to Alma.

She felt his breath on her face, Alma backed away. "I don't want to listen to this, George." Alma was twisting the hem of her shirt as if that could stem the tears that filled her eyes.

"It's the truth, Alma. That special time wasn't just after Maggie died. What about high school? Senior prom and that summer. First time for both of us. We're more than just good friends, Alma."

"George, please."

He was like Turkish delight then. You couldn't get enough of him. You liked the idea that someone wanted you. That someone would sneak around just to be with you. You delighted in teasing and tempting him.

"Then, end of summer after you got sick, you wouldn't see me anymore. That's when you got to be a saint, Alma. Said you had to confess to the priest. . . . that you didn't want to confess that again. Then Mack, when you started going with Mack. . . ." George shook his head and got back down on the floor.

Alma didn't want to think about that summer. Yes, she'd felt she'd become the whore the nuns said her mother was. Yes, she was attracted to Mack. He didn't have any of the weaknesses she had. He never pressured her for sex. He wasn't the touching or kissing kind. That made her feel less like a whore. Saint? Saint Alma the Pure? I went from whore to saint in one summer.

"It's that guy, isn't it? That architect. What's his name?"

"Tony? I hardly know him." The remark irritated her, but she was grateful for a change of subject. She wanted to think about them as friends, that's all, friends. "He is a nice man, but I'm not going to be marrying anybody, George. We're friends, George, you and me. We go back a long way. That's important."

He didn't reply. Instead he began assembling a crib. He was a better tinkerer than talker. His wooly, wild hair showed more grey than she'd noticed before. The lines on his face and around his eyes reminisced over the smiles and troubles of many years.

Warmth replaced the annoyance she'd felt since he arrived. He's a good man, I know that. He'd hate me if he knew what really happened that summer. Maybe he's right. We need each other. I do depend on him sometimes. Often. Nodding to herself. Often. Quite often. I'm capable of the lawn mowing, and the snow-blowing. And when I do, I do it to prove myself. I pretend to be annoyed or surprised when George does those things for me. But, if I am truthful, I sort of expect him to come riding up on his green tractor or with his snowplow. Sometimes, I hire someone before George gets to whatever needs doing, just to fool myself into believing I don't rely on him. Just to show him I don't need him. Just to prove to myself I don't need anyone. But what I say out loud is that I don't want to take advantage of his kindness. That he's under no obligation, he already has enough to do without worrying about me. That's the expected thing to say.

Together they constructed the second crib. They talked about Petra's engagement, George's opinion that Larry was a playboy, small tidbits of local gossip. But nothing personal, nothing intimate. George left after he finished with the cribs.

"Tell Grace, when you talk to her, Alma, to watch out for strangers offering help. She's a woman traveling alone and that's risky," he said as he left.

Alma guessed George didn't experience the same sense of freedom that being single brought her lately. So often now, she'd come home, fling her purse in the Lazy-Boy and kick off her shoes. She'd change her clothes, take off her bra and pull on baggy sweat pants and an oversized t-shirt, all soft cotton. She relished being alone. No demands, nothing to do that couldn't wait while she savored a moment of peace. Yeah, she missed having someone around. On bad days she thought even Mack was better than being alone. But that was seldom. Her bed felt empty sometimes. Part of her longed to curl up against a man who was her protector, her lover. She longed to be touched, caressed, to be aroused. Maybe George was right.

Alma cleared the table. She threw the soiled tablecloth down the basement stairs. She gathered a fresh smelling terrycloth towel and a bottle of homemade herbal shampoo and headed for the shower. She lingered with the warm water and rosemary scented bubbles until she felt energized.

Toweling herself dry, Alma looked in the mirror. She saw a two-dimensional Alma with the bathroom in the background as flat as if it were wallpaper, the tub to her left, a window shelf rose above and behind her. On her right the sink half cut off by the edge of the mirror. A footstool, paint worn by little feet trying to reach the toothpaste, caught her attention.

Where did that come from? That's the footstool I used as a child. Then, she saw her unclothed self again, tall for a woman, slim with the sagging of age evident on her skin, her breasts and upper thighs. Who is that woman? She's me. She's my mother. When did I get this old? How did I get to be this age and not know what I want to be when I grow up? I've not thought much about *being*. Maybe being available to the children. Being the one who tries to bring warmth to them. Taking care of my family, that's what I am, a care-giver. But what about my *being* and belonging to myself. I wish I could merge into my mirror-self like characters in the stories I used to read to the kids. If only I could do that, then I'd know all the answers.

Why? She taunted herself as she climbed into the bed and pulled the sheet over her goose-bumped flesh. Do you want to pretend some more? Do you want to hide? Hide away in a mirror-land of endless reflections of the same unchanging face? A world where nothing changes?

Stop it, she talked back to herself. Maybe, I could see myself, my real self. Maybe, I'd know where this feeling of unrest comes from, how to decide what would make me happy.

A strange lightness sifted through her. Alma felt sort of like she did once when she'd had too much wine: slow moving, dull-witted, not quite able to take it all in, her senses muted and her mind limp, as if dreaming while awake, pulled like a rag through a wringer to a different place.

When she adjusted, she found herself in an unfamiliar, cluttered chamber. The room exuded a sense that there could be stairs she couldn't see and secret passages long boarded up. The air tasted musty and felt damp.

A steamy shaft of light, filled with floating particles, drifted through the only window, small, close to the ceiling and partially covered by a tattered cloth. Invisible strands clung to her arms and crossed her face. She shivered and her mind minded not at all this strange turn of events. *If I pull those drapes back, I'll have some light.*

There was so much clutter Alma couldn't take two steps forward or in any direction. She was surrounded by stuff, though specific objects defied identity. She reached down and pulled a framed picture out of the heap beside her, as she attempted to clear a path toward the window.

Large curds of dust rolled off the glass Alma wiped with her hand. It was a photograph. An old black and white photograph. At first she thought it was an image of a seven-year-old Grace. *No, this photo is older than that; it must be my mother.*

The child in the photo gazed out at her with a joyous smile, a look that said *I'm special, a child of God, protected from all harm.* Alma stared at herself in her first communion dress and veil. Wonder filled her, and joy. *That was my day; I was the center of attention.*

She remembered Petra was behind her as the line of fluffy white girls and white-suited boys took hesitant steps up the long aisle toward the altar. Procession music bounded from the church organ. It seemed that all eyes gazed upon Alma. And she knew why. Sister Mary Cecilia told her she had the best dress. She tried walking the way Sister said, touching the heel of her front foot against the toe of her back foot. It was hard to keep her balance walking that way with her hands pressed palms together, especially when she heard Petra giggling behind her. But she did it because she felt holy, as if she glowed.

It didn't matter one bit that she'd have to give the dress back to Sister so another girl could wear it next year. Petra's mother was taking them to a place to get their pictures taken, and she'd be able look at herself wearing the dress anytime she wanted.

After the pictures, Alma went out to a pancake house for lunch with Petra's family. She had never been in a restaurant before; the smells and sights were wondrous. Alma had a big waffle with a giant mound of whipped cream and fresh strawberries. That tasted much better than the communion wafer that stuck to the roof of her mouth. Everyone in the restaurant looked at her and Petra. Some ladies she didn't know came over to their table to say how beautiful they looked.

I'd forgotten I was a child. I'd forgotten how I felt that day. Special. That's the way I think about my kids. They're special. Everyone thought I was special on that day. I see it there in the photograph. Inside of Alma a hollow opened, its edges pressing outward, a place that was once filled but its contents were lost. Waves of uncertainty and frailty submerged a need to search for that which was lost.

Her hand went to her chest, no longer naked, but covered with sequins and beads. She shook her head as if to clear it. This is the dress my cousin let me borrow for my high school prom. An I-am-so-beautiful aura swept her into delight. I loved this dress. Alma stroked the textured bodice of the strapless gown, fluffed the billowy skirt. I danced with everyone that night, waltzes, and jitterbugs, even the tango. I was a princess, a prize to be won.

She could hear the music. The DJ played all her favorites. She floated and twirled and shimmied about the dance floor with the dress flowing out from her body. A fragrant orchid encircled her wrist. Her long red hair bounced in a pile of curls studded with rhinestones. Her necklace and earrings glistened like Fourth of July sparklers.

George had taken her to the prom. So handsome in his tux, even though the sleeves were too short. He'd managed to get his hair to behave for once. George was angry because Alma refused to be a wallflower just because he wouldn't dance. He couldn't dance, didn't want to try. She let him kiss her that night and he'd felt better. And later, I let him... Change this picture.

She couldn't see it clearly, but she knew the gown's color was jewel-like, her favorite. Funny, I don't own anything that color now. I feel like I've said this before, that I don't own clothes in my favorite colors. I've been here before. I've wondered about the color of my clothes, none of my favorite colors.

An old, dusty mirror, cracked and marred, leaned against a rusty washing machine to her left. She could barely see in the dim light, but there before her in her mirror-world, she saw her seventeen-year-old self, in beaded, sequined jewel colors and her seven-year-old self veiled in white, now sad-faced, holding a broken baby doll. Underneath the sequins her aging body still sagged. She blinked to clear her eyes. All my selves live at once. No moment is gone, they're all here, stored away in layers like fine linens. The image in the mirror découpaged self upon self, upon self, the ones behind indistinct or completely obscured but decidedly present.

She beheld all the views of Alma. Will the real Alma please step forward? The mirrored images did not obey. Each stood its ground.

17

Crunching gravel, announced Grace's arrival days later. Petra had pulled in just moments before. Alma and Petra rushed to greet her. Alma's smile relaxed the tension in her face but not in her heart. Grace was Grace and her phone calls had demonstrated she'd not mellowed one bit.

The car door opened, releasing the clamor of confinement: children were crying, cat howling, radio blasting discordant sounds, and Grace shouting for quiet. The baby screeched louder because the cat, escaping its carrier, pounced on her as it dashed out of the car.

"The cat!" Grace screamed.

No one chased after the cat. Alma retrieved the shrieking Michaela from her infant seat. Petra seized Aaron, whose impulse was to follow the cat, now out of sight.

"Tome here, Tiddy," shouted the boy. Tears steamed down his flushed cheeks.

"I think he's got a fever," said Grace, rummaging through the diaper bag. "I've got a thermometer somewhere."

"No, no, Tiddy," cried the child. "Tome back. Me go home. Mommy. Me go home," he pleaded, struggling to get free of Petra's grasp.

"Let's get the babies settled," suggested Alma. "It's cold out here. Lunch and a hot drink? Then Petra and I will unload the car while you rest. Sound good?" Her jaw muscles worked as if they were bearing the weight of the squirmy bundle in her arms.

"No! I've got it under control," Grace said as a diaper bag fell from her shoulder and ejected its contents. Formula spilled onto the front steps. Wet foot prints followed Petra into the living room.

"Aaron, shut up, hear? I've had it with you." Grace threw the cat carrier across the room and stormed out to her car. The driver's side front tire looked dangerously low, as if the driveway had accomplished its revenge.

Grace returned, laden with more bags and suitcases. "Can I get some help here? The car's got to be unloaded." She threw everything on the floor and glared at her mother. "Well? Do I have to do this all by myself?" She kicked the diaper bag across the room and stomped out the door. It slammed behind her.

"Hold on Missy. We'll take care of these babies first. Stay outside. Don't come back in till you can be civil," said Alma, her tone not quite confident. "Where is that thermometer? Do you have some baby Tylenol?"

Grace tore open the door. "Come on kids. Back in the car. Aaron, go." Grace reached for Michaela who was whimpering in Alma's arms. "Go, go. In the car." She pointed at Aaron, who was clutching Petra's neck.

"No. No more tar." Petra unwrapped his little arms and put him down.

"You are welcome here, Grace. I'd like you to stay."

"Yeah! Right."

"But you're not welcome to rage and demand. Your children need attention and you need rest. But, if you want to go"— she handed Michaela over to her mother— "then it's better you go now."

Grace grabbed the baby and dragged Aaron behind her. She put the children, both screaming again, in their car seats and backed down the long driveway to the road. There she stayed for several minutes. She drove back to the house. The tire was flat.

Alma paced the living room feeling the old guilt for asserting herself. She'd sworn to herself that she wouldn't get back into that parental role again, yet here she was issuing orders.

"Come on. I'll fix some tea. Let her sit out there and simmer. Come in the kitchen where you can't see her," suggested Petra.

The tablecloth blossomed with bright daisies woven into sunshine. Fresh fruit blushed red and orange and purple in a wooden bowl. Lots of bananas; Alma knew babies liked bananas. Grace's favorite chocolate pudding cake beckoned from under a glass dome on the kitchen counter. Alma pressed the heels of her hands into her eyes. Stupid. It was stupid to pretend it could be different.

"This is your home, Alma. Grace is a guest here. You did the right thing."

"Petra, she's my child and I turned her away."

"She left of her own accord. She's an adult, Al, and she should behave like one. She has no right to be abusive to you or those kids."

The tea kettle whistled and chamomile released its scent as it grew cold in Alma's cup. The kitchen clock ticked loudly until the front door opened.

Words, completely foreign to her, came grudgingly from Grace's tight lips. "I'm sorry."

Alma longed to hug her daughter, but she knew that would not help Grace at all. "Your old room is ready for you. Rest. Petra and I can look after the children."

Grace obeyed, wordlessly, her red-rimmed eyes flashed defiance still, never making contact with either of the other women. For two hours there was peace. At first Aaron cried for his mother, but when he saw Alma's big bath tub filled with toys he was intrigued. Warm water and floating duckys soothed both children. While Alma bathed the babies, Petra rummaged through two diaper bags and a duffel.

"She crammed her life into these bags. Clothes, mostly baby clothes, formula already mixed and in bottles. That's great! So easy. Here's the thermometer, one of those ear jobs. Jars of baby food. Bananas, my personal favorite. Birth control pills—six packs, one open, half gone. Hmm, this is a new prescription."

"At least she has more sense than I did." Aaron sloshed a wave over the edge of the tub. "Diapers, remember? And something for his red bottom, that's what you're looking for, Pete."

"A speeding ticket, a pink pacifier. That must be Michaela's. Condoms. Only two disposable diapers, neither small enough for the baby. A mashed breakfast bar, diaper wipes, Xanax."

"What's that?"

"Tranquilizers. There's only two left. Another speeding ticket. One very bruised apple, a power bar. Oh my God, a gun. Holy Toledo!"

"Quit waving it around, Pete. Get it out of here."

When Grace awoke, both babies were sound asleep in their cribs and Petra had gone home.

"Got anything to eat?" Thank yous were not her style.

"I made your favorite soup, beef barley and some cornbread. Perfect for a cold evening."

"I don't eat meat much. Got eggs? I'll fix some scrambled eggs."

Alma resisted the urge to help. She poured a cup of tea and ladled a bowl of soup for herself. A heavy silence lay over the kitchen. Alma looked out the window, not knowing how to deal with Grace. The kitchen windows were closed against the cold. The trees looked barren except for a few stubborn leaves that fluttered in a wind that pulled winter behind it. The sky was a flat, lifeless, gray without the slightest hint of blue or wisp of white. A few deer were at the salt lick Tony had helped her position near the evergreens. She could give succor to the deer but not to her own daughter. How can that be, she asked herself? I love this girl, yet I've never been able to show it to her satisfaction. Alma remembered the day ten-year-old Grace had skinned her knee. The entire kneecap was raw and bleeding. Grace refused to allow Alma to help her, despite the apparent pain. Grace washed it herself, applied gauze bandages. When Alma suggested that kind of dressing would be painful coming off, the youngster went to her room and shut the door.

I wonder if she knows I had this fantasy about leaving Mack, but didn't—because of her, because her little life had begun? I wonder if she sensed that, if she knew that I, for a few moments at least, didn't want her? Petra suggested an abortion. I entertained that thought, for minutes only, but it was there, it was real, an abortion in my mind. Did that little clump of cells feel rejection? And in turn reject me?

Grace sat at the table with scrambled eggs and cornbread. Well, at least she likes the cornbread, thought Alma. The clink of her spoon in the teacup was loud and irritating. Grace's fork scraped annoyingly against her plate. Alma spooned soup to her mouth carefully for the sake of quiet, for something to do. What do I say? Petra was right. I want a better life for Grace than I had, a happier marriage. The refrigerator dropped ice cubes into the bin, the furnace whirred to ease the chill. Alma considered building a fire but dismissed the idea. It's too late.

"I know what you're thinking." Grace banged her dishes into the sink.

She never did clean up after herself despite the show of independence. Alma was corrected by the swoosh of water in the dishpan and the lemony scent that drifted her way.

"Really? What am I thinking?"

"You think I'm wrong to leave Cliff. You think I should try harder. That's what you did."

"That's what I did. Right or wrong, that *is* what I did."

"With a man who didn't care about anything, anything—except money, about not spending money."

"Your father is not the only person I tried harder with."

"Me? Oh yeah! Right." She grabbed the towel and dried her hands as if she were scrubbing a stain from them. "You were only interested in keeping the peace. That's what you think I should do, too."

"What do *you* think, Grace?"

"Oh shit!" Grace's hands rose and gestured at the air, then came to an abrupt halt, with a muted slap, on her thighs. She dropped into the kitchen chair. "See, see. I can't talk to you." She motioned with both hands as if handing something to Alma. "You . . . you . . . can't take responsibility for anything. You're always putting it off on me."

"Tell me what it is I need to take responsibility for." Alma's tension dissolved into a current of resolve. This is Grace's problem. I refuse to gather it, in all its fragments, as if it belonged to me. I'll listen, but I'll dig my heels into now and not go back to old ways of being.

"*You* want me to go back to him, go back to wondering if he'll come home with the news that he's been fired from another job because his boss was an idiot. Go back to yelling at each other and the kids crying because we terrify them. You don't think I should have left him to begin with. I can't be like that. I won't be like you." Grace was wringing the dish towel, twisting it around itself, around her wrist, untwisting, unwinding.

"I admit that was my initial reaction, Grace. An old habit I'm trying to break. What do you want? What will make you happy?" Alma asked, knowing she'd borne a guilt that didn't belong to her, had never belonged to her, and surely had no place in this moment. If I have sown the seeds of Grace's rage, it is Grace who has nurtured them. Alma went to the sink and rinsed her soup bowl; pieces of barley, threads of beef and little bits of carrot swirled down the drain. She plopped the bowl into the dishwater.

"I don't know."

"What do you crave for yourself?" What a strange question to ask, thought Alma. What do you crave? Alma became aware of her own primal cravings, as if they were new, but she recognized them as both familiar and alien.

"I don't know." Grace closed her eyes.

"You don't want to be like me, you say. Then don't be like me. Don't let half your life go by before you discover what you truly want for yourself, Grace."

"You and my father," —her voice filled with venom at the mention of Mack— "you taught me . . . he taught me . . . I needed to sacrifice my desires."

"But you resisted, Grace. You were right. Your father and I, we were wrong. You've accomplished a great deal. I have always been proud of the way you put yourself through school. You can shape your life to your desires. Have you noticed that you have the ability to do that?"

Grace's face was gaunt and pale. Darkness encircled her puffy eyes. Defeat defined her shoulders. She folded her arms across the table and put her head down.

Alma went into the bathroom and returned with her lavender-rosemary shampoo and a white fluffy towel. "Come on Grace, it's time for a beauty treatment." Alma cleared the kitchen sink. The Treatment worked when Grace was little, even when she was a teen. My secret remedy for comfort from life's harshness, though if I'd called it anything but a game, Grace would have rebelled at the idea.

"Mom, not now, I'm too tired."

Alma remembered how she wished she'd had someone to take care of her sometimes. Someone to comfort, even pamper her, if only for a few minutes. She nudged Grace's elbow.

"Come on Gracie. It'll help you sleep. Here's the shampoo, herbs right from the garden. Remember how we made it? You still like lavender, right? I'll get the rest ready while you wash your hair."

A muslin bag held the fragrant herbs: lemon balm, lavender flowers and leaves, chamomile flowers, rosemary and sage. When Alma went back into the kitchen to add skin-softening oatmeal to the bag, she was greeted with the scent of the lavender and rosemary suds Grace was massaging into her hair. Good, Alma decided, this is going to work. Mercifully, the babies slept.

Alma filled her huge, claw-footed bathtub with hot water that ran over the muslin bag, infusing the bath with herbal essences of relaxation and love. That's what Grace wants, someone to care for her, something she has rarely permitted. A cup of chamomile tea with valerian flowers, a bar of sunflower soap, and a candle beside the tub completed the preparations. Alma warmed Grace's bed with the new electric blanket. She soaked for half an hour then went wordlessly to bed.

Alma fixed her own cup of tea with an extra dose of valerian, but when she slid between the soft warm flannel sheets her mind filled with desire and her own yearnings raced through her thoughts unbidden.

In a dreamy white gown of flowing chiffon, she felt the strength and gentleness of a hand stroking the curve of her waist. They were dancing and he was leading sometimes and she at other times. A waltz in which their bodies touched but demanded nothing, only basked in pleasure and comfort and lightness. There was no music, just the warmth and rhythm of their bodies.

She could feel his admiration and desire, but they were in no hurry to end the whirling floating dance, there was lots of time to linger in this embrace. His warm hand moved to her back, slid up to her neck, his fingers in her hair, then down again to her waist. Caressing. Wanting only to embrace, to cherish. He held her and she pressed against him, feeling safe and warm and wanted. She knew exactly what she wanted and who she was and apologized not at all.

Morning brought whimpers from Michaela and the howl of angry cats at the front door. Alma lifted the baby from her crib and carried her to the front door to see what all the noise was about. On the way she grabbed a bottle of formula, the last one.

The forecast had been right, a coating of frost dusted Grace's car. OJ, Alma's orange striped cat, stood guard at the front door against an intruding feline who stood its ground, fur standing on end and tail erect, ears flat back, protecting the place where the formula had spilled. They howled and hissed and growled at each other. They didn't notice when Alma opened the door.

A screech from the bedroom startled them all. "Tiddy, Tiddy." Aaron appeared as if by magic and dashed out, sending both animals running. Aaron cried and Alma struggled with the squirmy boy and the hungry baby.

Grace came stumbling sleepily into view. She lifted the boy gently and murmured soothing sounds in his ear. "Let's find Tiddy's food, hurry, hurry. Tiddy will come to get her food."

"If you stand on the deck in back," Alma told Grace, "and open the can of moist cat food, OJ will come running. Then we can get Tiddy in. Is that really her name?" She settled in the La-Z-Boy with Michaela and clicked the TV on. "Sesame Street, do kids still watch that?"

"No, she's No-Name-Kitty. Aaron can't say it."

Big Bird appeared bright and bold as ever, distracting Aaron.

The cats will have to make peace with each other much the same as Grace and I will. Chamomile and bitter greens, both useful, grow in the same garden along with weeds and pests. Alma cuddled the baby; Michaela opened eyes of indeterminate color to inspect the source of this new voice cooing at her.

Later, when the children were napping, Alma and Grace descended the stairs to the basement.

"Wow! Amazing! I've never seen these stairs cleared. I can even see the cement floor in places." She paused, then sat on the last step. Her forehead furrowed as her eyebrows drew together. "This is where he did it?"

"Yes." Alma didn't point to the corner, it was obvious, if Grace cared to notice. That area was freshly painted and completely cleared. She hadn't wanted to enter that space to put anything there.

"I think I'll move those unopened boxes there. Will you help me? I dread going through those boxes, there must be more than a hundred."

Alma looked at Grace, who stared at the clearing as she moved toward it. I can't even guess what could be going through her mind. Grief? Regret that she hadn't come for her father's funeral? The old hatred? Guilt? Remorse? Relief that he's gone?

"I remember hiding in this corner." Her body made the empty space appear cavernous. "Never when we'd play hide and seek. Only when William picked on me. Or, if I was mad at you or *him*. I'd get behind his workbench... Where is it? The work bench?"

George had broken it down and burned it. He hadn't even asked. He'd been so angry at Mack that he apparently got satisfaction from slinging the ax at the piece. Alma didn't want to tell Grace about the blood stains that soaked into the wood. Not just blood either... The thought brought another flashback, complete with sound and brilliant color splattered on the walls and ceiling. Alma covered her face with her hands and tried to rid herself of the image.

"What's wrong, Mom?"

"I get these pictures in my head... Not just in my head. They're sort of projected out, as if I were there again, finding him... I see the blood and hear... post stress something or other, it's called."

"You found him?"

"Alicia and I."

"She didn't tell me."

"Did you ask?" Alma wished she could retrieve the words.

"No." Animosity lengthened and arched the vowel. "No. I didn't ask. I didn't call. I didn't come for the funeral," she said as if she were about to add *stupid*. "I suppose you'll spend the day punishing me for not coming to his funeral. Why should I? He threw me out." Grace folded her arms across her chest and widened her stance. Her eyes demanded confrontation.

Fatigue swam through Alma. She had no energy to resume the old argument. Too tired to stand, she sank onto an unfinished chair, the arms of which were missing. Aggravation replaced weariness.

Now, calm down, she told herself. She's feeling defensive. No sense arguing with her. She's your daughter. Alma tried to think of a way to divert a quarrel, but inner waves of agitation squalled.

A testy voice rose within Alma.

This is the way you've always dealt with her, Alma. Mack too. I thought you wanted to be free of this strife.

Isn't the relationship what's at stake here? She's my daughter and I love her, Alma fought with herself, struggling for control, heart beating faster, moisture coating her upper lip.

Love is not all chamomile and lavender. She's not a very nice person.

She'll run away again if I'm not careful, Alma argued back.

Placating her now won't result in the relationship you want. She will love you less, if you allow her to strike out at you.

Alma stood to her full height, hands at her side, fingers curled tight into her palms, as if clenched fists could restrain her tongue. Grace diverted her gaze, but only for a second.

"No one threw you out, Grace. You left," Alma said softly.

"You didn't stop me." Grace's ragged voice accused.

"Is that what you wanted? To be stopped? You were unstoppable." Is that what this is all about? She didn't want to go; she wanted to be stopped?

"You could have tried harder."

"You too, Grace. You could have tried harder, too. I made mistakes. A lot of mistakes. I am sorry that some of those mistakes hurt you."

Grace rolled her eyes. Her right leg moved to the beat of her agitation, heel tapping rapidly, forcefully. But she said nothing.

"If I could change the past, the kind of family we were, I would," Alma snapped her fingers. "Just like that, I'd change it. But I can't. If there's any punishing being done, it's you punishing yourself and trying to punish me."

Take a stand. That's all you have to do now. Work it out as you go along.

Alma resisted the urge to walk away, to leave this uncomfortable place, to avoid saying the things that were erupting inside. Hold your tongue, don't accuse, she instructed herself to no avail.

"I will not wallow in regret, Grace," shaking her head. "Or berate myself. I don't want to live in that misery, any longer. I want to make plans. I will break down walls upstairs for a studio for quilting and sewing. Maybe move out of this house all together. All of this stuff here, this junk, I'd like to burn it."

Alma heard herself as if the words were someone else's. And that's exactly what I am going to do. She felt stronger. She unclenched her fists and took a deep breath.

Grace sighed and shifted her weight to the other leg, throwing her hip to one side.

"I will not fight with you, Grace. If you need to talk about what happened, we'll talk about whatever you want. If you want to fight and punish me, you'll have to leave." An image rose in her head. The herb garden, with escarole and mustard greens, planted among the sweetness of thyme and mint, bitter to the tongue but tasty when mixed with sweet lettuce in a salad.

"I'm getting thrown out again!" Grace's hands chopped the air and came to a stop on her hips.

"Stop it right there. Right there!" She came close to calling her Missy again. "I will not accept that. If you leave this house again, it will be *your choice*, your decision. It will be because you prefer to live in the pain of the past. It will be because you'd rather leave than face up to the problems and work out our differences. If you are thinking that I will try to stop you or beg you to stay, I will not. I want you to stay. I would like to get to know my grandchildren. I hope we will have a future together, but not if the price is constant tension, blame, and accusation." Alma remembered the gun. "The gun. It must go, immediately. There will be no guns in this house."

"Oh my God! I forgot! It's in the diaper bag." She started up the stairs.

They heard the front door open. "Alma," called George. "Whose flat tire is that?"

"I put it in the freezer."

"Alma, you home?"

"Mommy, mommy," cried Aaron, little footsteps pattered against the hardwood floors.

Commotion reigned for the rest of the morning. Petra arrived soon after George. Breakfast and formula, lost pacifiers and flat tires, dirty diapers and clean clothes, OJ and Tiddy, reminiscing and reacquainting, all needed to be attended to. George and Aaron became fast friends, but only after George reduced his height by playing pony and riding the squealing boy around the house on his back.

"Tire's fixed, Alma," announced George later. "Where do you want these suitcases? There's more in the car, too."

Alma and Grace looked at each other, each waiting for the other to respond.

"Put them in Grace's old room . . . for now."

"Thanks, George." Turning to her mother, Grace said, "I almost forgot. I have a job interview this afternoon."

"Already? How did you manage that?" asked Alma.

Petra shook her head and glanced at her watch.

"I sent a resume to Cromwell Aircraft. I heard they're restructuring their management team. They called me."

"Congratulations, that's not an easy company to get into." Petra patted Grace on the back. "Great company to work for."

"How did they . . . They called you?" Astounded, Alma wondered: Can this be the same peevish, angry person who needed *The Treatment* last night? The same grouchy young woman who growled at me this morning? Cromwell Aircraft calling my daughter in California? Grace part of a management team?

Aaron yelled, "Diddy up, diddy up, horthy," as he and George galloped down the hall.

"They, Cromwell that is . . . or rather someone from Cromwell, came to the California company I worked for, did some consulting on a project I headed up. We worked together for months. They . . . he . . . told me there was an opening, recommended me to Cromwell. I'm pretty sure the job's mine."

She's involved with someone. Alma wanted details. Who is he? How involved is she? But she decided she wouldn't risk putting Grace on the defensive. Alma was strangely relieved. Good for her. She'll have comfort, counsel, a friend. Somewhere else to focus her energies. At the same time she was concerned. The old admonitions against divorce, adultery, mortal sin came rushing in, but were ushered out as fast as they arrived. If my daughter could be happy, really happy with someone else . . . Her thoughts were interrupted by the phone.

"That was Tony, he's on his way over. He has blueprints," Alma said.

"I have to go to work." George gave Aaron one last ride. The child screamed when Grace took him off George's back. "More later, cowboy. Give Papa Georgie a goodbye kiss." The child refused.

Papa Georgie? Papa Georgie? What is he thinking, Alma wondered? Grace eyed Alma. She tilted her head and asked a question without words.

George beamed at his new status. Now he'd elevated himself to grandfather-by-association.

"Not me. I called in sick. I'm here for the day." Petra took the sleeping Michaela from her grandmother's arms. "Shall I put her down?" But she didn't wait for an answer.

Grace searching Alma's face.

"Who's Tony?"

"A friend. He's an architect. He's building a hotel in town." Alma kept her eyes on the table she cleared.

"The blueprints are for what?"

"I didn't ask him to. We talked about it. . . .he . . . I don't know. He just made the blueprints for fun . . . I guess." She inspected the table cloth.

"Show Grace the sketch he made." Petra returned without the baby. "She didn't even notice I'd put her in the cradle. Where is that sketch?"

"How'd you meet this Tony person, Mom?"

Now I'm back to Mom standing again. She seems like a

different person: administrator, lover maybe. She's good with the children when she's rested.

"That's a story you'll enjoy, Grace." Petra laughed as she looked for the sketch. "Here it is." Her voice raised an octave. Her movements lost their usual fluidity. She retrieved the sketch from the top of the refrigerator. Dropped it, picked it up and dropped it again.

"A new refrigerator? Way to go, Mom!"

"Yes, and I'm ordering a dishwasher. A portable. That'll work in this kitchen. Who wants to spend time washing a stack of dishes like that?"

Petra's hands trembled as she spread the sketch out on the table. "Go on. Tell her how you met Tony."

"Petra! What is wrong with you?"

18

"This is beautiful, Mom. The person who drew this sketch has environmental scruples. That's what I've been working on: environmental impact studies."

"Environmental impact studies? You are full of surprises. Are you really my daughter?"

Petra spilled the glass of water she'd been drinking. "Oh shit! Damn, damn, damn." As if in fast forward, she raced around getting paper towels, mopping the table, then the floor.

"Petra!"

Petra sat down and smoothed her hair and checked her nails. "Are you going to tell Grace about that night you met Tony? I'll tell her." Petra told Grace how she had to force Alma to go Patsy's Pizza Pub that night, what they wore, how she practically had to shove Alma in the front door of the pub, exaggerating greatly. Alma filled in some details and embellished the part about the green-drinking-dragon-lady. The three laughed together in not quite a natural way, Alma thought. Tensions from unresolved issues blocked the ease of laughter, making it sound not quite free.

"You would not believe your mother, Grace," Petra prattled on. Wait till you hear this. She chopped down the hen house and set it afire. George had to rescue us." Petra batted her eyes so she looked like Raggedy Ann, her palms splayed out alongside her face, ear to ear thin-lipped smile.

"You told me about that, Aunt Petra, remember?"

Palms fell, mouth dropped open. "Hey! That was the day we found money stashed in the basement. In books and tins. You've found more since then, right, Alma?" Her words fell over each other and her voice rose to high C.

Alma swung sharply toward Grace. What, she asked

herself? Petra told Grace about the hen house? "What are you talking about?"

"Money? You found money stashed in the basement?" Grace stood up. Her chair scraped loudly. "My father hid money in the basement? How much money are we talking about here? I spent years wondering if I'd be able to pay the rent and he's stuffing money in the basement?"

"Lots. Thousands. Have you found more, Alma?" Petra was on her feet now, too, clearing the table, clattering teacups, and dropping spoons. "I'd better take this wet tablecloth off." She tripped over her own feet on the way to the sink.

"What do you mean, Petra already told you about it? When? When you told Petra about Micheala and didn't tell me?" Alma looked at Petra, who turned away and fiddled with the dishes in the sink. "Grace?"

Grace looked as puzzled as Alma felt. Her mind seemed foggy with confusion.

Stillness fell over the room. No more teacup clatters, no dishwater swishing. No humming of the furnace or refrigerator. Even Aaron, he'd stopped playing with his giant sized Legos and looked wordlessly from his mother to Petra to Alma.

"Well?" asked Alma.

Grace turned to Petra. "You didn't tell her? I never really thought you wouldn't tell her." Then to her mother. "No wonder you didn't know about Cliff and me."

Petra's hand covered her mouth. Her eyes widened and her forehead furrowed as her brows reached for the ceiling.

"Tell me what? Petra, you knew about Cliff too." Alma sat still. Stunning possibilities swirled through the fog, clear one moment, dim the next. "Tell me what? One of you . . .."

"It's no big deal, Mom. Every once in a while Aunt Petra'd write to me. That's all. Hey, I gotta go. I gotta get dressed for that interview. I need to leave here . . ." She looked at the clock on the wall. "Oh my God, in five minutes." She rushed out of the kitchen.

"I knew you sent her Christmas cards since she's been in California. You wrote to her too?"

"Yeah, a couple of times." Petra avoided Alma's eyes. She washed dishes thoroughly. Rinsed them carefully, inspecting them as she did.

"A couple of times? As recently as the hen house incident? And she wrote back to you?"

"Sometimes."

"Sometimes? You knew about her breakup with Cliff?"

"She told me."

"She told you, but not me." Alma stood and moved from behind the table, closer to Petra. "But you didn't think it was something *I* should know?"

"Mom." Grace called from the bedroom. "Will you put Aaron down for his nap?"

"No. You'll have to do that."

"I don't have time. I'll be late."

"Make time."

"I'll do it, Grace," said Petra.

"No, you won't. You and I have to talk."

"We can talk after Aaron's asleep." Petra looked directly at Alma with tear filled eyes. "We need to talk, Alma." Petra picked up the boy and tossed him in the air. He squealed with delight. "Time for your nap, little man. Come on, Aunty Petra will read you a story."

The doorbell rang. Alma sat at the kitchen table and put her face in her hands for a moment and took a deep breath. They probably didn't mean anything by it. It'll be all right. She tried to breathe out the sense of betrayal that built inside, that everybody's-been-invited-to-the-party-but-me feeling.

Who are you fooling? she argued back with herself. Petra has been in touch with Grace all along. Think about it. Last year she said something about Aaron. What was it? Oh, that he'd gotten some new teeth. Then she said she was only guessing. That kids his age . . ..

Tony opened the door a crack. "Okay if I come in?"

"Come in," her voice sounding a little grumpy. "Come

in," she said more softly, summoning up some faux enthusiasm.

"Forgot. No one rings the doorbell here." He had a black wool cap pulled down over his ears and a maroon Parka on. Large rolls of paper extruded from under his arm. His smile was filled with good cheer.

Grace flew down the hall into the living room and stopped short of careening into Tony. She looked at him, then turned toward her mother, her back to Tony, then back at Alma and crossed her eyes. Then announced, "I'm outta here."

"You need a coat. It's cold," said Tony, taking off a pair of leather gloves.

She looked at him as if he'd said something stupid, then at his gloves. "Poor animal, sacrificing his life for your comfort," she said, then dashed out the door.

"Who was that?" Tony placed his hand over his chest as if he'd been struck.

"My daughter, Grace. She arrived last night." Alma felt tired, confused, worn out from trying to keep everybody happy. She hadn't realized how much she'd come to appreciate the quiet order of her life. She'd thought she was lonely. She thought she *should* be lonely because she was alone, because everyone asked her if she were lonely, because Petra treated her as if she were lonely. After all, how could a grieving widow be anything but lonely?

"Your daughter. She's visiting?" He sat beside her at the table.

"She's moving here." Alma highlighted the events of the last twenty-four hours, leaving out details.

The chaos must have been evident to Tony. He raised his eyebrows and let out a long breath. "You need a break. Have you had lunch?"

It was two o'clock in the afternoon. "I don't know, did I?" Alma placed her finger at the side of her cheek and rolled her eyes upward as if searching the top of her mind for the answer.

"Come on," he took her hand as he stood, provoking her

response to stand. A moment of graceful unity. "Let's go down to my office to look at these blueprints. On the way we'll stop by the hotel construction site, I'll show you around. We can have lunch at Patsy's."

Without a word, she willed her eyes to leave his. She went to the hall closet and pulled out her jacket. Heading toward the bedroom, struggling to get the sleeve turned right side out as she pushed her arm through it, she said, "Petra, I'm going out."

"What? Is that Tony?"

"We're going out for lunch."

"You're leaving me here, alone? With the kids?"

"Yes." Looking at Tony, she said, "Let's go."

"How's your ankle? I see you're still limping a little."

Alma heard what Tony said, but she was distracted. Petra's not my friend, she's here more to be nosy than helpful. No, that's not true. Petra is here for Grace. To be with her. Petra *is* her godmother. They've always been close. Alma remembered the peals of laughter when Petra taught Grace to apply mascara. They'd experimented with eyeliner and false lashes. Petra favored Grace, though she brought supplies for both girls. Alicia lost interest quickly which was strange. She was more the mascara type than Grace.

They were getting in the car when Petra appeared at the door, Aaron on one hip.

"Hey, he'll never sleep now. When will you be back?"

"Don't know. I'll write you a letter." That was nasty, Alma thought. She smiled.

They drove toward town. Smoke curled from a few chimneys. They passed three women walking briskly up the hill, laughing as they went. I miss having girlfriends. Laughing with a group of friends. I'd forgotten how much fun that could be. I've lost contact with all of my friends, except for Petra. Sonya, we used to be good friends in high school. Petra! The thought of her makes me so mad. She tries to run my life for me. Why didn't I notice that before?

"She's been writing to Grace." Alma surprised herself,

that she'd spoken aloud.

"Who? Who's writing to Grace?"

"Petra. I think she's been writing to Grace for a long time. Here I am worrying about her, wondering where she is, if she's okay, and Petra's been writing to her all along."

"That isn't okay?"

Keep quiet, Alma. Since when do you go blabbing on about your troubles? But her disobedient words spilled forth.

"No. Of course not. Well, yes. I guess she had a right to do that, but why didn't she tell me Grace was all right?"

"I'm a little lost here."

"This morning, I found out Grace wrote to . . . or maybe called for all I know. Anyway, Petra knew that Grace and Cliff were breaking up. I didn't know until she was on her way here, a few days ago."

Tony looked as if he were trying to assemble the pieces of a mental puzzle.

Alma told him the short version of Grace's history.

"Do you know for sure that Petra's been in close contact with Grace? I mean, since Grace left home."

"No. I'm just guessing that from Petra's reaction today, when Grace let it slip."

"You and Petra are good friends?"

"Since high school. Longer."

"Eight years since Grace left home. That seems like a long time to keep such a big secret."

"Petra's not too good at keeping secrets, either. As I think back, though, there have been times . . . like when Grace went to Buffalo to finish her last two years of college, Petra mentioned something about her dorm room. When I asked how she knew that, she said that's what all dorm rooms looked like. What did I know?"

"You knew she was going to Buffalo?"

"Yes, Grace did call me, but rarely. At least when Grace lived here, in the area, neighbors would tell me they'd seen her here or there. Even Petra. She'd say, 'Hey, I saw Grace. She's working at Schneider's Bakery now. Can you imagine

Grace getting up at four in the morning?' She knew, Tony. She knew how I worried about Grace. She could have put my mind at ease."

"Petra's your friend. I'm sure you'll straighten it out. Talk with them. Both of them. Get some straight answers. You have to tell them what you're thinking. For your sake. My mom used to say, "Don't pick fights, Tony. But you must stand up for yourself, too. Be careful the wind does not blow through you." She loved poetry and that thing about the wind is from an Hungarian poet, Babits, I think. Hey, there's an unusual looking restaurant." He made a U-turn and stopped in front of the place. "Ever had lunch here?"

19

The one story building was like a neon sign without electricity, gilded in all the primary colors. There were cornices and columns where there shouldn't be any. Trellises, covered with brownish vines, climbed here and there. The walnut-stained, wood sign, a slice from the trunk of an old tree, boasted the name in rounded, broad gold letters.

"The Eggs Nest? No, it's new. It's been here about five years."

Large maples and oaks surrounded the structure, leaving only a narrow path to the parking lot behind it. From the back they could see that it was actually two stories and much larger than it appeared from the road. Inside, the place was even more exotic.

Alma looked around as if she were a tourist in a postcard shop. This old house had many rooms that wandered through this level. Each set up for dining. Magazine covers, greeting cards, old photographs, newspapers, and wrapping paper covered the walls and ceiling, from which hung model airplanes, Christmas lights and ornaments, ships in bottles, egg beaters, an old fan, an old-fashioned telephone and other objects that belonged elsewhere. Mismatched tables and chairs were placed well away from each other. Nothing matched, yet everything went together like flowers in a spring bouquet. They were the only patrons.

"Makes you feel like having fun," said Tony. "Take a look at this menu. Very sophisticated."

"I'm ready for some fun. I feel adventurous," said Alma, looking at the unfamiliar dishes on the menu. "I will order something I haven't eaten before."

A woman approached, tall, thin, dressed in an urban

slacks set, a gold necklace showing beneath the jacket, rings on each hand but no wedding band. She addressed Alma by name.

"Hi?" Alma responded, scanning her memory.

"I'm Rachel Rivers." She smiled warmly at Tony.

"Rachel! Oh for goodness sakes. I didn't recognize you. Gosh it's been years."

"Hi Rachel. I'm Tony O'Sullivan."

She gave him a dazzling smile. "Welcome to The Eggs Nest. You're the architect for the new hotel. Leave your business card. We have a weekly drawing for a free lunch. I own this mess." Then turning to Alma, "Sorry to hear about Mack."

Alma wondered just how much she knew about Mack. She wondered how it could be that Rachel had owned this place for so long and she, Alma, didn't know about it. She wondered why Sonya hadn't mentioned it, but then it'd been only recently that she had any conversation with her. She felt like Rip Van Winkle, awakened from a long sleep and everything was different.

"Thank you. I . . . Wow! You own this. All of this?" Alma made a sweeping motion with her hand, "It's so interesting. The way you've decorated. You ought to come by and look at some of the junk in my garage. It would fit right in. Oh," she opened her eyes wide and clamped her hand over her mouth. "I'm so sorry. I didn't mean to call your . . . belongings . . . junk."

"Don't feel bad. Most of it is junk. Cleaned up and polished but junk just the same. A few pieces are antiques. I enjoy collecting things. Junking, that's what I call it. It's my hobby. I accumulate so much, I either have to throw it out or do something with it. I can't throw it out, so I change this a couple of times a year."

Rachel and Tony talked about the restaurant that would be in the hotel. Rachel was saying she had a bid in to run that restaurant, wanted to partner with the hotel owners, something like that. Alma wasn't really listening.

It's playful, artful really, arranged like this, there's an

order to the chaos. I could take the bottles out of boxes, arrange them on shelves, thought Alma. Make a room downstairs, hang some things like Rachel has, arrange the furniture in interesting ways. I remember how nice the basement looked with fabric draping the walls. I could refinish some of the chairs.

"I refinished all the furniture myself. I get it from the dump, from garage sales," Rachel said, as if she knew what Alma was thinking.

"Rachel, do you ever see Sonya? At the antique shop on Route 209?"

"Sonya and I are still good friends."

They're still good friends. She felt left out. "Well, she says many of the pieces Mack collected are valuable."

"She should know. She's an expert. Did you know she used to have a shop in the city? Customers come from out of state, even from Europe. What are you going to do with it? Your stuff. Sell it?"

"I don't know. Maybe . . . This morning I felt like burning it." And just why are you telling her this? "I've given a few things to Sonya to sell for me. I don't have the same enthusiasm for . . . collecting. Stop by, have a cup of tea. Take a look. Maybe you'll find something you like."

"I heard from Sonya that you dry your own herbs for tea. She said it's the best she's ever had. Maybe you'd consider selling some to me, for the restaurant. My customers would enjoy it."

"Sell my tea? You'd buy it? I don't know. I'll think about it."

Rachel checked her watch. "Kitchen's closing soon to prep for dinner." She pointed out meals that were no longer available.

When Rachel left them, Alma said to Tony, "Rachel Rivers? She used to hang out with Petra, Sonya and me sometimes. But then she was skinny, straggly-haired and shy, kept to herself mostly."

"She's very a smooth, sophisticated business woman now. But you, you're real. I like the way you said you felt like burning the stuff in your basement. That's honest. I like that." he looked away, down at the silverware, as if he were embarrassed by his own boldness.

"I'm learning to be honest with myself."

"That's what I saw in you at Patsy's the night we met. An honesty. You were uncomfortable there and weren't afraid to show it. No one's ever thrown a glass of wine at me before."

They both laughed.

"Do you have enough dried herbs to sell?"

"That's interesting. I could grow more in the spring. Package them in jars according to flavor. I *will* think about it." They talked about the lunch selections.

"Shall I order for you?" Tony asked.

"No, I know what I want. I'm not sure I can say it, but I think I'll have no trouble eating it."

"Can I choose a wine for us?"

"I'd love a glass of wine with lunch," said Alma feeling a little reckless. "And if I like it, I'll write the name in my notebook and order it the next time I go to Patsy's."

She found herself nodding and ahh-humming automatically in response to the inflections in Tony's voice. He spoke about his brother who lived in Oklahoma and his sister who lived in Rosedale, his apartment in Manhattan. Great place, Manhattan, if she ever visited, he'd show her around.

She listened, she did. But another layer of thought ran through her mind as she listened. His smiling eyes were what attracted her attention and evoked a warm response in her, as if they assured her he could be a friend, maybe more than a friend. They smiled even when the rest of his face didn't. Sort of like Santa Claus eyes. Something else about him appealed to her, a quality she couldn't quite identify. He wasn't a particularly handsome man. His nose was shaped oddly, she noticed. Then she realized his moustache actually camouflaged a scar, maybe a harelip. I wonder what it would be like to kiss him. What would that scar feel like against my lips? His mustache. Would it be soft or bristly? Like the brush I use to scrub the mushrooms? She hadn't ever kissed someone who had a mustache before. Oh, Alma! What are you thinking, she asked herself? He takes you out to lunch and you're wanting to kiss him. A plate yielding the fragrance of curry jarred her from her reverie.

Tony ate slowly. He chewed his food carefully. Alma watched the way his mustache responded, moving up and down. He seemed to savor each bite, lingering over each mouthful, before slipping the next morsel in. Mack ate quickly, keeping his mouth full, swallowing partial mouthfuls to make room for the next spoonful, probably never tasting anything.

"Mmm. Perfect. The seasoning is just right. Fresh herbs make all the difference," said Tony, as he slid a piece of shrimp into his mouth, then licked a droplet of butter from his lower lip.

Alma liked him and she liked that she liked him, a sensation both pleasant and startling. "We don't want her to turn out like her mother." Voices of the nuns emerged from the edges of memory. Words overheard by a little girl too young to understand fully, until later when classmates made it perfectly clear. "Slut," they'd said. She could eat only half, not even that, of her lunch. Finally, she excused herself from the table.

The restroom was on the second floor, she assumed. Three times the stairway turned, so that at the top, Alma was unsure of which direction she faced. She wandered into a small bedroom and sat at an antique vanity table. The large mirror, framed in carved, organically shaped maple, balanced smaller mirrors hinged to each side. She faced herself in the center. Plain, she thought, attractive, but plain. The color in her cheeks was natural, as was her short red, silver-streaked hair. Her eyelashes and eyebrows were the same color, a shade lighter, perfect for showing off her green eyes. A thin white line beneath her right eyebrow reminded her of three long ago stitches. A few creases around her mouth. No, not plain. Unadorned, she thought.

A triptych of simple beauty, flawed, but authentic.

From the edge of her vision, the side mirror reflected a three-quarter tangential self. Bare tree limbs outside the window formed a tangled motif around her head. In the very same panel, without turning, she noticed a second reflection from the other small mirror: a shadowed profile, as if she were turning away from herself, three-quarters of her face invisible.

What matters is how you see yourself, she thought, as she met the full-faced image in front of her, not anyone else's idea of you. Can you see yourself as desirable? Can you admit you long to be touched?

She is acting, said her tangential self, like her mother. Luring some man into her life, so he can take care of her. And Grace, a married woman, look at her. What's she doing with the Cromwell man?

The truth is you are afraid, said a whisper, so softly that Alma faced the image, now no longer turning away. You're afraid of pleasure just like you are afraid to spend money. You used to like making love, being touched, having your desires satisfied. Remember?

I remember, said the smallest voice, in a guttural, primal tone. I want to be touched, kissed, lusted after.

See, said her tangential self. Kissing some mustache is just the beginning. Living in sin, that's what the nuns called it.

"Excuse me, this wing is private. If you're looking for the ladies' room, it's downstairs," said a voice that diminished as it left soft shuffling footfalls in the hall. Alma quickly found the restroom, then returned to her seat.

A dessert had been placed in the center of the table. Something moist and chocolate, with two forks. Tony seemed lost in the view just outside the window. Alma wondered if he was thinking about his deceased wife. He hadn't mentioned her since the night they met. His smile reached out and drew her into an embrace as she returned to the seat across from him. Alma knew what he'd been thinking about, but before either could say a word, Rachel joined them. As if it were a barely visible bubble that quietly burst midair, the moment was gone.

Rachel chatted for a while and promised to visit Alma for a cup of tea and bring Sonya with her. Interesting women, thought Alma. Each of them has her own business, each lived on the second floor of homes they'd converted. I'd like to get to know them.

She and Tony toured the hotel under construction, wearing bright yellow hard hats. The workmen greeted Tony warmly, asked him questions freely. They talked about problems as if they were buddies. Tony was clearly in charge, decisive.

Alma was having fun, as if she had a right to spend the afternoon so frivolously. Sonya's antique shop was on the way to Tony's office.

"Can we stop and look? Do you have time?"

"Sure," said Tony. "Maybe I'll find some furniture."

"For your apartment? How will you get it home?"

"Remember when I told you I wanted to open a pottery studio?" He parked the car. "I decided to do it. I'm looking at a piece of property west of town. And another piece outside of Rosedale. I'm going to build that A-frame like the one I sketched for you. The blueprints I have for you are actually a copy of the plans for my place, with some modifications."

They walked into the shop and were greeted by the gentle spicy scent of potpourri and the distracted smile of a saleswoman. She told Alma the owner was out of town on a buying trip, but that she'd try to help her if she had any questions. Buying trip, Alma thought, that would be fun.

Sonya had artfully arranged her merchandise. There were pieces as small as thimbles and as large as armoires and every size between. Antiques were displayed everywhere. On tables, walls, in glass-covered cases, on shelves, in cabinets and half-opened drawers. Books with yellowed edges and tattered corners were stacked neatly on the floor alongside chairs, that were grouped in cozy seating arrangements. China and glassware were arranged in place settings on the tables and in china cabinets. Alma imagined a three-generation family seated there, enjoying a holiday meal. What stories these pieces could tell, she thought.

She noticed Tony's hands, large, sure, steady with a dusting of dark hair. His long fingers were tipped with smooth, clean fingernails. He held a fragile hand-blown vase, the color of violets, up to the light, then gently replaced it on the shelf of a maple display case filled with glass bottles of every shape and color. "Beautiful. I'll buy this when we're finished looking," he said.

One room held at least as much stuff as Mack had. But here, it looked orderly, attractive, almost like a picture in a magazine, not at all like a junky basement. Even the pieces she'd given Sonya to sell, fit into the picture. The two browsers wound their way from room to room, till Alma had no sense of where the entrance was.

Vigor replaced the earlier fatigue she'd felt. She banished nagging voices, she noticed, only when she engaged herself, as she did in the antique shop. Had she somehow encouraged their presence?

Resisting the urge to return home, Alma went with Tony to his office. It was in a rundown looking building. The blacktop in the parking area was in disrepair. His office was littered with stacks of papers and files lining all sides of the desk and in the corners, along the walls, in the middle of the room. Alma was shocked. Towers of Pepsi cartons flanked the bookcase. Books, papers, a stack of dirty ashtrays, drafting tools, empty glasses and cups with dark stains, and long rolls of paper cluttered the shelves. What little that could be seen of the rug looked like it hadn't seen a vacuum in months. The curtains were dirty. Bits of dust and lint clung to the screens behind the smoggy glass. The air was infused with stale cigar smoke mixed with a floral cover-up.

She'd imagined his office to be neat, with walnut furnishings, brass desk accessories, and fresh flowers, with paintings hung over bookcases and credenzas. Maybe even overstuffed chairs and a low table in the corner. It would smell like freshly brewed coffee.

"Sorry, I should have warned you. This is the contractor's office and he lets me share it. Actually I have two drawers and whatever desktop space I can clear."

Alma was relieved.

"He's usually out at one construction site or another. He must have been here today," he said, fanning the air with his hand and wrinkling his nose. "I just need to get my glasses," he said, as he took them out of desk drawer. "You should have seen it when I first arrived." He shook his head. "Let's use the conference room."

That room wasn't much better, except that half of the large table was cleared and the smell of cigar smoke less noticeable. Tony rolled the blueprints out, smoothing them with the flat of his hand as gently as she would have hand-pressed a piece of fine fabric. She helped him. Their hands touched as they anchored the corners with Pepsi cans that had been lined up like a divider between the clean side and the cluttered side of the table.

"He must really like this stuff. He drinks it at room temperature. I can't wait to get out of here. I'm moving. I signed a lease on an office in Rosedale. I didn't think I'd be here long, but it looks like I'll need a satellite office. This hotel job has brought me several new clients."

Alma felt a burst of joy at that news. The more time she spent with this man the more relaxed she was with him and his comfortable ways.

"This doesn't look at all like the sketch," Alma said, tracing the blue lines with her finger.

"True, but it is the same A-frame I drew for you. Blueprints are not as pretty. This shows the layout of the rooms, and the wiring and plumbing. See how it's laid out? These are the rooms downstairs. Over here, see? There's the second level. That could be your living space, if you wanted." His lower lip curved around each word as he spoke.

He pointed out the features and explained how he'd

divided the space. Two bedrooms downstairs could be work rooms, say a cutting room here and a designing room there with drafting tables. He'd even drawn them. Two bedrooms upstairs: one could be a small sitting room with TV, stereo.

"Where is the kitchen?"

"Here's the refrigerator and stove."

"I don't think an A-frame is right for me, Tony." She felt awed at herself. Telling the expert, the architect, that his plan was not right for her. Knowing, with fresh clarity, what was right and going with it.

"That's a good way to bring the outdoors in. You seem to love those trees."

"I do. And maybe I will build something, if I can figure out how to pay for it. Just not an A-frame. I have a picture in my head."

Alma imagined a house with two floors and many rooms. Rooms that wandered, like in Sonya's antique shop but different, hers, her own. She could see white lace curtains responding to the breeze blowing through open windows. She could start small and add on.

"I have a house. I could do all of that in my own house. Why move? Add on a room for a studio. Another for drying herbs."

"You could do that. Might be less expensive. Might not. There is enough room on the west side without having to remove trees. Or the basement, plenty of room there. It would be expensive to break through cement block to make big windows, but it can be done."

"I won't let one more tree be sacrificed. I need to do something with the piles of logs, too. They need to be put to good use. I can't let them just rot there. And the junk . . . the collection, in the basement. I can't quite think of it as a collection, but I can't call it junk after today."

They talked for a long time about Alma's studio. What it would look like. How to use glass to make it blend with the environment. Tony made more sketches. With each succeeding rendering, the house became larger, had more rooms, a deck, even a pool.

"We are getting carried away, Tony. There's no way I can afford this."

"You're right, we need to erase the pool," he laughed, as if that were the only extravagance. "There's one way to raise money for your project. Sell it . . . the logs, the paraphernalia in the basement."

"No. No, I've changed my mind about that. I don't want to make money on that stuff. It would be like making a profit from the pain that is part of every damn log, every broken chair."

"Isn't that what Mack had in mind? To make money from the things he stored there? Wouldn't selling his stuff honor his memory?"

"No. That would honor his miserly ways. That would honor the suffering his fanaticism caused. That would honor my complicity in the unhappiness we experienced. Money, profit from selling it, would do that. If there is any honoring to be done, it will be to honor the future and I won't pay for that with profits from misery. I want to be disconnected from all that."

"Alma, you can never be disconnected from the past. It will always be part of you. I learned that when my wife died." His eyes darkened. "Remember the door jamb in your kitchen? I noticed the worn areas where kids frequently held on and pulled their way through."

Alma nodded, sad that she'd made his heart ache.

"The past is like that, it leaves a permanent impression. The only way to remove those imprints from the door jamb is to rip it out and replace it. That doesn't work so well with people. At least, it didn't work so well with me, after my wife died. You could paint over the wood and cover the damage. Or you could strip the paint off, and highlight the grain of the wood, flaws and all, with a light stain. The natural beauty shows through."

Tony looked directly at Alma and she allowed the look, their eyes accomplishing what they weren't quite ready for. The natural shows through, that's what is attractive about him. That's the quality I couldn't quite identify while we ate lunch.

"You didn't have any ugly stuff between you and your wife. Or at least you don't talk about it."

"We were married only a short time. It wasn't long enough to create much of a life together. She was sick most of the time. I resented her being sick. Instead of being supportive, I withdrew from her, anticipating grief. Holidays? Why make plans? Why start traditions? And after . . . For a long time I was angry at her for dying, and ruining my life. That's ugly. I needed to face the truth about myself."

Alma nodded.

"Whatever your relationship was, you both made it that way."

Alma nodded.

"You can take responsibility only for your part. You can cover it up with coats of blame, if you want. Or you can strip away the blame and let the natural beauty show through, color other relationships. You know what I'm trying to say?"

Alma nodded, but spoke not a word. She stood and stretched to release a growing tension that made her muscles tighten. Water from the cooler, as it gurgled into a cone shaped paper cup, distracted her from the urge to touch him.

When she turned, Tony stood right there. She bumped onto him. He put his hands on her shoulders to steady her. Lightly she touched his cheek. She held his gaze for a moment as she slid her hand around the back of his neck and pulled him toward her. His mustache was soft and bristly on her face, his lips moist and warm as they touched hers. He slipped his arms around her and she luxuriated in the embrace, feeling their bodies pressed together, smelling the tweed scent of him.

Tony's breath was hot and minty. With his lips and tongue he eased her mouth open. Passion welled up in Alma as she responded to him, pressing her hips against him gliding side to side, increasing his pleasure. He slipped his hand under her sweater stroking the skin of her back, the curve of her waist. Alma's breath caught as his hand caressed her covered breast. She arched her back as her hand pulled him close and her hips moved more urgently. He followed the curve of her breasts to the valley between them. With a little fumbling, he released the front clasp of her bra. Then she froze. He pulled away a little, but still held her.

"I know you're not ready yet. It takes time to trust fate, to hope that this time it will be different. It has taken me this long to care about another woman, to risk the possibility of loss. There's no hurry." He traced her lips with his finger.

Alma felt foolish, and aroused, and embarrassed, embarrassed that she froze, embarrassed that she initiated the . . . triggered the flow of passion . . . embarrassed and pleased and fidgety, and cherished, unable to catch her breath, all at the same time.

He kissed her lips. "Okay?"

She nodded, feeling awkward with her bra unclasped, wondering how she'd fasten it but not wanting to move or appear . . . what? I can't think . . . unsophisticated, like an unsophisticated country girl. But that's what I am, an unsophisticated country girl and that feels pretty good at the moment.

Alma touched his face, "Okay."

They held each other for a time, saying nothing, holding on.

"Did you ever strip paint from a piece of furniture?" he asked, still holding her.

"No." What an odd question to ask at a moment like this.

"It's a process. Unless you use harsh chemicals, you have to take one layer at a time to protect what's underneath. It takes time."

Alma said nothing.

"Are you okay? Have I offended you?"

She shook her head, then nodded. "I'm okay."

He released her, holding her still with his eyes. He looked down at his shirt. Then at the crushed cup in Alma's hand. A large wet spot darkened his chest. "Well, I see you're still throwing your drink at me. Wait here while I get some paper towels." He left the room laughing.

Alma laughed too. She fastened her bra, filled another paper cup and sat, feeling more relaxed then she had all day. An image of an old dresser rose in her mind. It was painted a color no piece of furniture should be. She saw her own hand apply something, with a golden paint brush, stroking the surface of a small area. The bristles moved back and forth until the color looked like it was melting. With a rough-textured white cloth, she wiped the color off, but some remained and she could see another color beneath. She continued working in the same small area, each time wiping the color off with a fresh clean cloth. When she broke through to the original surface, what she saw surprised her. A small section of luminescent white shone out from beneath her dirty cloth.

That's you, said her own voice. Imperfect but precious, lit from the inside, the pearl of great price. You've been many places. In each place, you covered yourself to fit the surroundings. That's no longer necessary. Now it's time to take off those layers. You're doing a good job of uncovering. Let it happen in its own time. Be patient, but let nothing interfere.

20

She nodded, shedding her jacket. That's just what's been happening to me since that day a few months ago. The day the laundry lay piled up near the basement door. She nodded again, hugging herself as she adjusted to the difference in temperature without the coat. I am not losing my mind, I'm changing it. Relief. Feel that? It's relief, dare to feel it.

Tony's return to the conference room startled her. His voice sounded too loud after the quiet place she'd been.

"I called a friend of mine," he lowered his voice as if he'd read her thoughts. "He's an auctioneer. He might be able to help you dispose of the things in your basement."

"I meant it, Tony. I don't want to make money from this."

"You won't. Listen. He does this kind of thing often. He has lots of ideas. Here's one. The bidders pay with time or dollars to selected local charities. Like the churches, the schools, the library, the volunteer fire department. They bring cash or credit cards and pay their donation to the charity, right then, before they take the item. If they bid time, representatives of the charities would be there to sign folks up for volunteer hours. Bidders collect their purchase when they've fulfilled their time commitment. The charity stores the goods for the volunteers."

"Hmm." Alma's eyes moved as if from one imaginary bidder to another. "What a good idea." She thought some more. "It's crazy. Who in their right mind would do such a thing? Give it all away?"

"You'd have to pay him, the auctioneer, and he's expensive. You could charge admission, a couple of bucks a head. People would pay just to take a look."

Alma gathered her thoughts from the walls, the ceiling,

from the towers of Pepsi cartons. "I'd get rid of, all of it."

"The community benefits."

Alma nodded. "Mack's gift to the community. He was generous in a way, in his own way. He was extravagantly generous when he gave trees back to the land. He'd save the best pumpkins for our Jack-O-Lanterns, before selling the rest."

"He's a genius, my friend is. Think about this. He suggested you sell a few one acre lots to finance your studio. Sell them at the auction. Eighteen acres, even if you sold ten half-acre lots, you'd still be far enough from your closest neighbor."

"That would be hard to do. Sell the land. I don't know."

"Think about it. Walk around the property. See if you can imagine other homes there. Are you getting hungry? Want to try Rachel's dinner menu?"

Alma looked at her watch, then out the window. It was already dark. "I didn't realize it was so late. I'm not at all hungry." She hesitated then decided. 'I have a situation to deal with at home. Another time, okay? Soon."

Grace's car was in the driveway, beside Petra's, when Tony dropped her off. He declined the offer of a cup of tea, saying he valued his life too much to risk it, going in there with Grace *and* a situation. He confessed he was not that much of a tea drinker.

Alma kissed Tony's cheek. "Perhaps I'll go through the process more quickly than you did."

Alma waited a moment outside the front door gathering her strength. She knew what she had to do.

Grace was on her before she'd even fully opened the door. "Mom! Where have you been?" She glanced spastically at her watch. "Do you realize what time it is?"

"Grace, shush," said Petra. "She's been worried about you, Alma. You were gone so long."

"And with a stranger," said Grace.

"We have something to say to you, Alma." Petra threw a keep-your-mouth-shut look at Grace.

"Before you do that, I have something to say to both of

you. First to you, Grace."

All three women were standing in the living room. Alma faced Grace. Petra sat in the rocking chair. The anger Alma experienced earlier had melted away. Conviction, if not courage, rose within her. Alma recognized the quiet inner voice that encouraged her and she knew it spoke the truth. No voice opposed her.

"Tony is a friend of mine, Grace. You were rude, very rude to him. You had no right to comment about his choice of gloves, or to speak so disrespectfully."

Grace looked as if she were about to speak. Alma raised her hand to signal, stop.

"A twelve-year-old would know better than to say what you did. I expect you to apologize the next time you see him."

Grace started to roll her eyes, then stopped, when Petra cleared her throat. She pressed her lips together, tightly.

This is the hardest part, thought Alma. "Next, as soon as possible, you need to find your own place. You have your own life and so do I. You may stay here as long as I see you make an effort to find a job and a place to live."

"If I walk out of this house again Mom, I won't be back." Grace shifted her weight. She looked as if she were going say more.

"If that's what you decide you want, then I'll respect your wishes."

"Grace, you don't mean that. Hush," said Petra. "She has a job, Alma. She starts next week."

"But how can I? I need someone to watch the kids."

"I will take them tomorrow so you can find a place to live. Tuesdays and Thursdays, you can plan on me spending the day with my grandchildren." The more Alma said, the less her heart pounded. "I'll help you find a babysitter, too."

"Right. Sure. And by what miracle am I to afford all this? Cliff emptied all the accounts and canceled the credit cards."

Grace sat on the sofa with her hands in her lap. Her

eyes defied Alma to continue.

Why didn't she tell me that? No wonder she slept in the car. Alma's resolve weakened.

Grace made her choice, reminded a inner calm voice. You offered her an alternative. It will take time, mending this relationship.

"I intend to give the money I found in the basement to you and your brother and sister. That money should have been spent on you when you were growing up. You can have a portion of your share tomorrow."

Alma held herself erect, her outer posture belying the interior battle, the old voice subdued but insistent.

"How much did you find?" Grace stopped pouting.

"In due time. You'll find out in due time. For now, be satisfied that you'll have enough to get you started.

"Petra," Alma paused and took a deep breath. Here is where the hurt was greatest. Alma paused, wishing for some miracle to make it unnecessary for her to continue.

Petra, her eyes glistening with tears, sat in a rocker, not moving, surveying Alma as if she were trying to read her mind.

Alma's eyes filled. Words caught in her throat.

"I am grateful for your friendship, Petra, for your help and . . . your spunky attitude. Even grateful for your bossiness. But . . . I've learned something . . . about the way I use gratitude. To avoid facing the truth. To avoid doing something about how unhappy I was. So . . . right now, I'm mixed up. Mad at you and at the same time grateful because you have maintained a link between Grace and me. She was able to come home to me, on account of your keeping in touch with her. Right now, I don't know if I should tell you off or tell you what happened this afternoon.

"The truth is . . . I feel betrayed, Petra. How can I trust you again? You knew where Grace was, that she hadn't been raped and thrown in a ditch to die, all those things I worried about. But you didn't tell me." The pain, as if being cut off from a lifeline and flung into an abyss, made it hard to breathe. That was all Alma could say.

"At first, I thought she'd come back. When she didn't, I admired her, Alma. She did what you couldn't. It took courage to leave, even more courage to stay away, when she had no money, when she worked two jobs while she went to school. Grace worked hard to make a life for herself. I didn't want her to give up, to come home. I actually hoped her example would motivate you to . . . I don't know exactly what . . . make some kind of changes. You were in such misery, all the while saying stuff like, 'I'm so lucky my tomatoes are growing so well.'"

Alma took her jacket off and flung it into the closet. Then she went into the bathroom. She splashed water on her face, combed her hair, and brushed her teeth as if it were morning and she was getting ready for the day. She felt stronger, that's for sure. Maybe a little wiser.

"I thought I was helping," Petra said. She'd made tea and they sat at the kitchen table. "Especially after Grace went to Buffalo. At least we wouldn't lose her, I thought. That was my reasoning. She's like my daughter too, Alma." Petra wiped her eyes.

Alma could believe that.

"That's true." Grace looked from Alma to Petra and back. "Don't be mad at Aunt Petra. It was me, Mom. I called Petra first. I'm the one who started the letter writing when I moved away from here. I made Aunt Petra swear she wouldn't tell you or *him*. I meant mostly him. I didn't want that man to know anything about me."

"She said if I told, she'd stop writing and calling. I was so afraid I'd lose her, Alma. If she ever got in trouble, she'd have somewhere to turn. If anything happened to you, I'd be able to tell her."

"I did, Mom. I made her swear not to tell you. But I didn't think she wouldn't tell you. I felt like I was keeping in touch with you when I wrote to Petra. I couldn't call here, he might answer. He might read letters. All these years I figured you knew what I was doing, where I was. I'm sorry." Grace hugged Alma, an aberrant gesture for her.

Alma returned the embrace with less than full enthusiasm.

"I couldn't talk to you Mom." Grace inspected the worn wood floor, the frayed area rug, kept her eyes downcast. "I've done stuff I'm not proud of. You can't talk to your own mother about that. I'm exhausted. I'm going to bed." She looked only at Petra, then left the room.

"Of all the promises you've broken, Petra, you decided to keep that one."

Petra, motionless in the rocker, said, "Alma, this was the most important promise I ever made. So many times I came close to telling you, so many times. Jeez, Alma. You're all pissed off over letters and phone calls. Grace is asleep so just between us, what would you have done if she'd called you?"

"That is not the point," said Alma in a controlled voice, quiet but not calm. "The point is that you deceived me. The point is that you decided what was best for my daughter. Had she called me as often as it seems she called you, I'd at least have known she was still alive." What business of yours is it, anyway? What business, may I ask? Alma wanted to scream.

"Typical. You can continue your hand-wringing role as grief-stricken mother. How about telling her, 'Come home Grace. I'll back you up.' Or what about, 'Do you need some money? I'll cash a check. How much do you need?'"

"Maybe, I . . ."

"Maybe, my ass," Petra shouted, then craned her neck to see down the hall toward Grace's room and lowered her voice and leaned in toward Alma. "Maybe your penny jar." Petra raised both arms, "Hallelujah, Saint Alma, salvaging pennies for the poor—but never a check, not any kind of real help, not enough for her to live on so she could work only one job while she went to school. Mack's check book? Ha!" She pounded the table with the palm of her hand. "No way. That would blow your image. As long as . . ."

"Blow my image? Now you're being like that Duke guy in Patsy's. Has psychoanalysis become your hobby too? Just shut up!"

"You shut up. As long as Grace was away, you could play the distressed mother and keep the peace at home. Not my fault, you could say." Petra raised her hands palms out. "Blame it all on Mack. Now, I won't let you blame it all on me."

"As usual, Petra, you're blowing it all out of proportion." Alma fought to retain a quiet voice. This is not what I had in mind, she thought. Not the I-am-me-and-I've-become-a-different-person-taking-charge-of-my-life conversation I intended. "She had a scholarship." Alma stood and walked away from the table, turned and walked back. "A scholarship," she said victoriously her jaw clenched, her arms held stiffly at her side, her hands tightened into fists. "She didn't need money. Drop it Petra. Just drop it." Alma looked at the clock on the kitchen wall. It was stuck in last night; she'd forgotten to wind it.

"How do you know what she needed? You were too busy planting tomatoes. She got another scholarship— for track. Did you know that? Do you know which job she was able to quit when she got that scholarship?"

Alma raised a fist pointing it at Petra then shaking it as if she had hold of Petra's collar. Rage opened her mouth to express itself.

"Shut up and listen," said Petra. "You know that lounge out on thirty-two?"

The fist sprang open. Above the hand she clapped over her mouth, Alma's forehead creased as her eyes opened wide then squeezed tightly shut. She sank into the chair shaking her head.

"Yeah, that one. Scholarships don't pay for everything. At least she wasn't stripping— but the outfit the waitresses wear!" Petra rolled her eyes and turned in her seat to look out the window. Her voice deepened, quieted. "I didn't know about that either. Someone told me after she'd already quit." She turned to face Alma. "I couldn't tell you. Maybe I was a little afraid of blowing your image too. You're the only real friend I have."

Alma hadn't moved, her hand still clasped over her

mouth, eyes moist.

Petra's eyes lowered. She was silent for a moment. "But at the time, all I could think about was her safety. I was afraid of what she might do to herself. She was feeling like a worthless piece of garbage at that point." Petra glanced down the hall again.

"Garbage?" Alma tapped her teaspoon on the table, feeling torn, wanting to tell Petra to get out and wanting to know the truth and not wanting to know it.

"Yeah. Dumped by her parents, dumped by her boyfriend. Then an abortion."

"An abortion?" Her hand froze mid-tap, then she dropped the spoon.

Petra nodded. "She was pregnant when she left that day. She didn't know it."

"Oh my God." Alma covered her face with both hands for a moment, trying to grasp what Petra was saying. *This can't be happening. This can't be true.* "And still you didn't tell me. What gives you that right to withhold something like that?" The tea cups jangled in their saucers when she slammed her fist on the table. *Yes,* you *could* have told me. Yes, you should have told me. "Psychoanalyze yourself for a change. Maybe you liked playing hero. Maybe you're the hand wringing hero."

"I wanted to. Shit! I wanted to. It wasn't just a promise not to tell. She threatened to kill herself if I did. I thought she just might do it. And now . . . after Mack. . . . I think she would have. In some ways she's so much like him. You remember what it was like for you."

"For *me*? What?" Alma placed both hands, palms down on the table as if bracing herself.

"Your abortion."

"*My* abortion? What are you talking about?" Alma's hand went automatically to her stomach. Like a closed window pierced by a rock, the wall she'd built in her mind shattered releasing an image of a wizened face looming over her in a darkened room, propelling her to another place.

The air smells of old cooking grease and apples rotting on a tree that keeps sunlight out. She is lying on a lumpy mattress on the floor. A thick gray spider web fills the corner above her. She hopes the spider is not near. On the wall across from her are open shelves crammed with dusty brown and green bottles, Mason jars holding gray curled leaves, dusty dried twigs protruding over the rims of others. There is a bitter taste in her mouth and she feels nauseous. She raises her head and the room whirls around her. She rolls on her side to get away from that face. In the little space on the floor, between the mattress and the wall, she sees curds of dust, some dead flies, and a few leaves from the apple tree just outside the window above her. She vomits on the dead flies.

"Ya tore. Ya waited too long. An' ya got ta wrigglin' around too." Alma turns. The old mountain woman, stooped as if she'd pulled weeds all her life, wipes her bloody hands on a dirty apron. "That poultice I plugged ya wit'll stop the bleedin'. Ya'll be scarred, a course, but that'll keep ya from doin' this again. Ah'll git yar friend."

The old lady ushers Petra in roughly, shoving her toward Alma. Almost falling, Petra kneels and reaches out to her friend then withdraws her hand as if she were afraid to touch her. Alma is still retching.

Petra whispers, "She's all right. My friend who told me about what this old broad does. She's a rough, tough old lady, she told me, but my friend was okay afterward. You'll be okay, Alma. She's had lots of experience helping farm workers, mostly migrants."

"Git her dressed an' leave. It's outa there, no more baby. A boy it was. I done all I kin. If ya say ya been here, I'll git mah son after ya. He'll beat cha bloody." She shakes her head, glancing sideways at the two, "Don'cha know there's ways a woman kin keep from gettin' caught up like this? Dumb white girls," she mutters under her breath, "don' know notin'." She fingers the wad of bills Petra gave her, licking her fingers as she counts, then picks up a bloody basin and leaves.

"Yeah, that abortion."

Petra's words jolted Alma back to her own kitchen. The brightness of the overhead light made her squint. An empty teacup held a scattering of tea leaves on the bottom. The scent of apples drifted from a wooden bowl on the table.

"Next day we were at Doc Galvin's. Remember that—you still bleeding and vomiting?" Hospital, he said. "No hospital," Alma had said, shaking her head.

"So he stitched you up and shot you full of medicine so you wouldn't get infected. But you did. He wanted to report that old witch, but we wouldn't say who she was. You wouldn't tell who the father was. Have you shut all that out of your mind? Have you been pretending all this time that it never happened?"

Dr. Galvin kept that secret, Alma thought, even when Mack brought me to see him after we married. A thickened hymen is not so different from scar tissue.

Alma was numb, her chest tight. She couldn't catch her breath, couldn't speak, couldn't think. Petra didn't seem to notice.

"You know what it was like, Alma. You felt like shit after that. That's how Grace felt."

One thought trickled into Alma's mind. *I would have been there, to help her through it, if I'd stood up to Mack.*

Alma bent over, feeling faint, lowered her head between her knees.

"Too long," said Petra shaking her head wearily, "I've kept too many secrets—yours and Grace's. I have told you about Grace's abortion over and over in my mind. I have rehearsed this so many times, telling you. It's like this movie in my head.

"We walk into the office," Petra said as if watching that movie. "Grace holding on to my hand, like a small child crossing a dangerous intersection. The room reeks like the stink of your body when you're scared, except when the door to the inner rooms opens. Then you can smell the antiseptic. The smell reminding us why we were there.

"A young couple, kids, hold hands. They squirm in their seats, eyes on their Nikes. The only other person is older, twenty-something. Her wedding ring catches the light when she rubs her nose, a gesture she repeats often. I noticed these things, but didn't really see them until I thought about it later, many times.

"I did," said Grace, interrupting the story, tears rolling down her face.

Startled, Alma started to rise to go to her daughter. Petra puts her hand on Alma's arm.

"I remember," said Grace, "their sneakers matched and they were the same as mine. I envied her, that she had a boyfriend who stuck with her. And the married lady, siting there like she was riding a bus, she wore designer jeans and had a suede jacket across her lap. I wondered if she were trying to hide her stomach, if it had begun to show she was pregnant. Mine didn't. As long as I kept looking at them, I didn't have to think about myself, about my heart pounding, about why my deodorant wasn't working, about why I was there."

"I prayed, Alma, and you know that is a rare thing for me." Petra picked at her cuticles.

Grace moved further into the room as if in a trance. She sat cross-legged on a chair. "The door opened and the young girl went in the back; the boy left. When he came back he knocked on the frosted glass. When it opened . . . I heard a cry from the back.

"Then I go blank, Mom. I don't remember much after the door opened again and a white uniform said, 'Come in please.' Except for, 'Yes, I'm sure. No, no allergies. You want me to put my feet up there? Take a deep breath, Miss, it will make you sleepy but you'll still be awake.'"

"I remember the old woman," Alma said, "she gave me something to drink, tasted awful. If that didn't work, she said, come back in two weeks. I came back." Grace looked all blurry through Alma's tear filled eyes. This is not something a mother wants her daughter to know about. Petra's right. Too many secrets. "There was nothing to breath to make me sleepy. It hurt, worse than having a baby."

The three women were quiet, each lost in her own thoughts. Alma remembering how worthless she'd felt. Remembering without feeling. Feeling nothing while tears left little wet round spots on her shirt. She'd avoided her mother. Avoided George. Got her own apartment. She hired on as a janitor in an office building, washing floors, cleaning toilets. She worked at night so she could take classes at the community college, but she never got around to enrolling.

Yeah, she said to herself, I know what it's like to feel like garbage. She understood why Grace stayed away, even before Grace said the words. She understood why Grace kept in touch with Petra. A way to keep the connection to her mother.

"I ran away because of my father, but I stayed away because of that abortion. I was too ashamed to face you. Too damn stubborn to admit he was right about Raoul." Grace was the only one who was dry-eyed. She bit her fingernails, already so short she worked her teeth over them trying to coax something to yield for her to chew on.

21

Alma climbed the uncluttered basement stairs with an armload of fresh smelling laundry. The basement was clean: fresh paint, bright lights, lots of room for storage. A long padded table draped with a delicate silk stood at the far end, near the bilco door. A dressmaker's dummy stood between it and a new sewing machine. She'd paint the rest of the house later this spring and renovate. She walked out onto the deck to fold the clothes.

The still low sun began to warm the crisp air. A breeze suggested warmer times to come. Her mini-forest was lush with new growth. Cardinals sang to each other, *Whooit, whooit, whooit* from the pine tree on Alma's left. *Cheer, cheer, cheer,* from the birch. Robins built a nest in the maple tree.

The light breeze rustled the new leaves and delivered a pine laced apple blossom fragrance right to the deck, *her* deck. She listened for the sound of the water rushing over rocks and fallen trees in the stream. Yes, she could hear the burbling. Melting snow on the mountain was a sure sign that winter was over.

A family of deer emerged from the trees and cautiously made their way to an apple tree at the far edge of the property. Too early, thought Alma. But there are lots of blossoms. You'll soon have more apples than you can eat. That is a nice family you have, she whispered to the buck, an old friend, with a deep scar on his right flank. I'm glad to see you have recovered.

The sun, shining through the geraniums, triggered no memories. The daffodils stood at attention next to the irises. No matter how harsh the winter, they returned each spring bringing new blooms with them. This year, she thought, there are so many, I'll have to separate the bulbs.

"OJ," she said to the orange striped cushion of fluff, as she snapped the wrinkles out of a clean white terry-cloth towel, startling the deer and the cat. "This sweet smelling air is so luxurious. I don't even care if the side lawn does look like the local flea market." She reveled in the silence, grateful for her home, her own place in the world.

Soon people were milling around outside: the auctioneer and his staff; her dear friend, George; new friends, Rachel, Sonya, and a few early arrivals. And Tony. Members of charitable organizations set up tables to sign up volunteers or take time or monetary donations as payment for the items they purchase. She'd join them later with pots of fresh coffee, Mocha Java, Tony's favorite, and hot herbal tea.

The phone rang. It could only be Petra this early.

"Hi, I'm on my way," said Alma's friend. Can I pick anything up for you? Stop at the grocery?"

"I need some coffee creamer. Not the flavored kind. Thanks, Petra."

"How did it go? What did they say when you gave them the money?" asked Petra.

"William, Grace, and Alicia were shocked to see the bundles of five-hundred-dollar-bills."

Alma had found $78,341 stashed in the basement. She divided it equally among the three of them.

"I told them to consider it a gift. That their dad had put aside the money for them. They were overwhelmed by the amount. One moment in total disbelief, the next excited . . . making plans to spend it, save it, invest it.

Only William was angry. 'He wouldn't give us movie money, and you expect me to pretend he saved thousands just for us?' "

"Oh Lord, that spoiled it for the others," said Petra.

"Grace told him to 'chill.' Alicia was happy to get the money, her husband was laid-off. They have gone through their savings. In fact, she said if he doesn't find a job soon, they might move back here. Grace thinks there's work for him at Cromwell. They are looking for welders."

"Did William refuse to take it? The money."

"For now. But I think he'll change his mind. I told him he was free to accept the money or not, just as he was free to choose what to build his life on bitterness about the past or this rare gift."

"And Grace?"

"She's still Grace. We tangle often, but so far, I'm holding my own. We're going to make it, Pete. Time, we just need time."

"This is a big day, Alma. Everyone in town is talking about it. How are you feeling?"

"I feel like a baby chick that has just broken free of its shell. Like I've been cramped, closed in a small space, arms and legs held in tight and suddenly I have room to stretch myself out. Throw my arms out wide, feel myself be open."

Alma could hear the driveway gravel crunching. People were arriving for the auction.

The sign posted at the entrance to Alma's driveway read:

JUNK LOTTERY

**Saturday from 8 a.m. to 4 p.m.
ANTIQUES, COLLECTIBLES,
BRIC-A-BRAC, TOOLS, FIREPLACE WOOD,
FOUND OBJECTS.**

Proceeds to Charity.

22

I open my eyes onto the moonlit darkness of my room, surprised, for the moment, at the arm stretched across my breasts. A smile begins in my soul and slowly finds its way to the corners of my salty tasting lips. A stillness, like a cozy quilt, fills the room. This noisy old house is creak free. The wind, too, is at rest, the trees quiet. The birds haven't yet sensed the approaching dawn. The soft breathing beside me seems to fluff the hush. I can feel the air is cold, but I am warm in my bed. Better than warm. I am content, peaceful, and loved. I am not too Pollyannaish, I'm not too sensitive, I am not too anything. I'm just me. I would lie here delighting in the knee that has just slid onto my right thigh and the sleepy mummers of contentment that blow softly in my ear. I would, if my bladder weren't refusing to be ignored. I carefully slide out of bed. I spy my nightgown on the floor and the empty condom wrappers, gifts from Petra.

The cold of the floor, the chill on my skin, rush me into the bathroom then back to bed. Before I wiggle myself back under the arm and knee, I remember the window I opened last night to let fresh air in, frivolously allowing heat to escape. But I don't close it. Outside the trees are bare with no apparent signs of life, but I know better. Inside, rings trace their history, mark the trying times, isolate the trials from the new growth. Inside life rests. And the fireplace, I should check that. Instead I slide in closer, careful not to dislodge the arm that caresses in response to my movement. Fire's probably out, it was almost there when we left it. The smile has crept onto my face again; I can feel it seep into my mind. I love to sleep with the window open in the winter. I love not worrying about the last burning ember when sleep is waiting. A gentle awareness flows from the smile. These things I enjoy like I'd savor the first apple pie of the season, not as if I've been deprived, but as if I've been anticipating.

A little patch of moonlight shines on the letter from Mack, one he wrote when he failed a suicide attempt. That letter has set me free. I have no need to reread it. There may be others that have gone with the books and maybe not. I know this: he loved me in his own way. Suicide was entirely his own choice. I know that again, more deeply as I shed layers of guilt, layers of false assumptions about both of us.

I imagine putting his letter in a gilded, glittering box on the mantel. Inside I've put his love and my respect for what was. I place a golden lid on the box and push it aside.

I look at the face beside me, grateful that he is so comfortably familiar. Shall I marry him? Do I want to be married? To anyone? I don't know. Tacked on the wall, the sketch for the studio is lighted by the first glimmers of sunlight. Do I want a studio? I don't know, maybe a small cottage. Well, Alma, what do you know? Do you know what you want? Indeed I do. I want my life to be about this moment, moment by moment, with the past contained and the future free.

I snuggle in, aroused by the smell of tweed and the brush of moustache on my cheek.

Mickey Getty attended Florida Atlantic University and studied writing there. She has been the recipient of several awards: The National League of American Pen Women Second Place Letters Award, the Thomas Burnett Swann Memorial Scholarship, the Florida Atlantic University World AIDS Day Literary Expressions Competition several years in a row, and the fiction award from the Pennsylvania Writer's Conference for "The Birth of William," an excerpt from *The Junk Lottery*.

She and her husband live in Reading, Pennsylvania. She is currently at work on two new novels: *The Gift of Sin* and *Soot*.

If you like the work of Mickey Getty, we recommend:

Manual for Normal (Rebecca McEldowney)
Guardian Devils (Rebecca McEldowney)
Soul of Flesh (Rebecca McEldowney)
Bad Apple Jack (Gregg Fedchak)
The Broccoli Eaters (Gregg Fedchak)
Love Among the Tomatoes (Gregg Fedchak)
The Big Five-O Cafe (James Wolfe)

Other excellent fiction

1001 Nights Exotica (Cris DiMarco)
1002 Nights Exotica (Cris DiMarco)
Bones Become Flowers (Jess Mowry)
Breed of a Different Kind (Walt Larson)
Crossing the Center Line (Jackie Calhoun)
False Harbor (Michael Donnelley)
Gathering in the Mist (David Bromden)
Heir Unapparent (John Harrison)
Judah's Luck (Walt Larson)
The Junk Lottery (Mickey Getty)
Little Balls, Big Dreams (James Wolfe)
On a Bus to St. Cloud (Patrick Brassell)
The Sitka Incident (Walt Larson)
Soldier in a Shallow Grave (Gerald Cline)
Storm on the Docks (Walt Larson)
Strong Medicine (Walt Larson)
Visibility (Cris DiMarco)
Willy Charles, Esq. (Walt Larson)